ALSO BY NELSON GEORGE

FICTION

Night Work

Show & Tell

One Woman Short

Seduced

Urban Romance

NONFICTION

Post-Soul Nation

Hip Hop America

Blackface: Reflections on African-Americans and the Movies

Buppies, B-Boys, Baps, & Bohos: Notes on Post-Soul Black Culture

Elevating the Game: Black Men and Basketball

The Death of Rhythm & Blues

Where Did Our Love Go?: The Rise and Fall of the Motown Sound

Nelson George, coauthor

Life and Def: Sex, Drugs, Money + God

THE ACCIDENTAL
HUNTER

A Novel

NELSON GEORGE

A TOUCHSTONE BOOK
PUBLISHED BY SIMON & SCHUSTER
New York   London   Toronto   Sydney

TOUCHSTONE
Rockefeller Center
1230 Avenue of the Americas
New York, NY 10020

TOUCHSTONE and colophon are registered trademarks
of Simon & Schuster, Inc.

For information regarding special discounts for bulk purchases,
please contact Simon & Schuster Special Sales at 1-800-456-6798
or business@simonandschuster.com

Designed by Jan Pisciotta

Manufactured in the United States of America

10   9   8   7   6   5   4   3   2   1

Library of Congress Cataloging-in-Publication Data
George, Nelson.
    The accidental hunter : a novel / Nelson George.
        p. cm.
    1. Singers—Crimes against—Fiction. 2. Women singers—Fiction.
    3. Bodyguards—Fiction. 4. Kidnapping—Fiction. I. Title.
    PS3557.E493A64 2005
    813'.54—dc22   2004056265

ISBN 0-7432-3552-5

*To Coffin Ed,
Grave Digger,
and Easy*

CHAPTER ONE

NIGHT DIDN'T NOTICE the first Kawasaki Ninja in his rearview mirror as his black Explorer cruised Brooklyn's Belt Parkway toward Manhattan. He was too busy savoring a fantasy of his own making. Only a few years ago Night was a professional boy toy for lonely widows and aging ladies, his body a commodity enjoyed in the privacy of pricey condos and high-end hotels.

That was another life. Sitting behind the wheel of his ride Night listened to a CD made off the sound board of last night's concert in Atlanta. Screams of black women filled his ears, along with the sound his voice, crooning smoothly through the R. Kelly produced and penned ballad "When Darkness Falls."

As he luxuriated in his voice Night glanced over at Tandi Lincoln, sleeping sweetly in the passenger seat. She was a striking cinnamon lass with curly bronze hair and the well-maintained skin of a pampered black American princess. Years ago she'd dumped Night when she'd been advised of his old profession by a playa hater. Losing Tandi had always tugged at his heart, so when celebrity arrived (via his record deal) Night worked diligently to woo her back. There were plenty of women available for a dark chocolate R&B love man, but Night's gigolo days made him jaded about women, sex, and all the accompanying bull. Tandi had vibed him when he had nothing and no one, and he needed the assurance of that kind of love. For the gig at the Fox Theater, Night had flown her down to Atlanta, a city that was home base to one of the nation's finest collections of African-American women, a gesture to demonstrate to her (and himself too!) how important she was to him. After the gig they'd gone back to the Four Seasons and, with the conviction of a woman who knew she was adored, Tandi had loved the singer so intensely they'd almost missed their flight home the next afternoon.

He glanced out of the driver's-side window toward Coney Island, where the Wonder Wheel floated cars through the Brooklyn sky as it had for decades. As a child Night had taken the D train out to Coney Island to lie on its eroding, crowded beach and indulge in bad fried food. It was another blast from his past, years of poverty and hunger and anxiety. He thought of his mother's death and his father's belligerence and the uncertainty of his youth. When you were poor and black, he mused, you never knew what the fuck could happen next. You never felt in control of anything—least of all your life. He squeezed the wheel of his big, sturdy ride, happy that was all finally behind him.

Night only really paid attention to the first Kawasaki Ninja after he passed Coney Island. The bike and the driver's helmet were white and lime green. On his body was a lime-colored, leather Rocawear tracksuit. The biker weaved his way through the light late-night traffic until he was abreast of Night's car. Night thought the driver just wanted to drag race, which would have intrigued him if Tandi wasn't in the ride. As this thought amused Night, little groups of Japanese-style motorcycles began appearing in his rearview mirror. First he spied three. Then there were five. Then four more. By the time Night's Explorer cornered the tip of Brooklyn and was in the shadow of the Verrazano Bridge, there were fifteen bikes either beside or behind Night.

Obviously this was one of those ghetto bike clubs that had popped up since DMX featured the Rough Ryders club in one of his videos. All summer long these posses roared through the city, intimidating drivers fearful of the futuristic funk these motorized gangs represented.

Night wasn't afraid—not really. But he was becoming real concerned. If any of these untrained, risk-taking fools somehow jammed into his car, Night, the one with the money and visibility, would take the weight. Any accident or, God forbid, a smashup would automatically be his fault. Next to him a bike popped a wheelie. One kid stood up on his bike and did a handstand while rolling at sixty miles per hour down the Belt Parkway. Night attempted to maneuver his way out of the pack but found that instead of giving him space, the pack grew tighter around him. The green-suited biker accelerated a bit and moved right in front of his ride and dangerously close to his front bumper. Night pressed the center of his steering wheel and beeped loudly. The lead biker beeped back, closely followed by the horns of the other fourteen bikers in a frightening, sardonic chorus.

The blaring horns woke Tandi and, looking out of the window, she immediately saw that Night's SUV was stuck in a cornfield of Japanese motorcycles. "What's going on, Night?" she asked.

"Just some hip-hop bike motherfuckers," he replied dismissively. "They just making some noise. They got nothing better to do."

The lime-green biker slowed down, forcing Night to reluctantly decelerate. Two of the bikers on the driver's side began driving dangerously close to him, while the bikes on the passenger side slid over to the right, creating a narrow passageway. They wanted Night to move to his right, which was precisely why he didn't do it.

"You think they're fans, Night?" Tandi asked innocently.

"That's probably it," he told his Tandi, trying to downplay his own anxiety. Night knew they weren't. The women who bought his records drove Saabs, not Kawasaki Ninjas. Besides, he'd kept his windows up and he doubted they could see through his tinted windows in highway light. But this was an expensive ride, so he might have just been the wrong SUV on the wrong highway on the wrong night. He'd let his driver go home at JFK, happy to be driving himself again after three months of riding in tour buses, limos, and jeeps around the country. Now he was contemplating pushing the pedal to the floor and blasting his way through the bikes before things got serious. But he'd thought too long.

There was a loud tap on the driver's-side window. Night turned and found the long barrel of a Desert Eagle automatic aimed at his face.

"Oh, my God!" Tandi cried as Night struggled to keep his emotions under control. The biker with the gun motioned with it for Night to roll down his window. Night, frightened into obedience, followed instructions.

"Next exit!" The voice was low-pitched but female—definitely female.

"Night," Tandi screamed, "don't do as they say! Keep driving straight!"

"No, boo, it'll be all right. It's just a carjacking. They'll take the ride and we'll be all right. Just keep it together and we'll be all right." Night's voice was as calm as he could make it, but his heart was beating double time. Led by the lime-green biker, Night guided his car toward an exit for Red Hook, a section of Brooklyn with waterfront warehouses that was, at night, dreary and relatively isolated.

For the first time in several miles Night noticed that the CD of his performance was still playing. He heard himself seducing several thousand willing women. It was the voice of a man in complete control of his environment. It was a beautiful illusion that he suddenly had to let go of. He clicked off the CD player, took a deep breath, and followed the lime-green biker down the exit ramp.

CHAPTER TWO

D HUNTER, DRESSED in black from boots to turtleneck, sat behind his battered mahogany desk as his small brown eyes focused on the woman in front of him. He always liked giving this little talk and worked hard not to let it sound too rote.

"The rules of D Security are very simple," he explained to Mercedez Cruz. "We don't disrespect the clients or the customers. We don't curse and we don't instigate. We take for granted that people want to feel safe even when they forget how to act." Mercedez shook her pecan-colored head to acknowledge she was listening. "We're more Dr. King than Malcolm X." He paused for her to chuckle, but she didn't. Mercedez just looked with black, piercing eyes at the broad, brown man sitting across the desk from her. Clearly, Mercedez didn't waste smiles, which D always felt was a good trait in the crowd-control business. One introductory don't-even-think-about-it stare could prevent a whole lot of mayhem later. D continued: "If someone gets abusive or threatening we get backup and move in a wave. First we make a show of force. If that isn't effective, we move together and subdue with a minimum of punching, swinging, and stomping."

She'd been recommended to D by Mike Daddy, her sometime lover and the full-time barber to the black elite (P. Diddy, Chris Rock, Derek Jeter). When Mercedez walked in (at 10:45 for an 11:00 A.M. appointment), D's first impression was that she was too slight for the job. Then she took off her red 3rd Down jacket and D saw her taut shoulders and arms, and fingers that were unusually thick for a woman's. "For the most part," D observed, "the people we encounter are out for a good time. We don't wanna get in the way of that good time unless they constitute a physical threat to others or are verbally abusive. If they are just acting stupid and no one minds, that's fine."

Mercedez's résumé revealed a degree in criminal justice from John Jay and gigs at health clubs as a trainer. She was a sexy little hard rock who'd grown up in Brooklyn's Pink Houses, a place where you develop a third eye for trouble. When not tending to her six-year-old son, Damian, she worked as a bodyguard/trainer for several female R&B/hip-hop divas, which could be lucrative but erratic, because when the singers weren't about to tour, they often replaced sit-ups with Krispy Kremes. Mercedez was now seeking a job with steady hours and better cash flow.

"Now," D continued, "we'd be bringing you on to specifically help us police female customers. As you know, women can be tricky. If a lady wants to ho out with a man in a men's room stall we let her, but we don't let men in the ladies room. That's not acceptable. If she throws a drink on her boyfriend, fine. Women do that and then make up with the fool ten minutes later."

"I know about that," she said with her first smile.

"But a man throwing drinks at women? He's got to go."

Mercedez mentioned the name of a prominent female pop star she had once trained who was now notorious for getting drunk and passing out on VIP room sofas.

"If stuff like that happens," D replied, "first we talk to whoever is with her and try to get her out of the club that way."

"What if the bitch is alone?" Mercedez was not feeling this lady.

"Number one, Mercedez," D said evenly, "she's never alone at a club. Number two, she is sometimes a client herself, so she's never a bitch to D Security."

"I hear you, D. Everybody can't be as wholesome as that Bridgette Haze, I guess."

"That's right, baby. Naughty but nice like Haze is a good way to go. Look at poor Janet."

"Well, baby," she replied with her second smile, "I'll definitely try to do that. Baby."

Now D chuckled and asked, "Can you start tonight?"

"Yeah."

"Cool. Fill out those forms and I'll give you the guided tour."

The black man in black and the wavy-haired Puerto Rican woman moved out of the small, dark office through the even smaller reception area where a hard, black leather sofa sat under a Miles Davis *Kind of Blue* poster, and into a conference room. There was a long conference table, six chairs, two landlines, and innumerable paper plates and plastic forks. A big chart was mounted on one wall, listing employees and clients in neat black columns. The room stank of herb, bootleg designer cologne, and bronchitis spray—the last item crucial, since respiratory diseases were endemic to night club security. The other three walls were covered with a haphazard collage of concert posters, flyers, promo stickers, and food menus taped, glued, stapled, and pounded into the plaster and atop one another. There was a framed photo of D and some of his bouncers outside the Supper Club the night D Security had handled its first party. Next to that was a large autographed poster of Night in a stylish overcoat and apple jack cap.

D was writing Mercedez's name on the duty roster when she gave Night's poster an affectionate glance and asked, "Do I get to protect him sometime?"

"You never know," D replied with a smile, once again impressed by his old friend's ability to attract women. He continued, "You know that club on Broome where they hold the 'Tea Party'?"

"Oh, yeah, that spot's hot."

"Report there around 8:30 and ask for this man." D pointed out a bald, big-shouldered white man in the Supper Club picture. "That's Jeff Fuchs. He runs that location and needs someone just like you."

"Shit," she said matter-of-factly. "Everybody needs somebody like me, D. But it's what they want in return that's the problem."

"I hear that."

She gestured toward the picture and then at D. "You gotta wear black to work here?"

"It's not a rule," he replied, "but it can't hurt."

Mercedez gave D a firm handshake, pulled on her red jacket, and left his office with a noticeable swagger.

Back at his desk, D clicked on his ebony Apple G3 and went over the night's work roster.

D Security had the usual complement of ten at B.B. King's tonight for a blues concert, which means they'd encounter one or two overlubricated barleyheads, but otherwise it was a rocking-chair gig. Jeff's team was, as usual, working Emily's Tea Party, which meant D would have to go down for a minute and act important. The key meeting of the day was to be at Bad Boy, where D was to see about providing security at an album-release party for one of P. Diddy's baby acts. That could be a big payday, though sometimes it took a while for payment to flow down from Big Baller Land. Before D headed uptown for the sitdown, he'd call to confirm, since at Bad Boy time was elastic.

Now that Mercedez was gone, D checked various pieces of technology for messages. On the office answering machine: a grown woman's voice. Gruff. Ethnic New York. Officious. Just doing her job. "This is Teresa from A.S.S. There will be an envelope left for you with the receptionist per Mr. Calabrese's instructions. Good day." If Mr. Dante Calabrese truly had his way, I'd be ass out, D mused, so fuck him, and thank you one more time, Mr. Bovine Winslow.

On the cell: Static. Cell phone? Plane phone? Her voice.

Light, Preoccupied. Sexy. Comfortable with itself. Too comfortable with me. "Mr. D, it's Miss Ann. Are you ever gonna wear that red Versace blazer I got you? I know it's a little bright for your narrow taste, but you need some color in your life. So are you gonna wear it?"

Next message: white voice. Black inflection. "Where you at, son? Need an extra man for tonight at Emily's Tea Party. Actually an extra girl would be good. That crazy sista from the Bronx isn't just frisking—she's copping feels. Bitch gets more play than me, which is fucking with me since she's God damn ugly. Get at me, dog." Jeff Fuchs in full wigger effect. With Mercedez in the house that request was handled.

Next cell message: Sour. Brittle. Anxious. Proper. British and black. And D's for as long as he cherished it. "My lovely, where are you? I need you at the club. E-A-R-L-Y. Okay? M-O-N-E-Y is owed. I know you know, my lovely, but I need to suss out my finances. The Crunch check is late. I design all these sexy workout things for them and still they treat me like a bald-headed stepchild. But then sometimes so do you. You know how I get. Please. E-A-R-L-Y. Love." Never, ever should have sexed Emily. That was a mistake. He knew it. But then, if D could rewrite history, he'd start a lot further back.

Not only had he slept with her, but, worse, he'd borrowed money, too. Money was always trouble. Combine that with sex and you've let the Devil into your bedroom. D had spent a lot of time around people with so much money that nothing their greedy souls desired was out of reach. He'd seen people—close friends, intimate acquaintances, and customers—who lived as if money were endless as air and just as easily acquired. D himself had never once enjoyed that carefree exhilaration. All he knew was that mundane feeling when the already small denominations in his wallet shrank with every glance at the trendy eateries, couture clothes, and tech-toys-for-boys he desired.

His baby business was grossing dollars, but net was something else. Paying overtime. Giving advances to build loyalty. Just keeping the cash flow tight. Vendors were slow with checks. Payment often came in sixty-day cycles, while rent and telephone bills came every thirty days. All of it was draining D Security's meager resources. Business had been good when they began four years ago, but the novelty of D Security had worn off. The business was based on intimate relationships with vampires—people who worked nights, thrived in darkness, and had breakfast after 1:00 P.M. Tough to count on people like that, D knew, 'cause he was one of them.

Around 2:30 someone called from Bad Boy to say the meeting would have to be rescheduled. No surprise there. D decided to head home and take a nap. He lived on Seventh Avenue and Seventeenth Street, just above a bar called Merchants, where every couple of days he stopped in for a mohito, one of the few vices he allowed himself. Although it was only midafternoon, D's place was as dark as 11:00 P.M. The walls, carpet, bed, shades, the clothes scattered about—all variations on black. Coal black. Charcoal black. Inky black. Blue black. Plain old ebony. For D, his apartment was sometimes a womb, sometimes a crypt, sometimes a dungeon—depending on his mood. On one wall was a small square of white. A framed letter from his mother that D read at least once a day. "The Lord," she wrote to her youngest son, "gives each of us a gift. Something that says we're special. It can be strength. It can be in the mind. It can be our smile. But the Lord also gives us a burden for us to overcome. Our time on Earth is about learning our gift and overcoming that burden. Often it's easier to see our burden than our gift.

"You know how the Lord has burdened me. But I'm clear now: My gift was to be a mother and to know and feel the things only a mother can. No matter what has happened, I'll always know what it is to carry life in me. That's what I was given. Now you got to go out and find the thing the Lord gave you. That's what your life's about now." D wasn't sure if he totally believed his mother. He often wondered if he truly had any special gift other than being big and brown and occasionally frightening. Still, he read it every day, like a prayer. Despite his misgivings about the message, it gave him a sense of comfort, as if his mother were hugging him, whenever he asked for one.

Framed next to that letter was a blurry Polaroid snapshot of his family. A weary, chubby woman in a bulky red sweatsuit stood farthest to the left. Her arms were folded around a teenage boy whose long, skinny limbs and glittering gold chains distracted from the sneer on his gaunt, brown, obsessed face. At the other end of the photo was another teenager. This one was younger, with a handsome face and a God-given smoothness. The arm of a caramel shorty leaned against his body, desperately trying to claim him, though this young man would prove impossible to snare.

In the center of the photo stood a firm, muscular, large-bodied young man who damn near blotted out the sun. He wore a tank top and big, baggy basketball shorts and cradled a trophy in his large hands. He smiled with all the confidence a powerful man should. Around his neck dangled the legs of a seven-year-old boy, whose hands held on to either side of the big-bodied young man's head. If you thought the little boy looked dizzy, you'd be right. The little boy was dazzled and in-toxicated by the view from Matty's shoulders. It was a view from on high he'd later grow into. That summer day was one of the few from D's childhood he didn't want to forget.

D was never comfortable being the baby of his family, since a baby has no responsibilities. The baby is the one watched over, the one coddled and protected. Now D had outlived his baby status. Now he was a protector, a guardian, the one who made others secure. Yet in this world, who was really safe?

D reached into his medicine cabinet and pulled out his plastic pill dispenser. Sitting on the toilet seat he counted out fourteen tablets: ten Viracept, which were protease inhibitors; two Combivir, which were ACT; one Claritin for his sometimes leaky sinuses; and one Zovirax to prevent herpes outbreaks. He'd been taking this HIV regimen for three years now and, so far, he looked as healthy as Magic Johnson. Which is to say, if you didn't know D was HIV positive, you wouldn't.

He took his tablets into the kitchen and turned on his blender. After tossing in bananas, strawberries, apple juice, and a protein drink called Metrix, D slid several of the pills into his mouth at a time and gulped down his juice drink.

With his body on his bed and his eyes closed, D let the medication flow through him and listened to the city outside his apartment—the cabs, the trucks, the folks down at the bar right below him, and the grocery store on the corner. D felt his senses tingling, like Spider-Man in a comic book, as his organs and his blood accepted the potent cocktail of medication. The disease had made him incredibly conscious of his body—every ache, every pain. Even his breath seemed important now. There was nothing he could ever take for granted again.

After fifteen minutes he got up and slid into his third-best DKNY suit; a Gap turtleneck; sharp, shiny, retro-sixties Italian boots; his favorite Dolce & Gabbana distressed-leather trench coat; and a Kangol worn backward—all of them a proud shade of midnight black. D strode briskly out into the chilly embrace of a suddenly soupy, gray, late winter afternoon.

At Seventh and Thirty-second Street, D reached his destination, the office suites of A.S.S. (Athletic Sports Services), where D had expected to pick up a check. Instead, he found himself sitting on a wooden facsimile of a New York City park bench in A.S.S.'s lobby, flipping through *Sports Illustrated, The Wall Street Journal,* and NBA press releases. A.S.S. was in the business of squeezing 10 percent from the sweat of black gladiators, so the walls were adorned with huge photos of the agency's clients dunking, shooting, and otherwise hanging in NBA-authorized air. Forty minutes after his arrival, D was summoned from the bench and ushered into the presence of A.S.S.'s prickly coach. As the agent for two dozen NBA studs, Dante Calabrese fit nearly into the category of white men comfortable with black folks. Same as D's man Jeff Fuchs, except that Jeff wanted to fit in, while Dante was obsessed with cashing in.

D sat uncomfortably across from the agent and took inventory. He had a big head covered with thick, dark brown hair, matching eyebrows, tiny black eyes, and a mouth that would have seemed small if it wasn't always open. His suit was expensive. So was his watch. But it wasn't his looks or his gear that made Dante a player. He made sure he knew which SUVs were cool and where the black elite dined in each NBA city, and he maintained an active working knowledge of current slang. Although he could sound goofy saying "off the chain" or "def" or whatever young black folks were into that particular summer, Dante was self-aware enough to run his awkwardness into self-deprecating humor. Calabrese's goal was constant—to calm the psyche of young African-American millionaires. "Yo, dog, my man is funny" or words to that effect were what he sought. This attitude disarmed his cash cows and made them feel vaguely superior to their agent, an illusion Calabrese found extremely useful.

If a player's folks were working class or worse (which most were), Calabrese employed the ghetto glamour of flashing rings, fancy cars, and illegal cash payments. If a player's parents were middle class, he talked education, wise investments, and future business opportunities. If a player made it to "the show," it was stroke, stroke, stroke their egos like he was captain of the Harvard rowing team.

If you were D—an interesting but highly marginal personality in the athletic orbit—Calabrese didn't feel obligated to wear a mask. When Calabrese asked, "How's the party security business these days, D?" he expected this black man to respond, "Yo, shit is phat. My spot is blowing up." Instead D, as professionally dispassionate as he could sound, reported, "Well, Dante, the business is growing. We're picking up more accounts. I'm hopeful things are about to go to another level."

Calabrese acted as if this information was important to him. D knew where he was driving, so he took the wheel. "So, you wanna know why, if business is good, do I need five thousand dollars from Bovine?

"Well, Dante, I've put out a lot of cash to get D Security going. I'm still in debt to several vendors for the uniforms, overhead, and, of course, I pay lots of insurance. I'd just rather owe Bovine money than five guys named Vinnie." Calabrese loved Mafia jokes (he watched *The Sopranos* incessantly), so that was an ace. Still, there'd be no check without a lecture.

"D," Calabrese said with the gracious smugness of a rich man, "I get it. It's the cost of doing business. I understand that. I totally get it." Then he glanced over at his G3 screen. "But looking over Bovine's file, I see this loan will bring what you owe him in excess of fifteen thousand dollars."

"To $15,045," D said.

"That's right, D. That's a nice sum of money. Not outrageous, but a nice sum nonetheless. Now, you've been a really special friend to Bovine since he's been in New York. You've helped him in so many ways."

"I really like the guy."

"I know," Calabrese conceded. "But at some point I feel you either have to formalize this relationship—"

"Formalize?"

"Either come to work for Bovine to pay back this debt or simply be his friend and stop borrowing money. This in-between stuff has to end. You're a businessman now, D. I'm sure you understand." An envelope appeared out of Calabrese's pocket and D's eyes followed it like an alcoholic's do a drink. "Get back to me on this, okay?" D nodded affirmatively as he took the envelope and signed the upscale IOU form.

If Bovine hadn't okayed that request, Dante Calabrese would never have said that. What they wanted was a full-time bodyguard/flunky/hangout buddy who'd handle everything from the dishwashing to condom purchases. D had done that in college for a pal and for Bovine when he first hit New York, but he'd outgrown that role. That's what D Security was about, having his own thing, building his own empire. He didn't want to work for anyone anymore now—least of all an NBA star. Still, he wanted to maintain the Bovine connection and knew Calabrese's words were a threat. The potential for Bovine's next check was at least $70 million to $80 million. Calabrese didn't want anyone to affect the flow. If D was back on Bovine's salary, Calabrese could control him and muffle his influence. Right now, despite the loans, D was too independent, too much his own man and too close to Bovine to suit Dante.

A stop at his bank. Moving money around in his D Security and personal accounts. Then over to Thirty-third Street off Eighth Avenue and the players' entrance to Madison Square Garden. The guards checked him in with a nod and a smile. An elevator took him up to the arena level, where he walked through a long passageway and then stood in front of the court. Down at the Eighth Avenue basket of the world's most famous arena, under the white championship banners and the retired numbers in the mostly empty building, Bovine Winslow moved without the ball.

Drop step right. Spin move left. The hustle. The electric glide. The Bankhead bounce. Bovine Winslow was deep into the choreography of his game. "Yo, D," he yelled as his friend stood courtside on the polished wood, just outside the charmed rectangle. Bovine stopped his dance and went over to D. "I don't like these guys, D." Bovine spoke in the lovely southern drawl that graced sneaker and pizza ads all over local TV. "These boys from D.C. go too far." Down at the Seventh Avenue end of the court, two Washington Wizards, garbed in the team's patriotic-colored warm-ups, tossed up shots, joked, and cut unamused glances down at Bovine's dancing.

Watching Bovine's ritual pregame dance, D saw once more why men envied and women lusted after the Knicks forward. In a league of tall, well-constructed bodies, Bovine's physique was a conditioning coach's dream. Shoulders as broad as Karl Malone's; waist as taut as Evander Holyfield's; his ass a tight, pointy weapon used to pound low-post opponents into submission; long, sturdy legs with the tapered ankles of a sprinter; all of it adorned in a shiny onyx coating.

Strangely, Bovine's remarkable body was also his curse.

People never took his pain seriously because all the world could see was strength. They didn't think the knees, elbows, and low blows of opponents hurt Bovine or that the bites, scratches, and groins of women, greedy for his sex, could scar him or cause discomfort. He'd mumble, "Everybody acts like I'm not a person," yet no one took his mild complaints seriously because Bovine was everybody's cock diesel fantasy. No one acknowledged Bovine's vulnerability, and after a while, tired of being ignored, he just did his solitary basketball dance and brooded.

Later, sitting on a stool in the Knicks locker room—sanctuary, sweatbox, and changing room—Bovine continued, "The Wizards are the worst team in the league for disrespecting a brother. You shouldn't invite them to our party and around our honeys. Sounds right to me, D." That was classic Bovine: "Sounds right to me."

The phrase had already been used in a Knicks radio spot, sampled for the hook on a Mary J. Blige record, and exploited in two sneaker commercials. Not to mention the line of black SOUNDS GOOD TO ME T-shirts D was hawking via Korean vendors, flea markets, and the Internet to help pay bills.

D really wanted to get into his conversation with Calabrese but knew this wasn't the time. Bovine had pulled out his blue Sony Walkman and slipped in tonight's selection, Ice Cube's classic *AmeriKKKa's Most Wanted*, a recording perfect for moving Bovine into the mental combat zone he'd happily reside in for the next three hours. It wasn't the time to talk business with Bovine. It was time for D to work the room—the room being Madison Square Garden.

D gave Tea Party comps to the Knicks backcourt and the Knicks Citi Dancers, except for the Asian girl who had tried to stick her tongue in Emily's ear at a party last month. D gave no comps to the press-room security guards or sports writers. D gave no comps to women wearing pearls. D did give comps to any lady in leather pants. Throughout the pregame warm-up, D surfed the lower-level seats for "fabulous" people of every description.

At the Garden on a game night, D was a third-tier celebrity. Players were level one. Celebrities level two. Level three were folks in the mix with a small portfolio. Just as D watched for the kind of client Emily wanted (record bizzers, models, Wall Streeters with style, media types, classy groupies), D too was watched. A black man in a black suit and shirt strutting around the Garden, nodding to ushers, shaking hands, and kissing cheeks. You might not have known who D was, but you knew he was in the mix.

Which was why D was always gazing at "the Mack." At least that's what all the season-ticket-holding brothers called him. Game after game this old white man with a short white Afro sat courtside with a stunning array of women. Between his always impeccable taste in companions and his righteously retro hairstyle, the Mack was one of the most identifiable figures in the high-profile world of Knicks courtside VIPs. D, however, knew more about the Mack than most people. His name was Ivy Greenwich and for three decades he'd been one of the biggest managers in pop music. He was Night's manager, which was why D knew his backstory, but they'd had only fleeting contact. If he was at all known to the masses, it was as Bridgette Haze's manager. That little white girl was a huge star. D didn't care much for her music, though he did think Haze had a pretty big ass for her race.

On this evening the Mack was accompanied by Danville, a bronze beauty whose long body was encased in hip-hugging jeans. D'd met her one night with Beth Ann, which seemed connection enough to make a move. After shimmying past security guards, vendors, and corporate types gawking at Danville's gams, D strode over to the happy couple. Danville had only a vague memory of D but knew all about Emily's Tea Party. Equally cool was that the Mack had heard of it too.

"I've been meaning to get down there," the white Afroed man said in a voice that somehow blended Brooklyn with Birmingham, Alabama. What a striking sound he made—ethnic New York with a southern drawl. "Danville tells me a lot of her friends go there."

D confirmed that and added that Ford, Elite, and Zoli models who turned up got free admission. "Sounds like my kind of place," he replied suavely, as Danville playfully elbowed him.

"You know," D said, "you manage a friend of mine?"

"Really. Who's that?"

"Night. We go way back. I've done security for a few of his shows. I have a company." D pulled a D Security business card from inside his suit and handed it to Ivy.

"Ahh," Ivy said. "I've heard of you guys. This is your company, huh?"

"Absolutely. We've been in business a couple of years and we handle security at many clubs in the city."

"And you're good friends with Night?"

"Oh, yeah," D replied. "In fact he told me he'd be coming down to Emily's Tea Party tonight."

"Ah," Ivy said again. "'But you didn't speak to him today, did you?"

"No," D said. "In fact I haven't heard from him since he did that show in Atlanta. But as you probably know, he's in love these days and taken to spending a lot of time in bed."

They both chuckled, though D noticed Ivy's laugh sounded forced. Since they'd started talking about Night, there'd been a subtle shift in Ivy's posture. The Knicks and Wizards were moving onto the court, so D excused himself. As he was about to walk away, Ivy took hold of his sleeve and pulled D's face close to his. "We need to get together and talk a little business, D."

"That would be my pleasure, Ivy."

Just before the opening tip, D moved into his seat seven rows behind the Eighth Avenue basket, where he had a clear eye line toward the Knicks bench, where Bovine's game face was already penciled in. This was Bovine's fourth year in New York and, not coincidentally, D's third in an expensive seat. Bovine's back had proved broad and D had climbed aboard, just like his teammates. It was Bovine who'd given him the seed money to open D Security, a debt D deeply wanted to repay, though who knew when?

D pulled out his two-way and sent a message to Night: "You coming tonight? D. P.S. Finally met your manager.

Sounds like it might be ready to put my company down. Lace me. Peace." Night didn't return the page, but Emily E'd him repeatedly throughout a closely contested first half. At half-time break D pulled out his cell and prepared himself for the reprimand. To his surprise, Emily, sweet as English tea cake, reported that her answering machine was filled with RSVPs and that the club's phone had been buzzing too.

"My lovely," she shouted, "our little spot is quite hot." To hear his tart English woman (or was it his English tart?) sound sweet as dripping honey felt like a revelation. It didn't last. "Did you get the money?" When D reported that he'd visited Calabrese, she said sharply, "You should have brought that check right down to me immediately and not carried it around like a trophy. You've owed me that money for months. Just what do you do with all your money?" None of your business, D thought, though what he said was, "Emily, I see some of the players' girlfriends. Let me comp them before they get away." She said, "Get down here as soon as possible." It was a plea that sounded like a command and D hung up slightly pissed.

Right after D clicked off, his two-way quivered and Fly Ty's number flashed on. D sighed and stared out at the court, looking but not seeing. Can't deal with him tonight, he thought. Maybe tomorrow. More likely the day after that. Or the day after that. What does he want now? Memories can be like razors on your tongue. One nick, and no bandage made could stop the bleeding. No Fly Ty tonight. Hopefully none for a while.

Back in unreality, Bovine led the Knicks in a furious fourth-quarter comeback. The Wizards did their best to deny him low-post position and, when that failed, they tried doubling him quickly. But Bovine's footwork was better than theirs. With three minutes left the Knicks got him the ball in the left box. Bovine sprang to the baseline, ducked as low as high-top sneakers, and then sprang through the arms of two Wizards defenders for a hardy two-hand jam. And one. Game over.

By the time Bovine had showered, met the press, and slipped into the olive Armani Emily made him buy on a day they'd all gone shopping, it was 10:30. Bovine and some other Knicks were heading up to the West Side and the Shark Bar. Middle-class, monied, and quite happy to let you know it, the Shark Bar's clientele was a local who's who of soul-food-loving African-Americans. Bovine and company were treated with the special deference black folk reserve for athletes and entertainers. Businesspeople passed over their cards. Jeeps were offered for lease. Blockbuster video franchises were dangled. So were free haircuts.

D skipped the Shark Bar and hailed a cab on Thirty-third Street. On the way downtown, D pulled out a bottle of Phat Farm's Premium, squirted some in his hands, and, like Roy Scheider in *All That Jazz,* smacked both sides of his face with cologne and announced, "It's showtime!" Next stop, Emily's Tea Party.

CHAPTER THREE

THE TWIN TOWERS used to loom over Wall Street as monuments to commerce and government hubris. Their destruction had caused incalculable trauma, an ongoing war, and a recession that still rippled through the city. When Emily's Tea Party opened its doors a few blocks from the WTC site, eyebrows were raised and doom was predicted. Who would want to party so close to such tragedy? Emily replied, "I will offer high tea, muffins, and all the new-school funk they can handle. The spirits in the air here need to get their groove on too." And apparently, she was right.

Outside Emily's party there was that wonderful milling about, that semicircle of anxious, well-dressed people and an aura of pissed-off impatience, that announces New Yorkers are dying to get in. Moving through the crowd, D was cajoled, cursed, and pawed, and he savored each ego-enhancing step of the way. Jeff Fuchs, D's bald, buff, butt-ugly white homie from the Bronx, yanked aside the velvet rope, tugged at D's arm, and confirmed the obvious: "It's off the chain!"

Just inside the door, standing by the money box like a sentry in a long, slinky, sky-blue satin dress and talking with her usual firmness into a cell phone, was Emily Anekwe, the round-hipped British-Nigerian girl who was the evening's host, the party's inventor, and D's eternally antsy girlfriend of the moment. "Of course, Damon," she said into the cell, "your booth will be saved. But only three people, my lovely, okay? Love you." She clicked off and gazed at D balefully through small brown eyes and then stretched out a long, yellow hand tipped with dramatic crimson fingernails. D pressed an envelope that contained $1,250 in cash into her hand.

"I thought," she said sharply, "you were giving me a check?"

"I cashed it," D answered quickly. "That G puts us even, plus you got some interest."

Emily surveyed him suspiciously, counted the money quickly but thoroughly, and then somehow slipped the envelope into her dress. Now looking impish and pleased, Emily smiled and kissed D so deeply that the heavy aroma of the Cuban cigar she'd smoked a half hour before filled his lungs. When she was through, Emily took his arm, popped a cigar in her mouth, and escorted D to her Tea Party. Out of the corner of his eye, D noticed Mercedez going through the designer backpack of a young lovely. She was acting as if she hadn't noticed D kissing Emily, but he got the feeling she hadn't missed a thing.

As a designer, Emily's specialty was urban prep in the style of Phat Farm and Sean Jean. As a club impresario, this spunky product of England's industrial north had a deep affection for the rituals of upper-class British society. So she'd had the space done up with portraits of the Queen (Elizabeth), Princess (Diana), and Kings (the boxers Lennox Lewis and Prince Naseem). "High tea" is a crusty English tradition that involves strong tea and sweet cakes. Emily had taken the silverware, the food, and the genteel formality of these high teas and used them as the organizing principle for her party. Drinks were served in kettles and teacups and the staff, from DJ to bartender, wore Edwardian frocks.

For the moment this ersatz formality was working, attracting an intriguing blend of Europeans, downtown hipsters, and Wall Streeters looking for a thrill. Nothing this extreme could last long, but while the flame was burning, Emily was gonna throw on logs. "It's still early," she said, "but it's already been a good night, my lovely."

Emily looked particularly sexy this evening, her English accent flowing out of her wide Manchester mouth in the most alluring way. "Maybe we can slip out early and go to my place."

Despite her lusty vibe, D was noncommittal. Ever since she'd picked him up at Kinko's—she at one computer, reworking her résumé, he next to her designing a brochure for D Security—their lives had been bound together by a mutual interest in night life and money. D wasn't in love with Emily, but he had mostly enjoyed their year and a half together. Emily wasn't deeply in love with him either; just a very enjoyable level of infatuation, though D's dark moods and mysterious ways often irritated her. And then there was his "condition," which actually made him vulnerable in ways Emily found strangely attractive.

Once inside the Tea Party, D's eyes combed the room for drug dealers, those always reliable barometers of a spot's heat. Where there were alcoholic beverages, loud music, and the promise of random coupling, there was sure to be a dope man around. Party people wanted easy access to their illegal substance of choice, and the dope man (or woman) would, like any user-friendly service, be accessible to his clients. The problem with drugs at a club was not consumption, it was distribution. At an upscale joint like Emliy's Tea Party, your dealers had to be discreet, well dressed, and unassuming. No one dealing out of stalls. No coke set out on the tables by folks nostalgic for the eighties. Just a regular flow of transactions done with a minimum of visibility and flamboyance.

Which was why D gave Patrice Floyd a comfortable kiss on the cheek. "I'm saving you some," she said seductively. Patrice was a chunky but funky sista in a brown dress and boots, her brown hair streaked with a rainbow of colors. When not macking white men, preferably of French or Italian heritage, Patrice worked downtown parties, providing drugs (E, crystal meth, coke, herb) in exchange for small, tightly rolled bills.

"Leave my man alone, Ms. Floyd." This was, of course, Emily.

"I was talking about chronic," Patrice replied, "you uptight, half-white creature." Emily and Patrice were "friends." So, like two brothers playing ball, these girls talked plenty of trash.

"Patrice," Emily continued, "don't you ever offer D anything again without checking with me."

Patrice, sassy as a TV maid, replied, "You just afraid he's gonna ask me for a freebie. Well, don't you worry. When it comes to my stuff, everybody pays." For some reason this made them both giggle. D checked out of that conversation and noticed a guy clocking him. Light skinned. Maybe black mixed with something else, like Emily. Bald head. Loop earring. Just-got-out-the-joint pecs. A tough, sexy-looking brunette with outer-borough attitude sipped gin and juice with him. D had seen him at the Tea Party before, but tonight the dude's vibe was strong, like he was making up his mind when to step to D. He was either a thug or a cop, and D figured he'd know which pretty soon.

At a table was Attak, the old rap star ("old" in rap was twenty-seven), who still kept his hand in by managing a few acts but now spent more time acting—he'd just taped a highly touted sitcom pilot out in Cali. He was sipping champagne with two healthy Mary J. Blige dress-alikes who recorded as Sudden Pleasure and were at that moment being sweated by Mayo, a tastefully dreaded older record executive. D didn't like Mayo very much—he'd tried to stiff D on a bill a few years back—but Mayo had actually had two positive impacts on D's life: He'd once produced some tracks for Adrian Dukes, who was and always would be his mother's favorite singer, and D had met Beth Ann through him. Mayo and D had one of those classic New York night life relationships: They traveled in the same social circles, dated from the same pool of women, tolerated more than liked each other, and never had any contact during the day, which was fine with both.

A couple of Washington Wizards towered over a group of hangers-on by the bar. Tom Brookins, their star forward and one of Bovine's least favorite people, was looking pretty laid-back for a guy who'd just been schooled at MSG. When D told Emily who Brookins was, she floated over to offer him a booth, some complimentary drinks, and much professionally flirtatious conversation.

D was about to head to the manager's office in the back when he spotted Ivy Greenwich and Danville, just out of his Silver Shadow, entering the club. Behind them, holding hands and staring at each other like a romance-novel cover, were Bovine Winslow and Bee Cole, the music-video director who, word on the street said, was about to bust out with her first feature film. She was at least ten years older than Bovine, but no woman D knew projected more raw sensuality than Bee. Nice rebound from Beth Ann. It made D smile.

"Clear out a booth for them," D said to Emily, but she was already kicking a group of unhappy low-level hip-hop executives out of the Tea Party's largest booth. After some maneuvering, the booth filled with Bovine, Bee Cole, Ivy Greenwich, Danville, Emily, and D, creating a half-moon of hyped-up energy that combined music, fashion, and sports figures linked by mutual admiration, accomplishment, and sex appeal. D thought of his man Night and how much he'd have enjoyed being in this mix. He was gonna say something to Ivy but saw him locked in conversation with Emily and Danville and, instead, took a sip of the champagne Ivy had ordered. As a general rule D didn't sit like this with customers, but Ivy could be a source of business, so some schmoozing seemed prudent.

Other party people rolled up on this booth, seeking the validation that a smile, an introduction, or, Hail Mary, full of grace, an invitation to sit down would mean. Emily, chatting away, was in an Eden of her own making. She lived for moments like this and, to a degree, D did too. Ivy had been seated two people away from D, preventing any substantial networking, though they did pass a few innocuous words about the game. Once it became clear to D he wasn't really gonna get a chance to chat up the manager, the security man decided to excuse himself.

"My lovely," Emily wondered, "where are you going?"

"You know," D said coolly. "I am in charge of security at this club. It might be nice if I checked in with the management. Besides, I need to go to the restroom."

For the benefit of the crowd, Emily got fresh. "You know I don't like anybody else holding it but me."

"Even me?" he replied.

"Especially you," Emily said. "After all, my lovely, I don't always know where your hands have been." This generated a few titters from those at the table. D just turned and walked away in the direction of the restroom and then veered off into the manager's office.

Vinnie Del Negro, the manager of Emily's Tea Party, was behind his desk, talking to his wife on a landline. When Vinnie saw D, he reached into the top drawer of his desk, pulled a book out of his top desk drawer, and handed it over to D. It was now 12:30 A.M., which meant D still had two and a half solid hours to protect and serve those partying. So, D began his scrutiny of safety at the Tea Party by flipping open his copy of Chester Himes's *The Quality of Hurt* and, as had been his recent ritual, dived into the late writer's misadventures and caustic worldview. There was something decadent, debauched, and compelling about Himes's expatriate journey across Europe that made D linger over these passages as if walking through a dark, enticing dream. When D was a child, he'd spent a lot of years curled up with books, escaping where he was and the limitations of his adolescent body.

But now, his twenty-first-century physique, like that of his pal Bovine, inspired respect and, sadly at times, responsibility. So sometime after one o'clock, as Himes was listening to James Baldwin explain to Richard Wright why he wanted to borrow money despite dissing the older writer in an essay, Jeff Fuchs's voice could be heard on the office walkie-talkie. "Yo, we gotta problem, son! Your man Bovine is in a beef!"

Out in the center of the dance floor, Bovine stood facing a liquored-up Tom Brookins, who was shouting invectives about Bovine's mother and ancestry. There were a few people between the towering duo, chief among them Mercedez, who stood before Brookins like a terrier challenging a Doberman. The whole room was watching, happy to see some love-it-live NBA action they didn't have to pay Garden prices for.

As D stepped between them Bovine, his southern accent now thick as gravy, shouted, "You stay the fuck away from my woman!"

"Your woman!" Brookins snorted like a bull. "Man, that Beth Ann is just a skinny piece of ass. She gives good head though, partner!"

No jock was gonna dis Beth Ann on D's watch. So D snatched his left wrist—a crucial part of a body the Washington franchise valued at $70 million—and twisted it around and then behind the player's back. Brookins went down on one knee. D leaned over and whispered, "This could be a minor sprain that a little ice could address or a Ewinglike season-ending injury. Your call."

"Fuck you!" Brookins cursed. D twisted his wrist back a bit harder. Brookins's eyes watered.

"D," said Bovine, "let him go."

"I will, Bovine," D said coolly. "I will." D loosened his grip a bit and looked around. Jeff had Bovine on lockdown and, to D's surprise, Mercedez was all over the other Wizards player. Nice.

"Let him go, D," Bovine said again.

"In a minute, Bovine." To Brookins, D whispered, "We're leaving now, okay?" The player didn't speak. He nodded. D guided him out the door where Jeff, an old hand at these scenarios, had already alerted their limo driver. Out on the pavement, D let Brookins go. "Have a good night," he said as pleasantly as possible.

Brookins rubbed his left wrist with his right hand. He spat out the sentence, "Fuck you, you busta!" Whatever, D thought. He heard Bovine yelling at Brookins from the door. He walked back toward Bovine. Mercedez was escorting the other player out. D smiled at her. Then her jet-black eyes narrowed, and she came toward D, low and quick, and then went down. She went past D real low and extended her right leg. Mercedez's right foot hooked the ankles of a charging Brookins. The NBA player fell like a redwood, his face about to catch concrete. D caught Brookins by the shoulders before his mug kissed the curb, though that already sore left wrist broke his fall.

"Please, Mr. NBA star," D said to Brookins, who lay on his stomach before him. "Go back to your hotel before you hurt someone. Namely your silly, nonfighting, motherfucking self."

Despite the pats on the back and the "You-the-Man!" bluster that D received back inside the Tea Party, the head of D Security was not happy. Number one, any time you have to use aggression instead of conversation, the situation could go against you. D felt he'd reacted too quickly and probably should have guided the jock to the door while he continued to talk smack to Bovine—and not laid a hand on him. Just because the beef was over Beth Ann, D had let things get funky.

Number two, Mercedez had almost seriously injured an NBA asset. If this got out—which in some barely factual way it was sure to—it could get the Tea Party banned by the league. Moreover, despite saving Brookins's mug, this incident could still lead to some legal action. D Security (namely him) could not afford a lawsuit.

Number three, Bovine hadn't told D that Beth Ann had been sleeping with Brookins, which, obviously, was the source of his hostility. D vowed to do a better job of keeping up with black celebrity gossip. Knowing who's "doing" who was quite helpful in heading off trouble.

"I'm going home," D told Emily.

"Okay, my lovely hero. I'll meet you there in an hour."

"No, Emily," he replied too forcefully. "I just need to chill right now, okay?"

"No, it is not. But I know how you get when that skinny girl's name gets mentioned."

"Come on, Emily. You saw what just went down. It's not about her. Chill with that."

"Would you have done that for my honor, D?"

"What do you think?"

"A man," she said tartly, "is known for his deeds. Not his rhetorical questions."

D told Jeff to call him if any cops showed up and then walked out of the club. Didn't say good-bye to Bovine or Ivy or anyone. He just headed out of the Tea Party and into the empty lower Manhattan streets.

It was about 2:00 A.M., and despite his expensive black leather jacket, black suit, and boyish smile, D Hunter decided not to take a cab. The fact that D was six-foot-three, broad-shouldered, and thick had made him somewhat fearless about places others tried to avoid. So he walked up to Church Street and went into the Chambers Street A train station. He'd always felt comfortable on the subway—not safe, exactly, but not fearful either. After a loud, blaring night of security work, the relative silence of a deserted subway station brought calm.

The uptown platform was empty save for a pale, dingy

homeless man around age fifty who'd wrapped himself in newspapers and blankets and squeezed his feeble body under a wooden bench specifically designed to prevent people from sleeping on it. This guy had ingenuity, D thought, and smiled in admiration.

Around 2:45, three black teenagers in a mishmash of urban survival gear (beige Lugz, Triple Fat goosedown jackets, jeans sagged around their ankles) flecked with red (bandanas, baseball caps) came onto the platform. They had the loud, loose energy of young men determined to find out how much they could get away with. The loudest one was a small kid with the restless movement of Flavor Flav but none of his humor. The middle kid seemed surly and held his mouth open as if breathing were a chore. The biggest of the three was a man-child with a baby face that belied his large shoulders and hands. D moved behind a pole at his end of the platform and watched as they gazed contemptuously at the homeless man, as if his unfortunate circumstances suggested a weakness they could not stomach.

"Yo, son," the smallest teen said to the largest, "I finally found your daddy!" The other teen laughed and the big boy, clearly not quick-witted, mumbled a weak comeback. The smallest guy, who D heard the others call Coo, got a malicious look on his tight, mean face as he looked at the papers wrapped around the homeless man and then reached into one of his sagged pants pockets.

Out came a crumpled matchbook. He lit one match and threw it in the general direction of the homeless man. That match fell harmlessly to the floor.

The biggest teen, known to his mother as Raymond and to his fellow Bloods as Ray Ray, seized upon this moment to regain his honor. He took out his lighter and then sat on the bench as the homeless man slept unknowingly below him. "This nigga stinks!" he announced and then began lowering the lighter.

"Don't do that!" D Hunter spoke with force, but he didn't shout. It was a strong, flat statement. Not a demand, really. Just a very firm statement. Still, it startled Ray Ray, who immediately clicked off the lighter. Coo and Tone, the mid-size teen, sized up the speaker. D now stood near the stairs, his hands in his jacket pockets, his eyes locked on them. Coo had a hearing coming up on Monday about an assault on a classmate, a pocketful of marijuana, and a girl waiting for him in Washington Heights who'd just gotten off her job as a barmaid. He didn't need the static. Still, you couldn't let some old nigga dis you.

"Who the fuck ya talkin' too?"

When D Hunter spoke, he knew there could be a problem, but it wasn't his nature to be an innocent bystander. Instead of waiting for the three to gather themselves, D walked toward them. Slowly. Calmly. "No need," he said, "for you brothers to get in trouble over some dumb shit." D ignored Tone but kept his eye on Coo and Ray Ray, who was only an inch or so smaller than him. He knew if he could cool out the smaller kid, things wouldn't have to escalate. He wasn't packing, but having his hands in his pockets didn't let them know that. D was now close enough to smell the homeless man himself.

D was smiling when, out of the corner of his left eye, he saw Tone reach into his pants pocket. He immediately recognized a box cutter in the teen's hand and knew that, as a general rule with young boys, box cutters traveled in packs. So with a quick sidestep left, D moved toward Tone. Using his left palm to brace himself, D went down and swung his legs around, smacking them right into Tone's midsection. Both the box cutter and the teen went flying backward off the platform and onto the tracks.

D landed sideways, his leather jacket scrapping against the floor as Ray came at him with a size thirteen raised boot. Twenty-first-century kids are deficient in the old urban skill of boxing; those with deft hands are more likely to DJ than throw blows. But the rise of big, heavy boots as inner-city fashion had elevated stomping. Now it was an essential part of any fight. Pushing a man down and then stomping him senseless was a primary fight strategy of the hip-hop generation, and this kid was determined to display his skills.

As Ray Ray raised his left boot, D reached out both his hands and yanked his assailant's right leg. Ray Ray, both feet in the air, flipped up and back, landing with a solid thud against the cold concrete platform. He grabbed the back of his head in pain, emitting a childish wail and crying. "Coo!" he shouted. "Help me, Coo!"

Alas, Coo was gone. Just as Ray Ray crashed to the platform, Coo had turned and jetted up a staircase, leaving the fate of his two friends in the hands of this surprising adult.

"Bitch-ass nigga," D said under his breath, as the rumble of an incoming uptown C train filled his ears. He looked over at the platform where Tone was struggling, groggy and glassy-eyed, to get to his feet.

All the lights were green at the Chambers Street station when D jumped down onto the tracks, grabbed Tone around the waist, and with one motion, tossed the teen onto the platform.

On the ride uptown on the C train, D sat next to two boxer cutters, five bags of herb, a two-way, a beeper, $323 in cash ($52 of it bloody), a couple of wrinkled condom packets, and one worn-out wallet. He looked down at his treasure and then up at Ray Ray, who held D's black handkerchief to the back of his neck.

"This wasn't at all necessary, Ray Ray," D said to his new acquaintance.

"I know. Coo is always startin' shit."

Tone was slumped across from them on a seat, looking menacingly at D but too sore and defeated to do anything about it.

"Why you ain't call the po po?" Ray Ray asked.

"I don't think it would solve anything," D said. "You and your brother just need to start hanging out with a better class of Blood."

"How you know we brothers? Half-brothers really. Most people don't see it."

D grunted. "I just know." He was silent a moment and then told Ray Ray, "You know you could get a real job, Ray Ray. One that paid all right, was steady, and could give you a little action. Even a little authority."

"I know you ain't the police."

"That's right," D agreed. "But I am in the safety business. You know, Ray Ray, the world as it is now; everybody wants to feel safe. What I do is help them. Maybe you can be of assistance some day."

The burly teen just looked at his enemy/benefactor as if he were crazy.

Back in his apartment in the hours before D closed his blinds, he pressed PLAY on his CD player and slid on the blinders to cover his eyes. He lay in bed smiling as music filled his little room, obscuring the stale aroma of static air, funky socks, and take-out Thai food. D was transported to a place where he felt loved, where complex problems were solved by laughter, and the air smelled of yellow roses rubbed against lover's wet thighs. No confusion. No road-blocks. No money problems.

In this state there was a sense of elevation and peace that allowed D to lie motionless for hours. The two-way was off. The phone was off. Manhattan's hum, constant, exciting, and ultimately maddening, disappeared when confronted by the bass-and-drum grooves that rolled over his body. Time stopped. At least D felt it did, which was all that really mattered anyway. Some long-ago girlfriend called this place D's dungeon. Maybe when she became a woman she'd understand why D loved the stillness of his music-filled room and how hard it was to share.

D reveled in his CD-equipped dungeon. Once in this mood, he measured his movements closely for, if this was truly a dungeon, he wanted to feel his chains, to feel his flesh strain against them. Mostly he played moody mid-nineties music made by morose, obsessive Brits—Tricky, Portishead, Seal, Massive Attack. On certain nights he'd throw on some old-school alternative—Nirvana, Alice in Chains, Pearl Jam— music by the depressed junkies of rainy Seattle. Almost no rap. None of those juvenile male R&B singers. None of those groups singing songs for black-girls-who-have-considered-suicide-when-da-nigga-forgot-to-beep. D avoided the music of black people defined by clichés.

It was one of the many reasons he still played a lot of Adrian Dukes. Not that there was a lot to hear. The man only made two albums. Still, Adrian Dukes moved him. His voice made D remember and forget and feel strange and smile, and then D started crying, one crystalline tear after the other. Adrian Dukes wasn't Otis or Teddy or Marvin or Aretha, though who knows what he could have done if he'd lived longer. Yet Dukes had had his own thing—a voice that was as salty and sad as a drop of water from the big brown eye of a black baby boy who suspected that the best part of life was over the moment he'd left the womb.

Dukes reminded D of his brothers. He reminded D of his mother. He reminded D of his family's living-room closet, and somehow that made D feel safe. D played the music of Adrian Dukes as if his songs were hymns, or maybe they just sounded that way because Dukes had the voice of a choirboy. Maybe it was because he'd committed suicide at twenty-seven, leaping out of a Manhattan hotel room and into the footnotes of R&B history.

For all those reasons, D's mother had played Dukes's big hit, "Green Lights," religiously.

Green lights
(As far as the eye can see)
Green lights
(Yet you're still so far away from me)
Green lights
(Make your voice stop calling me)
Green lights
(You are the love I could never keep)
Green lights
Green lights
Oh, yeah, bright, bright green lights

Adrian Dukes had taken Zena Hunter to an elevated, pretty place, far removed from the cold, calculating streets of Brownsville, Brooklyn. D remembered the nights that Dukes's "Green Lights" played on the living room stereo. He'd crawl out of bed to watch his mother on the living room's love seat with the ripped, already yellowing plastic covering. She'd be by the window facing the parking lot in her powder-blue bathrobe. A Kahlúa and cream sat on a glass holder on the marble living-room table, Zena's face silhouetted by lights from the project building across the parking lot. So many nights, that's what D saw as he crouched in the hallway with his cheek pressed against the wall.

Once in the elevator after school, Mrs. Sumner, their next-door neighbor, had remarked, offhandedly, maybe, but with some malice, that his mother played that Adrian Dukes too much, that his song poured through her wall like a damn leak. "Don't you want her to listen to something else, too?" she asked young D. He'd just shrugged the way kids do when they're too young to dis adults and then helped Mrs. Sumner carry groceries to her door and walked down to his family's three-bedroom apartment, empty because Ma was at work, pressed play on "Green Lights" with the bass knob on ten, and pulled out one of his mother's Heinekens. He'd sat by the window where his mother usually sat, hoping that maybe one day, as that song flooded her apartment, Mrs. Sumner would find the same comfort in Adrian Dukes his mother did. And if Mrs. Sumner didn't, D figured he could live with that.

CHAPTER FOUR

THE POINT GUARD had pretty legs. It was not often D could say that about someone bringing the ball up court, but this particular afternoon at the Reebok Sports Club, he couldn't lie. He loved the way the shorts hung from the point guard's thighs.

So D wasn't happy when a knucklehead investment banker with a bad toupee tried to post-up his point guard, the lovely Mercedez, by shoving his butt into her stomach and swinging his arms too liberally. The ball swung the banker's way and, with undisguised glee, he prepped to school Mercedez. As he turned to fake, D made his move. By the time the banker began to release the ball, D was airborne. With outright malice, D came across and smashed the ball right into the banker's mug. Down went the banker, his nose a rosy red.

"Sorry," D said, "I got too aggressive."

"You sure did." This wasn't the banker, but Mercedez, who'd caught D's elbow in the head. The investment banker glared and stared, but after a brief pause for the cause, they finished out the run.

"Were you trying to help me or hurt me?" Mercedez asked as they left the court.

"I guess you'll never know," D replied.

"All I know," said Jeff, who'd been playing with them, "is that he lets me get posted on the regular."

The Reebok is a super-yuppie gym on Manhattan's West Side. NBA-quality court. Every damn fitness machine imaginable. Scores of trainers. Two restaurants. Four floors. Upscale but not snobbish clientele. Sprinkled in among the white collars are rap stars, ticket scalpers, loan sharks, and private investigators.

Jeff loved the Reebok because the few sistas who worked out there tended to be models, record executives, or personal trainers—three types of women he related to easily. Jeff ran with Mercedez and D, though ball wasn't his passion. He was addicted to Reebok's Jacuzzi.

"Jeff," D warned, "you are gonna turn into a prune."

"True," he answered, "but I'm gonna be the most chilled-out motherfucking prune ever, son."

After showering, Mercedez and D met in Reebok's cafeteria-style dining area for smoothies fortified with protein. Mercedez sat down across from D and, out of the blue, said, "You know, D, you're full of shit."

"Okay," D replied, "what did I do?"

"You gave me that speech when I got the job about being laid-back and not using violence, but I see you definitely go for yours."

"Mercedez," he replied, "I do mean what I say. I shouldn't have touched Brookins. I should have spoken first. And you really shouldn't have tripped him. You know, if you'd let him attack me, I'd have had a possible assault charge to hold against him."

"So what you're saying is I should have let him jump you?"

"Kinda," D said thoughtfully. "At least then I'd have some leverage if he tries to sue me or the company. Listen, I'm not mad at you, Mercedez. It's just that we have to be smart about what we do. This company is still young. It's not even walking yet. I'm not full of shit, but my judgment isn't always as good as my philosophy."

"But," a voice said, "it's a lot better than it is used to be." It was Jeff, his skin flush from the Jacuzzi. "This man tries to act all calm and shit, but you know, there's a lot of bully in him. I bet he used to take plenty of lunch money when he was a kid."

"Nah," D said. "I was a quiet kid. Read books."

"You believe him, Mercedez?"

"Yeah, I do."

"Thank you."

"You know," she went on, "I get the feeling there's a little boy inside this big guy."

"Oh," Jeff groaned. "If you're gonna talk like this about this dusty motherfucker, I'm leaving."

"No, we're all leaving," D said. "We have a meeting and since I own the company, I need to be there."

In the cab downtown, Jeff and Mercedez started talking about what they did New Year's Eve 1999. She had been dancing to merengue with cousins at a house party on the

Grand Concourse. Jeff had worked, watching the back of a pop star as she and her pals did white lines in a Midtown hotel suite.

"What about you, D?" she asked.

"I just visited with some family," D answered. "Real low-key. To me it was just another night at the end of a day. It didn't change anything. Not for me it didn't."

Jeff, an often excitable guy, took issue with D and rolled into an explanation of all the changes the new century had brought forth, from Internet billions to 9/11. D just got quiet and gazed out the window.

There were already two members of D Security waiting when they arrived. Within fifteen minutes, three more of the team had arrived. A half hour later, ten men and two women piled into the conference room. Once a month, the staff of D Security gathered together to catch up and compare notes. Danny Wallace, a burly, slightly effeminate bouncer from Hollis, talked about the latest trend in drag queens—black guys dressed as Britney Spears. Jeff Fuchs talked about the growth of the Bloods gang and how it was affecting security at hip-hop parties. When it was D's turn he talked about money: "Between salaries, insurance, medical, overhead for the office, and miscellaneous, we're in the red for the third month in a row." The room was quiet and then Jeff, trying to lighten the mood, said, "Sowhatshasayin'?"

"I'm saying the concept of D Security is sound, but we simply need to bring in more business."

There was a lot of discontented grumbling after D's announcement. Some wanted to lose the office. Others suggested charging more. They all agreed on one thing—whoever brought in new clients received a 10 percent commission on the deal. Afterward, when only D and Jeff were left, they sat in D's black-walled office. Jeff's right leg pumped up and down as he spoke.

"Yo, son," he said in a high-pitched, rapid tone, the relaxation of the Jacuzzi long gone, "we can't let this go down. If this company closes up, I got to go look for work again. You know that can be hard for me." Jeff had a small but pungent criminal record that included breaking and entering at a sneaker store when he was twenty (he was going to hawk the overpriced footwear for wholesale prices) and robbing a cabbie at knifepoint two blocks from One Police Plaza ("by the time I got up my nerve, we were already downtown"). Not the résumé of a hardened thug, but certainly not that of a white-collar employee either. Between his stint in a methadone center, his white-Negro accent, and his high-school equivalency diploma, Jeff was a white man with limited prospects.

Besides, handling the door at Manhattan night clubs gave Jeff prestige and power he both adored and needed. Although not incredibly lucrative, club security was steady, and you met stars and young women in really tight dresses. "D, I know another way we could make some paper." D could tell by Jeff's hungry expression that he wasn't going to like the suggestion. "We could just start taxing some of the dealers at the Tea Party and the other spots. We don't have to carry no weight—just tap the flow."

"Life's too short," D said, sounding as final as a coffin closing. "I'm not getting my hands dirty. Neither are you. We can build D Security into a real business, Jeff. We can get out of entertainment and eventually provide guards for banks, malls, the works. Everybody these days is afraid of everybody else—fuck what the crime stats say. The whole world wants to feel safe and no one does. We just need to stay afloat to capitalize on it. Taxing drug dealers will just pull us down."

Jeff, to D's surprise, just sat back and let him talk. When D was through, his friend just sighed. "Sorry I brought it up, D," Jeff said. "I know how you feel about being safe and all that." Jeff was going to let it drop, but then anger flashed in his pale blue eyes and his voice filled with jailhouse passion. "But if we really need to get a little dirty to stay in business . . . Don't be proud, D," he said. "I want to stay legal. But you and I both know not everybody legal is clean. Surviving is what it's really about."

"Living is the thing, Jeff," D countered. "Survival and living are not the same thing."

"The man in black wants to live? Then why do you dress like a motherfucking undertaker?" It was an old tease but one that Jeff never tired of. And D replied as he always did:

"This way I never have a problem matching."

"Whatever, D. I'm out." Jeff stood and put on a bloodred Philly 76ers baseball cap. "Yo, son, you hittin' Mercedez yet or are you planning to hit it?"

"Double no."

"But you know she's feelin' you?"

"And what about you? You're feelin' her, aren't you?"

His pale friend, going out the door with a thugged-out swagger, shouted over his shoulder, "Nigga, please!"

CHAPTER FIVE

THREE DAYS AFTER the Knicks game, D was chilling at Emily's Tea Party without Emily, who was home meeting a design deadline for Phat Farm. She would have been happy to know her boyfriend was watching her club for her, though not too thrilled with his companion. Her name was Luna and she was a long-limbed fashion stylist of indeterminate national origin with reddish hair. When D asked, "Did you say you were Irish and Cherokee or Vietnamese, Senegalese, and Spanish?" Luna's reply was, "Yes," which meant she either didn't understand his question due to the music or was not as swift as she was attractive. Either way, D left it at that. The only reason he didn't excuse himself was that he figured his potential client would be amused.

Ivy Greenwich slid into the club around 12:30 A.M., just as his assistant had said he would. He was alone, which was surprising, but otherwise this was that same commanding, cajoling, crisply dressed dude D had long admired from a distance. As D was admiring Ivy's beige suit and sky-blue silk shirt, instinct led the older man to kick game to Luna. After all, he was solo, which made him uncomfortable, and for a true club crawler, the night was young and tender.

Ivy worked the girl with more than just indiscriminate desire. Like most paid players, Ivy understood how to drop science about his bank without flatly stating, "I'm rich, baby." Like all old players, Ivy attempted this feat without revealing his age. Also like all old players, Ivy vainly believed he looked at least ten years younger than he was. A young player can ramble on about his virility, and his presence will do the rest. An old player must make it plain that his juice, when properly squeezed, can do wonders for worthy females.

So, before D's conversation with Ivy began, he kicked game to Luna with all the guile you'd expect of a white-Negro Mack Daddy. With his largeness established at the table and Luna vaguely smitten, Ivy finally focused on D. "I like the crowd here," he began. "It's a hip thing, but it's a pop thing too."

"Emily," D answered, "will be flattered you said that." Seizing the moment to sound sage, D replied, "Hip black shit becomes pop over time. Something starts underground. Something or someone introduces it outside the core audience and from there it eventually penetrates mall America."

"I agree," Ivy said, as if he were endorsing D for president. "That's my problem now. I have something that's already mall America, but it wants to be hip."

"You talking about Bridgette Haze?"

"I am, indeed. When I signed her, she was fifteen, had played *Annie* in six productions, and just wanted to be the queen of every mall and state fair in America. I had Debbie Gibson for the new millennium. Not as suggestive as Britney, not as nasty as Janet. Kinda Olsen twins, you know. Sweet, cute, fun, and sang well enough. Two CDs, three major tours, fifty fan websites, one Christmas special, and a Sprite campaign later, she's twenty-one and wants to move to New York and become the white Mary J. Blige. What do you think of that?"

"Well, Ivy, I'm no expert," D said, "but from what I've seen, that can't be done with a hard sell. You can't just drop a load of money, make a few videos, and expect tastemakers to respect her. You got to reposition her by giving her some edge."

Ivy nodded and said, "I know. Let people know she dislikes certain things and loves others. Let her be seen wearing the right designers. To be pop, you've got to be fuzzy, you know, but to grow and develop, you have to redefine that fuzziness so that you're shifting as the culture shifts. Mary J. Blige used to be too edgy for mass America—now she's Aretha Franklin for people who don't know any better. Bridge could become something new—but it has to be an evolution, not a revolution."

"Excuse me." It was Luna, who'd fallen silent during the talk. She stood up and announced, "I'm gonna go dance."

"Really?" Ivy said. "Well, save one for me. I'm coming out there after ya."

"I'll be out there then, waiting," she said, clearly not expecting Ivy to come. With a lecherous grin, he watched her multiculti body sashay away.

"Lovely young lady," he said, and then shifted gears. "We

have a problem, D." His southern-by-way-of-Brooklyn voice emphasized the word *we*.

"This Bridgette Haze thing isn't a problem for me," D replied, confused at where this was going.

"No, I'm talking about Night. You told me you were tight with him. I checked up and found out that was true, that you're like my client's guardian angel. So what I'm about to say to you is between friends, right?"

"Okay, what's going on?" D said with deceptive calm. "I haven't heard from Night in a week and that's unusual."

"He was kidnapped, D. He and his girlfriend were on the way into the city from Kennedy after coming in from Atlanta. They want two hundred thousand in hundred-dollar bills to be delivered on Sunday, or they'll kill Night."

"What do the police think?"

"The police don't know," Ivy said, clearly embarrassed. "The FBI doesn't know. No one knows except some people in my organization and now you."

"Why is that?"

"If it gets out that kidnappers snatched Night, I believe it'll set off a rash of copycat crimes. People these days are followers. Snatch a kid, drop a bomb, or whatever, and ten other people have set up websites about it and made some asshole a minor celebrity. I'm not allowing the crooks or the FBI to hype this out of proportion. I just need someone I can trust to deliver the money and receive Night. After it's done, then I'll bring in the bulls."

"I'm not sure that's the right call, Ivy."

"It's my money they want, so it's my call. Look, D, I saw

you handle yourself with that egoed-out NBA player. You are the perfect person to handle this because you're cool under pressure and you care about Night. Plus I'll pay you ten Gs. What do you say?"

In the big scheme of things, ten thousand dollars wasn't much, but it would still cover a multitude of bills. "Of course I'll do it," D answered, "but again, I gotta say I'm not sure this is the right call."

Ivy was about to say something when he started coughing—a deep, hacking ejaculation that seemed contemptuous of his aging body. After struggling to suppress the cough, Ivy excused himself and wobbled toward the restroom. D now had a throbbing headache and a stirring in his stomach. Night was like a little brother to him, someone to protect and guide and laugh with. He'd looked out for him many times, but this was another level of risk. It made D queasy. It made him re-member.

When Ivy reappeared, the aging mogul looked refreshed. His voice sounded stronger and there was new color in his cheeks. Strong chemicals were at work. "Where's Luna?" he asked, as if he wanted to banish his short illness from D's memory.

"Remember," D said as he surveyed the man, "she went dancing."

"I'm a great dancer," Ivy said as he sat back down. D saw that his eyes had a glowing, faraway look. "From the camel walk to the Bankhead bounce, I've danced many a woman right into my bed."

D looked at Ivy oddly and was trying desperately not to

laugh at his new meal ticket's childish boasting. The strain was showing on his face. "D," Ivy said, "I'll bet you one hundred dollars I can dance that exotic young lady—"

"Luna."

"Yeah. That I can dance Luna right into my bed."

"Like you said, it's your money, Ivy, and you've got a lot more of it than I do. In other words, I've seen how you roll, so I'm not betting against you."

"I like you, D," he said. "You speak your mind when you need to and you kiss ass when it won't hurt." He winked at D. "Help me get Night back on the DL and there's no telling what we'll work on," he said conspiratorially. The two men shook hands, and then the well-medicated Ivy strode toward the dance floor in search of Luna.

Heading to the manger's office and Chester Himes's autobiography, D spotted the same young, light-skinned black man who had been clocking him the week before, now leaning against the bar and talking to two other men. They were looking out at the dance floor where Ivy was dancing with all the confidence of an unself-conscious fool. Bald head. Small, dark eyes slanted like those of the model Tyson Beckford. Lips had a petulant, know-it-all curl. He caught D glancing his way and turned to face the bar.

D was contemplating going over to him when a small hand grabbed a big hunk of his ass. "What are you doing here, Emily? Did you finish the designs?"

"I needed a break," she replied, "and what better one than my party."

"I hear that," D said. Then he leaned over and hugged

her deeply, craving some physical affection. He was still shaken by Ivy's revelation.

"I must come late more often, my lovely. You aren't usually this forthcoming with the public displays."

"I need you to tonight, Emily," D whispered in her ear.

"Oh, my," she said. "I do have a deadline after all, but I'll try to squeeze you in."

Sometime just before the crack of dawn, D was wiggling like an eel out of water. For the first time in a half hour, his eyes looked up from Emily's yellow visage and toward the bedpost he held with his left hand. "AHHHHHHH!" His shout of pleasure went on so long it drowned out the Toni Braxton oldie on the radio. Emily didn't seem to mind. She just gazed at him, grinning like a bookworm acing a spelling bee.

His right hand let loose of Emily's wet behind and flopped down on the bed, tired from alternating squeezes and caresses. His back had arched like a cat's when he came. Now, as his cry died, D lowered himself atop her. For a moment, D shut his eyes. Blissful but still very aware, D reached down and slowly eased himself out of Emily, grabbing the ends of the two condoms he wore and removing himself from her in an orderly fashion. It had taken months for him to get used to wearing these layers of latex, and even now, aided by a liberal sprinkling of K-Y jelly and a very careful entry, he felt guilty coming inside Emily. It was dangerous for her, but she wanted to feel him, and every now and then, his male needs overwhelmed his sense of safety. Here he was protecting people for a living and yet he regularly put Emily in mortal danger.

Still, once he'd rolled over and placed the two condoms in a tissue, D lay there wondering how Emily had gotten so good. Was I that good a teacher? he thought, or had Emily been doing extra homework?

"D, how are you?"

"Oh, I'm good, baby. I'm always good with you."

"No." She was insistent. "How are you?"

Now D opened his eyes. Emily's head rested in her hand and loomed over him. "You think much about your family?"

"Sweetcakes, why are we gonna have this conversation now?"

"Because you never talk about them. I think that maybe that's why you're so distant."

"Emily," he said sternly, trying to cut this convo short. "I'm fine. I've dealt with it, okay?"

"But you being an only child. I think—"

"Emily." He spoke in a quiet, hushing tone. "Baby. Thank you so much for caring. No one else does, you know. I mean, you have been so understanding about all my issues. In my heart I know that you care about what I'm thinking and how I feel, but now, while I feel so satisfied, is not the time to talk about this."

D reached down and took Emily's breasts in his hands, rubbing his palms against her nipples, slowly, and licked the sweat off her neck and shoulders. "Are you sore?" he whispered.

"No," she whispered back, her mouth on his ear. "Not if you aren't."

Now they were back in a groove and, for the time being, D's lies were obscured by passion. He moved one large hand to her thigh and the other under the bed. He pulled out her mechanical toy and laid it on the bed next to her as he kissed her neck, lips, and face. After she put up with his condoms, he owed her. As he moved his face down her belly and one hand squeezed her nipples, D clicked on her sex toy. Emily began to breathe heavily. He smiled as he reached her belly button.

CHAPTER SIX

THE LAST TIME D had sat on a bench in Union Square Park it was a different time of year and a different time of day but otherwise, the circumstances were sadly similar. In both cases he was holding ransom money to be delivered to kidnappers. In both cases his friend Night was intimately involved. In both cases members of D Security were scattered around the park to provide backup. That day, a few years ago, when Night was still a gigolo and D had just started his company, D had been sitting next to Beth Ann waiting to spring a trap on a trio of menacing Israeli drug dealers and Night had been the reluctant middle man on the deal. That had been an emotionally tangled scenario involving love denied, money owed, Ecstasy sold, and lots of thwarted passion. In a way, today's transaction would be a lot cleaner. I give you cash—you give me missing R&B singer.

But that last time, D had had official backup. The police had been kept out of this one, and he still worried that would be a terrible mistake. D absently rubbed the black Nike gym bag slung over his shoulder as he watched a young Puerto Rican nanny pushing a little white boy in a stroller. Then he heard the rumble of multiple motorcycle engines. He looked behind him and saw a fleet of motorcycles coming across West Sixteenth Street. Turning back around he saw another squad rolling down from Park Avenue South. Suzukis, Kawasakis, and Hondas rolled up over the sidewalk and up walk ramps into Union Square, sending pedestrians and birds scattering. The nanny grabbed the child in her arms and cradled him to her body. D stood up and stood straight with his arms folded across his chest. People ran. There was much screaming, though most of it was drowned out by the roar of fifteen bikes. D just stood and waited. They had to be coming for him.

A lime-green Suzuki came around the curb from the left, and a black bike rolled toward him from the right. They both stopped on a dime in front of the impassive black man. The rider on the black bike pointed to the lime-green one and, in a tough, woman's voice, ordered D to "Get on that bike!"

"Where's Night?" D asked, and then tapped the Nike bag.

"Get on his bike!" she ordered again. The rider on the green bike now sat with his arms folded, parodying D's stance and radiating his own aura of cocky confidence. In the distance the sound of police cars could be heard. Already members of this bike posse were scattering, a few heading in the direction of the Thirteenth Precinct, on Twenty-first Street, to create a diversion.

"This is your last chance!" the woman on the black bike screamed. She looked over to the man on the lime-green bike.

He nodded, and without another word, she kicked off her engine and sped toward Fourteenth Street. The remaining biker turned his ride sideways and gunned his engine. D knew this was it. He hopped on the back of the bike, put his arms around the driver's waist, and suddenly found himself blazing down the steps in front of Fourteenth Street and right into Broadway's narrow lower Manhattan corridor.

"Where are we going?" D shouted gamely into the ear of his silent driver, but he just buzzed down into the Village without a word. Behind them he heard the whine of sirens and the dirty rumble of motorcycles amid the city's regular traffic chatter. Somehow they managed never to stop at a light, busting through intersections and just missing cars like a sprinter over hurdles. D felt as if he'd left his stomach back on that park bench and was quite amazed he hadn't tossed his lunch up on some unsuspecting pedestrian. The bike made a quick, illegal turn at Prince, made a rapid series of turns on Crosby and then Broome, and, suddenly, they were on the bargain-shopping strip on Delancey Street headed right for the Williamsburg Bridge. From all sides bikes appeared, like fighter planes returning to formation. Except this was Manhattan, not the wide blue yonder, so every pothole and bump vibrated through the bike and right into D's tightly clenched butt. He was contemplating whether he would throw up or shit first when the lady in black rolled up on their right. Despite the collective bike roar, D swore he could hear her laughter when she saw his face.

They all actually stopped at the last light before the bridge. The lady in black looked around to inspect her troops. She gestured "okay" to D's driver. The light turned green and they all blasted off onto the Williamsburg Bridge. Under other circumstances, the ride over the bridge could have been fun. The wind in your face. The view of the city. The power of the engine between your thighs. But D was an uneasy rider being taken who knows where for what dubious purpose. D didn't think they'd kill him. They could have run him over in Union Square and jacked the cash. D was sure he'd be alive at the end of this wild ride, but he sure didn't think he'd be healthy.

Once in Brooklyn, the bikes scattered again, most of them disappearing down several streets until all but the lady in black and the lime-green driver had split off. Driving in tandem and stopping at all traffic lights, the duo negotiated the journey from Williamsburg, around the Brooklyn Navy Yard, and into DUMBO. D had grown up in the BK but had never really spent any time in the area between the Brooklyn and Manhattan bridges. D tried to note the street signs but wasn't sure they'd mean anything later.

Just a block from the waterfront, they came to a big, brown-brick warehouse. In front of a green door, Night and Tandi sat blindfolded with blue bandanas tight around their heads. They were handcuffed to each other and to a door handle. D's driver stopped in front of the pair and, without any urging, D hopped off and went over to his friend. D pulled off the bandana and asked the obvious questions. As Night said he was all right, D noted that his eyes were red and glazed, like those of a man who'd been toking some hellaciously strong chronic. Tandi possessed the same Buddha-blessed look with her blindfold off. When D turned around, he saw that the lady in black was holding a Desert Eagle automatic. "The money," she said crisply.

"The key," he replied.

The lime-green biker reached into his jacket and pulled out a small key. D took the Nike bag from around his neck and walked it over to the lady in black. He tried to peer under her visor. If Night and Tandi had not been behind him, D would have snatched the helmet right off her head and punched her lights out. Instead, he noticed she wore a white turtleneck, which covered her skin. D thought she was black, but she could just as easily have had the voice of a white girl who'd grown up around black folks.

She snatched the bag out of his hands, looked inside, and did a quick count. Once satisfied, she nodded to her teammate, and the lime-green driver tossed the keys up in the air. By the time they'd come down and D had turned to free Night and Tandi, the engines of the kidnappers' bikes were roaring. They took off in opposite directions. D's eyes followed the lime-green driver down the street. He smiled. I think I know you, motherfucker, D thought. I bet it's you.

That evening, the light disappeared softly over Manhattan. From Night's apartment in Trump Plaza, Central Park spread out green and fluffy with the beige and gray stone structures of Fifth Avenue rising behind it like thick candles on a lovely, dark, lime-flavored cake. D gazed out at this gorgeous scene but couldn't really appreciate it. It wasn't simply that he'd stood there before (he had, and often), but that the sight was no diversion from the shouting going on behind him.

"D, man," Night pleaded, "come over here and talk some sense to Ivy!"

On either end of a cushy vanilla-colored couch sat Ivy, in black velour Sean Jean warm-ups, and Night, in a number 34 Boston Celtics white and green basketball jersey and black shorts. Ivy was rolling a fat Philly blunt as Night gestured and spoke. "Tell him we need to call the police and let them know how this went down. We can't let them get away with this."

"And what makes you think the cops would catch them?" Ivy said. He licked the tobacco leaf lovingly, rolled it around in his palm, and passed it over to his client. "Sure," Ivy continued, "if we brought in the FBI, maybe, they could run these kids down. But I believe if word got out that you had been snatched, it would set off a whole chain reaction of copycat jacks. Nobody has any original ideas anymore. You do something foul; five other people wanna get in at the same party. You jack a beat; somebody jacks the same beat. You snatch a child; somebody else snatches a child. If that started happening in show business, it could get out of hand quick, fast, and in a hurry."

Night puffed on the Philly, reflecting on Ivy's words. He wasn't convinced of Ivy's logic, but then Ivy was THE MAN—he had years of experience and Night had only been in this game a minute. He didn't necessarily want to butt heads with the man who'd put him on. D sat down quietly on the love seat across from the couch, observing his old friend and current employer, trying to balance his integrity with his financial need.

"C'mon, D, what you think, dog?"

"Ivy," D asked, "did you have any indication that this might happen?"

"Of course," Ivy said dismissively. "I get messages all the time that a bunch of motorcyclists are gonna kidnap one of my acts."

D, ignoring Ivy's sarcasm, pressed on: "You're telling me your office doesn't receive any threats against your acts?"

"No," he replied, "I'm not telling you that. There are a lot of crazies out there, D. You probably know that better than I do."

"So you ignore them?"

"Listen," Ivy said, "we shouldn't have this conversation in front of Night."

"And why's that?" Night wondered.

"I don't want you getting paranoid. You need to be focused on singing and performing and being a sex symbol. That's a full-time job, as you've discovered."

Night said, "So these guys get away with snatching my ass and damn near blowing out my eardrums?"

"No. We will eventually bring this to the attention of the police. But if it gets out there too early, as police investigations involving celebrities always do, it disrupts what we're building. You are a star, not a victim, and I don't want the media viewing you that way."

Night agreed with that, nodding as he pulled harder on the blunt. He held on to the joint, studied it in his hands a moment, and then sucked again. He didn't offer a hit to either of his companions.

"Besides," Ivy said, "I have a better idea."

Night's cell played the melody to Marvin Gaye's "What's Going On," and he picked it up from under his bare feet. "Hey," he said, and from the tone of his voice it was clear Tandi was on the line. "Yeah, yeah," he said, then stood and retired to his bedroom with the cell to his ear and the Philly in his other hand.

"You're holding back, Ivy," D said once Night was out of earshot.

"A little," Ivy admitted. "I'd gotten a couple of calls on my cell that caught my attention and they caught my attention because they had my cell number." He paused, measuring D a moment. "You still think there's some connection between this guy who hangs out at Emily's Tea Party and the guy you rode with."

"Yeah, there was just something about how he carried himself. The shape of his body. I watch people all the time to see who will and won't cause trouble, and he struck me as trouble. I've already let all my people know that if he shows up at any place we do security to let me know."

"Okay," Ivy said, leaning forward. "I got a proposition for you. I want you to provide some bodyguards for Night. They'll be on twenty-four-hour call."

"Definitely doable."

"And I want you to go look for that guy. Obviously, keep your eye out at clubs but, maybe, check out any bike clubs."

"I'm not a detective, Ivy. That's a different job."

"Shit, your name is Hunter," he said, laughing. "Don't be reluctant. A businessman knows when it's time to expand his services and his portfolio."

"I don't know," D said in reply.

"I'll pay you twenty-five thousand dollars in cash—off the books, tax free—to just go around and ask questions." Ivy began rolling another Philly. "You can use your team to do that, but I have a special cake gig for you, D."

"Cake gig?"

"Yeah, nothing but icing and vanilla flavor."

"Okay," D said. "What is it?"

"It's just hanging out with a sweet young lady for a couple of months." Ivy turned his attention to wrapping the marijuana inside the Philly blunt tobacco and then rolling it between his palms.

"I'm not a baby-sitter, Ivy."

"Don't worry, D. She doesn't wear diapers. It just looks like she does."

The manager lit the Philly, took a hit, and leaned back with a smile.

"Green lights as far as the eye can see!" Night walked back into the room singing the lyrics to the song. "The whole time those motherfuckers just played that song twenty-four-seven—pumping it into the room they held me in. Don't know what it was supposed to mean, but I'm sure it meant something." Night started singing again as he plopped back down onto the sofa.

"I remember it from when I was a kid," D said. "My mother used to listen to it all the time. 'Green Lights' by Adrian Dukes. It was probably her favorite song." D turned to the suddenly silent Ivy. "You used to manage Adrian Dukes. Do you think there's some connection?"

"Forget it," Ivy advised. "It was some old cut they got off some Rhino compilation. They picked out some old shit just to fuck with Night." Ivy sat up and passed the Philly to D. "It's a stupid joke, that's all." D took a hit and then passed the Philly to Night.

"Green lights," Night sang. "Green motherfucking lights." Then he took another hit and laid his head back.

After leaving Night's apartment, D went downtown to his office to begin preparing for D Security's move into body-guard work and private investigation. It was an organic shift, one D had wanted to do in a year or so when the company was on firmer financial footing. Yet here was an opportunity, a sad one since it was caused by a friend's misfortune, but one he'd be a fool not to take advantage of. After talking with Jeff about deployment and looking through his papers to judge the insurance and legal ramifications, D exited 580 Broadway while debating whether to get something to eat or cab it up to his apartment. D's preoccupied mind was why he was so surprised when two white males in Today's Man suits exited a car and flashed badges.

"What's this about?" D shouted as he was cuffed and stuffed into the backseat. Detective Bernard Bernstein, a ro-tund man with a puffy, pink face, spoke to D in a high-pitched bureaucratic voice:

"A friend in Brooklyn wants to see you. He knows you've been busy, so he figured you'd appreciate a lift."

Now D got it and asked casually, "Do I really need the cuffs?"

"Well," Bernstein replied, "it'll make us look good when we bring you in."

"Come on," D replied.

"Sorry," Bernstein said back, "but to be honest, he told us to cuff you."

D rolled his eyes and tried to make himself comfortable on the hard seat. He put his head on his chest and dozed off and didn't really wake up until he was seated inside the detectives' room in a police precinct in Brownsville, Brooklyn. D cooled his heels by watching bored cops, fearful parents, and the sullen poses of teenagers fronting lethal minds.

"Come with me." Bernstein lifted D out of the chair and moved him along as a butcher does a rack of beef. Inside an office, looking comfortable behind a battered metal desk, with a pipe in one hand, a phone in the other, and Jesus on the cross on the wall behind him, Detective Tyrone Williams, aka Fly Ty, glared at D, who returned the favor. The detective motioned with his head and Bernstein deposited D in a metal straight-backed chair.

Bernstein uncuffed D and exited wordlessly as Williams said into the phone, "No, I haven't yet interrogated the witness, but I will soon." A pause. "Oh, yes, he'll cooperate." A pause. "Yes, I'll get back to you presently." Williams shook his woolly walnut head as he hung up.

"Now, why did you tell me to beep you all those many months ago," he began roughly, "when, young man, you had no intention of ever returning my pages?"

"I got busy," D said with attitude. "When did you get your own office?"

"See," the detective continued in his same tough tone, "the things you learn when you communicate with your relatives."

D corrected him. "We're not blood, Fly Ty."

He corrected D. "One, your mother made me your god-father. Two, don't call me that again. It's Detective or Tyrone and nothing else or I'll lock up your all-black-wearing ass."

D countered, "You suggested becoming my godfather. It wasn't even her idea."

Williams put a fresh match to his pipe and came back with his all-purpose reply: "Jesus Christ brought us together, Dervin."

"It's D, Fly Ty."

"D. Okay," he said, grinning.

Bernstein opened the door. "Excuse me, Detective. We think we got the perp in the Tapley shooting. Anderson is with him in interview room C."

"Tell him to start without me." Williams stood up. His belly, once flat and firm, now round and ample, pressed against his white shirt and tasteful blue- and gold-speckled tie. Not as slick as he used to be, D mused, but still better put together than his coworkers. When Williams sat on the front of the desk, D noticed his Italian loafers. D half smiled, remembering how Fly Ty's good taste always made his over-bearing nature easier to take.

"Dervin Hunter, you are running away from your past. I understand that better than anybody except you and your mother. I even respect it 'cause you've been so successful in doing it. A lot of people try and can't. To a degree you've managed to do it. I guess my role in your life is to bring you back to it every now and then."

"Your role?" D snorted. "Listen, I never asked you for shit.

You started coming over. You reached out to me and I took what I could use. But my life is my life."

"To a degree you're right. But—"

"But what?"

"I promised your mother a long time ago I'd watch out for you." Williams spoke, as always, quite earnestly, but D was determined not to be swayed.

So D said, "Please, man," and tuned to gaze out of the room's dirt-smudged window. Through it he could see the Tilden projects a few blocks away.

"Okay," Fly Ty agreed. "You're a grown man. My promise probably means nothing to you right now."

"Good guess, money."

Williams had been interrogating arrogant young men for years, so D's attitude meant nothing to him. It just led him to shift gears. "So let's talk about why you're here." He leaned back and grabbed a police report, which he then offered to D, who, now looking at Williams, took and opened.

There was one eyewitness account of a fleet of motorcycles surrounding a Jeep on the Belt Parkway about a week ago. There were several reports about the bikes in Union Square, the mad dash through the Village and SoHo, and the journey over the Williamsburg Bridge. Makes, models, and a couple of license plate numbers were recorded. Most telling for D, there was a color photo, apparently taken by an innocent bystander with a disposable camera, of D holding on for dear life to the waist of the biker in lime green.

"I believe that's you, Dervin."

"Could be," D replied. "I'm not sure."

"You two sure do look comfortable." Williams chuckled at his own joke. "All this material came my way because the original crime, whatever it was, apparently happened in Brooklyn and, apparently, ended in Brooklyn. It looks to me like someone was kidnapped and that you, Dervin, delivered the ransom money. I'm not sure who was kidnapped, but considering your associations, I figure it was someone in the entertainment business."

"Your guess is as good as mine, Detective," D said, giving Fly Ty some slight respect for his instincts and investigative skills. Williams pulled another file off his desk. He took the first out of D's hands and replaced it with the second.

"Somehow, I believe Ivy Greenwich is involved."

"Why do you say that?"

"Look at the file."

This file wasn't as full. It contained reports of incidents of reported threats against various recording acts—all of whom were somehow associated with Ivy. There was even a missing person's report filed by Tandi Lincoln's father. He'd later called in to report her return—with no explanation. D read them over quickly and observed, "None of this seems to involve Ivy."

"On the contrary, Dervin, they all do," he said, "yet neither he nor his office has contacted the police about any of this activity. We learned about all this via the artists themselves, their families, or friends. Looks to me like he's trying to avoid a real investigation of any of this. What do you think?"

"I don't think anything, Fly Ty. I barely know Ivy. I know that Night just came home from a road trip and I assumed Tandi was with him. That's it. That's all I can say."

Williams just looked at him a moment and then removed the file from D's hand. "Okay," he said. "Be that way now. But you'll come to me soon. I know that and so do you." He sat back behind his desk and lit his pipe. "So what about your mother getting married?"

"It's her life."

"You know this cat?"

"Not really."

"Do you want me to look into him? I could."

D got up out of the chair and put his hands on Williams's desk. "You had your chance." D leaned in and looked the graying man in the eyes. "It didn't work out. Maybe, at the time, it couldn't work out. Buy yourself a tux—I know it'll be a nice one—and come to the wedding. That's all you need to do."

"Dervin, I've known you since you were a child. I know how you think. You think this marriage is a joke, just like—"

D's laugh made him stop.

"What?"

"This," D responded, "is not about you. It's about my mother being happy. End of story. Whatever feelings you have for my mother or about her marriage, don't throw them on me." There was no way D was going to give Fly Ty the satisfaction of knowing he, too, felt uneasy about his mother's marriage. It would have made the detective feel good, something D tried to avoid at all costs. "You had your chance back in the day, Fly Ty. Move the fuck on."

Williams got up and got right into the younger, bigger man's face without a trace of fear.

"Boy, I will put my foot so far up your ass I'll be walking on your lips, so watch what you say to me. Do you understand?"

"Yes," D said calmly. "I do."

D turned to leave. From behind him Fly Ty said, "God bless you, Dervin," as harshly as that phrase can sound.

Outside Precinct 77, Dervin found himself back on the streets of Brownsville, a place he had once called home. Twenty-first-century Brownsville was in much better shape than the neighborhood that had molded him. Sure, tall, ugly apartment-style public housing and many decayed, ill-managed tenements from Word War II still dominated the area. Public housing, aka "the projects," were still hemor-rhoids on the ass of mankind—ghettos in the sky that crushed the spirits of generations of poor folk. The genius idea of blowing up dilapidated projects, something that had been happening around the country since the eighties, had not yet been accepted in New York.

At least the tenements were gradually disappearing. In their place, tiny, inexpensive two-story homes with waist-high fences, narrow driveways, and compact lawns were appearing. By no means palatial, these houses nonetheless gave people a sense of ownership and pride. There was even more recreation than before. Over on Powell, where a bar-bershop and an Arab-run grocery store had once anchored a block of crumbling gray buildings, there was now a baseball diamond and real grass. The people who resided in the Ville were still the working poor, but there was a fresh sense of possibility in this part of New York so very far from "the city."

Despite the new life in Brownsville, D still carried the burden of the old one. For him, pain walked on these streets like the Devil in the blues song. Instead of air, D breathed in the panicky scent of evil. D walked down Livonia Avenue, his personal crossroads, where the elevated IRT subway put a ceiling on the sky and he'd barely survived his childhood.

While D strode Livonia with a fake bop, his eyes greeted every corner with barely suppressed anxiety. Brownsville wasn't his world anymore, but then D had never owned the Ville. In fact the Ville owed him a debt it would never repay.

Unconsciously, he headed straight toward the center stage of his nightmares—the corner of Livonia and Stone (now Mother Gaston Boulevard), where the Samuel J. Tilden projects began and his youth ended. Up in 315 Livonia, apartment 6C, with its beautiful view of the parking lot, where the train rolls by like clockwork, was where the Hunter family used to live. His father. His mother. His brothers and D.

He stood on the nondescript corner of that poor and obscure community and listened as the elevated IRT train rolled over, toward Manhattan. He stood there and started crying. He didn't wipe the tears at first. They just rolled down his wide, brown cheeks and fell onto his black shirt and leather jacket. A Kawasaki Ninja motorcycle came blazing down the street. A young black man in a garish, multicolored top and pants rolled by, the roar of his engine replacing the sound of the train in D's ears. He wiped his tears with his sleeve, gathered himself, and lumbered down toward Rock-away Avenue and the subway station. Pain was useful, he'd learned. But only if you could turn it into something, only if you could help someone. Time to do that, D told himself. Time to give someone the illusion of safety.

CHAPTER SEVEN

PASTIS IS A FANCY French bistro in what used to be known as the Meatpacking District, below Fourteenth Street and west of Ninth Avenue. There are still a few remaining rack 'em and pack 'em enterprises located there, but now they vie with clubs (Lotus), designers (Alexander McQueen), and art galleries for the area's soul. Pastis is just far enough away from the subway and street traffic of the city that celebrities and semicelebrities stop by all the time to see one another and munch on the well-prepared cuisine. Plus, the kitchen stays open late.

Around 11:00 P.M., D entered and walked past the long, boisterous bar and the crowded tables packed tight on the white-and-black-tiled floor over to the host stand under the archway leading to the main dining room. Eden, a tall, raspy-voiced bottle blonde with a punky cut and squinty eyes, gave D the once-over. Then he kissed both her cheeks and told her who he was meeting.

"Oh, she's here," Eden said with a frown, "but come with

me anyway." Eden guided him down the far aisle, past the restroom and Monica Lewinsky, who was laughing loudly at a female pal's story, to a large corner table. Ivy sat next to Bridgette Haze, who was smaller than D had imagined and, in her own sharp-featured way, more beautiful, too. That didn't mean she looked special, though. She could have been any of the million or so adorable little girls who are guided by ambitious, needy parents into talent shows, beauty pageants, and hours of tap and vocal lessons. From the time she popped out of the womb with her big blues and precocious laugh, on through the day she performed her mother's favorite song, "You Light Up My Life," at the first-grade talent show, little Bridgette had brought all these expectations on herself. At some point, around age seven, she'd accepted her status as (family) star and worked to live up to the role in which biology had cast her. Bridgette Haze was barely twenty-one but was a veteran at the fame game. She was no different from the millions who wanted the keys to the kingdom—the only thing that set her apart was that she had, against all odds, unlocked the door.

On the other side of Bridgette was a woman with brunette hair who looked like Bridgette, but slightly older, rounder, and sadder, despite the smile she aimed D's way. Next to her was Bee Cole, looking poised and paid and ready for anything. Squeezed next to her was Bridgette's publicist, a lanky, attractive black man in his mid-thirties named Rodney Hampton. He had sun-kissed skin, short hair, and an expensive beige shirt. At the corner nearest D, sizing him up with an unappreciative eye, was a burly white man with badly dyed blond hair, piled with mousse for that spiky white-boy style, Oakley shades, and an awful brown leather biker jacket, which D assumed was supposed to make him look tough.

"A cute guy can't get to be a hot guy," Bridgette was saying to Bee, "but a hot guy can fall back down to be a cute guy."

"Yes," Bee replied, "a hot guy can be cute if he's too boring or stupid. But an interesting guy can become hot if he's got some conversation and style."

"I agree," the singer said, then she turned and looked at D and then at Ivy, saying with her eyes, "Who's this?"

"Bridgette," Ivy said, "this is the man I spoke to you about. D Hunter."

"Sounds like a video-game character," she observed with a giggle. The woman sitting next to Bridgette smiled indulgently at her sister's joke and continued surveying D from head to toe.

"No, I'm a real guy," he responded, "though I do play video games." D actually hated PlayStation and its ilk but figured Bridgette probably didn't, so a little lie seemed in order. Ivy introduced D to the table. The woman with the appraising eye was Jen, or Jennifer Haze, four years older than her star sister and attractive whereas little sis was beautiful— same features but everything was just a little too far apart or a little too close together, just centimeters away from being fine. She owned a travel agency back in Virginia Beach that existed primarily off tidbits from her sister's table.

D knew Bee, of course. In fact, he'd have to have a serious talk with her at some point about the incident at Emily's Tea Party. At the corner was Hubert Humpries, Bridgette's longtime flunky-bodyguard-valet. Just over thirty, beefy, and decidedly country, Hubert was close to Bridgette's father, a football coach in Virginia, and had been designated the parents' spy, who kept them up on her moves and mood. D didn't know much of this when he sat down, but by midnight he'd either been told all this backstory or deduced it from the conversation.

"Tell us about yourself, D," Jen said, as plates of strawberry shortcake were delivered to the table.

"What would you like to know?" he replied, volleying her question back and glancing at Bridgette, knowing instinctively that big sister was speaking for little sis. Star etiquette dictated that a surrogate would ask all the potentially embarrassing little questions the star wanted answered.

"I've briefed everyone on your professional background, D," Ivy interjected. "I think Jen just wants to get a better sense of your personal background."

"That's right, D, let's get personal." It was Bee doing her Bee thing.

"Sure," he replied, and rather pat, gave the table his standard bio: born an only child in da BK to a working-class family of small means on the nicest block in the ghetto; attended St. John's University, majoring in criminal justice but, due to his father's death, left school early and started gigging as a bouncer at various clubs, which eventually led to his opening D Security. The ladies seemed impressed or, at least, comfortable with D's neat little fairy tale until Hubert, who'd been quiet during D's talk, asked, "So when did you get out of the joint?"

"Excuse me?"

"When'd you get out 'da joint?" Hubert said in a faux black accent. "Guys like you work the door at clubs 'cause you're big, got a record, and can't get a job doing anything else. Well, you better come clean, because we can't have any ex-cons hanging around. I don't care what her manager thinks about having some New York dawg watch her back up here. You probably got some dead homies—"

"Excuse me?"

"What, bro, you can't hear? I said dead—"

Yeah, it had been a rough day, but this was a job interview. So there was no reason for D to react violently to Hubert's silly speculation. Without thinking but with incredible physical calculation, D leaned over and pinned the country boy's arms to the table and leaned his face close to his accuser. "For the record," he said in a hoarse whisper, "I have never been in jail, dog, but I do know people who have. Some of them are friends of mine. And I have some dead homies, too. None of it is at all funny to me. If I was you, I wouldn't joke about it."

D pushed Hubert back into his seat and turned toward Ivy and Bridgette. "I should go now," he said. Everybody just stared at D, even Hubert, who was stunned by the swiftness and soft ferocity of D's action. "Yeah," D said absently. "I should go." Embarrassed by his anger and how easily a jealous man's words could sting, D knew he'd blown this gig, for both himself and his employees. Just as he had that night at Emily's Tea Party, he'd shown a very short fuse. He wondered if it was some new reaction to his HIV medication.

Were the meds altering his behavior? Perhaps he needed to change his dosage. He was rising out of his seat when Bridgette grabbed his right arm.

"I need to go to the restroom," she said. "D, why don't you make sure I get there safe." D really wanted to go, but the small white hand wouldn't let go of his wrist. Even as Ivy slid out of his seat and Bridgette moved into the aisle, she maintained contact with D, locking him in place as securely as if he had on handcuffs. D turned and led the singer up the aisle, past a gawking Lewinsky, and into the restaurant's co-ed restroom. In the main area was a long white sink and, on either side, doors to Hers and His toilets. Instead of going through the Hers door, the singer moved over to the sink and began washing her hands.

"You're quite a dramatic man, D Hunter." D quickly apologized for his unprofessional behavior. "Hubert must have struck some kind of chord, huh? But that's not your fault. If my parents didn't insist, believe me, Hubert wouldn't be here. I'm told he's my father's second cousin but I just think he was inbred with a jackass." She began drying her hands. "So you didn't do a thing Hubert didn't deserve."

Two khaki-pants-and-blue-shirt types came in, loud and boisterous. They spotted Bridgette and were about to open their mouths when D stepped in front of her and gave them his well-practiced, highly intimidating glare of death. Reluctantly they walked through the His door with no comment.

"Hubert doesn't have that effect."

"It's just a trick," D replied. "I'm a regular David Blaine with my eyeballs."

"David Blaine kicked it to me one night in L.A.," she recalled, "but he's gone out with too many singers already, and card tricks don't impress me. " She moved closer to D. "Ivy wasn't sure you'd want this job. Who would, you know. 'Spoiled pop diva seeks summer rental of New York bodyguard.' I could have hired ex-Mossad or off-duty cops, but I don't like guns around me, or ugly men. I want to enjoy New York City. I want to taste all that flavor everyone talks about on their records. I want to make better music than I've ever made before. That's all. Just come hang with us tonight and see if you're comfortable."

"To be honest," D said, "it's really about you being comfortable. It's just a job for me. Either I can do it or not. My comfort is not an issue."

"Very pragmatic, D," she replied. "Okay. But you should know my sister thinks you're cute and she has very good taste."

It felt to D as if every eye in Pastis was on them as they exited the restroom. Who was this big black man with America's sweetheart and what were they doing in the restroom? Even their table companions were curious and/or stressed that some communication had gone down that they weren't privy to. Hubert stayed quiet, glowering at D when he had the heart to look over. Bee was awaiting a reply from Night, on her two-way, to her question: "Tell me everything about D Hunter." Jen Haze drank from a glass of merlot and observed D with interest, occasionally whispering things to her sister. Only Ivy seemed sanguine about D's presence, as if everything were fitting his design.

D looked out of the dining room toward the bar. He

smiled at Eden and then saw a stylish brown-skinned black woman in a white-and-green dress, wearing an iced-out cross around her neck, looking his way. She locked her brown eyes with D's, not flirtatiously but with a willful intensity that suggested familiarity and contempt. Then she turned away. Was that the pistol-packing lady on the bike? It felt like it, but there was no other evidence. Just a hard look from a brown lady.

As Bridgette, Ivy, and the others prepared to leave Pastis, D's eyes searched the tables for some indication of trouble. European art types talked about Damian Hirst's latest installation; a moody man shared vino with a dark, thick woman; sundry swells in finery enjoyed hearty late-night meals. Of course, they were all cracking occasional glances over at Bridgette Haze's table, looking for that observational tidbit that would fill out phone calls next week. D didn't detect any threat in the dining room. And the presence of that intense woman didn't, by itself, constitute a threat. She could have been just scouting the terrain—maybe she was scheming on Lewinsky.

Responding to a question from D, Ivy said, "We have an Escalade outside being driven by Tony from TZL." Tony was the owner and top driver of a celebrity limo company. Like D, Tony was another black man with a dream. He'd started his service highly undercapitalized four years earlier, his only asset being his credibility after five years of chauffeuring for others. Now he had a slew of big clients, including a contract with Ivy's company. Perhaps, if he'd been driving Night from JFK, the kidnapping might never have happened. In a crunch, Tony would keep a cool head. That would be a major plus if they had to dodge bikers on Broadway.

"Let Hubert go first," D said to Ivy, "and I'll take the rear." Ivy was pleased by the authority in D's voice. His outburst at Hubert had been disturbing, but Ivy had been around enough artists over the years to know the quality of performance wasn't predicated on mental stability. Besides, Ivy knew that the same dark, emotional brew that made D dangerous made him easier to control—should the need arise.

Outside the restaurant, a few paparazzi had gathered, as had a few hard-core autograph hounds with photos of Bridgette Haze. Stars like Bridgette rarely traveled unnoticed, which was why it was so difficult to keep them safe. It was one of the reasons D had been slow to move into this area of the business. It was hard to make quick, silent moves with them, which made them as vulnerable as a child walking to school. Fortunately, as D surveyed the streets, he sensed no danger. Hubert stood next to her as she signed autographs while moving toward their waiting car, the sign of a celebrity practiced in the art of career and security maintenance. D was watching Bridgette enter the Escalade when he heard the rumble of a motorcycle. The sound came from the right of Pastis. He and Ivy briefly locked eyes, and then D, like a ballet dancer, turned to his right and moved sideways to peer down the block. A single old-school Harley-Davidson rolled up the block with a middle-aged white male in a shining black helmet in command. D stared at him with a shark's dead eyes and then entered the Escalade. After exchanging greetings with D, Tony said, "Nice hog, huh?"

D agreed. "There's something comforting about that kind of bike."

The driver then turned to Ivy. "Where to now?"

"Take us to DJ Power."

An hour later Bridgette Haze was living a dream come true. She'd been nominated for a Grammy. She'd headlined arenas all across America. She'd bedded a couple of the hotties of the WB. But right now, in a Times Square studio (in the lobby of which Tupac had been shot all those years ago), Bridgette was feeling like Mary J. Blige. She was singing over a beat made by Power, whose gritty tracks had made him the truest hard-core producer since Premiere (or even better, Swizz Beats).

She stood with headphones on in the vocal booth. From where she stood Bridgette could survey her entourage. There were many of the usual faces: her manager, a scheming ancient-school man with crazy hair who was two seconds from being fired if he couldn't get her label behind this new direction; her sister, who sometimes felt like a much-needed security blanket and too often felt like a shadow lost in Bridgette's shade. The new faces were way more intriguing. Power, of course, was a gift from God. All those endless Swedish nights, cutting poppy tracks in Stockholm, had been profitable, but none of that music banged like Timbaland or the Neptunes. She'd enjoyed two CDs' worth of this, but now Bridgette's inner R&B diva was calling, and that bitch had to be satisfied.

Speaking of satisfaction, Bridgette gazed over at D Hunter, who sat in the back reading a paperback by some obscure writer named Chester Himes. While she'd loved R&B, Bridgette had been raised in Virginia Beach, thinking one day she'd scoop up Brad Pitt (fuck that *Friends* bitch!). But there was something comforting—and intimidating—about Mr. Hunter. She'd loved that he got up in Hubert's grill—he was a pain who still acted as if Bridgette were fifteen. She could see that D was a brooder, as if he were carrying some dark secret, which thrilled the lingering adolescent romantic in her. Most men she encountered talked too much, either about themselves (to impress her) or her (to kiss her ass). He didn't seem anxious to talk at all—a quality Bridgette had come to value in men. Let some other girls seek out men who could express their thoughts. Give her a guy who'd protect her and listen to her and regularly rock her world. Jen had nudged her under the table about D already—which could be good or bad. Jen was way more complicated than she was. You never quite knew where she would come from regarding men. A talk was in order.

"That's hot to death," Power enthused over the studio speakers. "Ain't nobody heard Bridgette Haze blow that! Let's try the second verse one more time, all right?"

"No problem," Bridgette replied.

New York, she thought as the beat dropped, is gonna be fun.

CHAPTER EIGHT

"**S**o you really know how to ride?"

"Son, I told you I could. I can't do that trick shit but I'ma learn, no doubt."

D had gotten to the office early to prepare for the big meeting with the D Security crew. He was to unveil the deal he'd cut with Ivy and how that would expand the company's services, their duties, and, happily, their paychecks. When he'd gotten off the elevator, he found Ray Ray sitting outside the D Security door nodding his head to the D.J. Clue mix tape in his CD player. The young man was looking for work.

"I'll follow a nigga. Collect money. Take a head out if I have to, but it's gonna be a legal gig," Ray Ray said earnestly, oblivious to the illegal nature of the activities he'd just volunteered himself for. "I'm not trying to go to jail, son. Fuck that."

D wanted to help the kid out but had no ideas for his would-be protégé until he glanced at the copy of *Motorcycle* magazine lying on his desk. Ever since the ransom drop, D had been boning up on motorcycling, trying to identify the bikes that had taken him on his wild ride through the city. D had asked Ray Ray if he could ride, beginning the conversation.

"Okay, Ray Ray, let me get back to you. I think I have a job for you, but if you can't really handle a motorcycle, you're ass-out." D watched Ray Ray exit, his large frame both hulking and goofy, a child in a man's body, and smiled, remembering himself and the long, awkward journey a big man has to grace.

By the time the first of the D Security staff began arriving, the conference room was ready—the Chinese food had been delivered and he had Sade's *Love Deluxe* filling the space with good vibe. Unlike the company's last, tense meeting, he had great news to announce, and it was received as such.

"As long as the bitch don't try to dress like me, we'll be cool," was Mercedez's reaction to having to spend time with Bridgette Haze.

"Night's cool with me. Maybe I can knock off a couple of his groupies, son," were Jeff Fuchs's thoughts on being on Night's watch.

The only negative feedback, and even that was measured, came from Danny Wallace, who wondered, "Do we have enough qualified people to stretch ourselves like this? We'll be covering our regular gigs, plus working in this bodyguard thing. Staffing is one of our problems now."

"At most," D assured him, "it'll only be for a month. I can't see Bridgette Haze here much longer than that. By the time the Source Awards come around, we'll be back to normal."

After high ratings and security misadventures in Los Angeles and Miami, the Source Awards were coming back to New York for the first time in years. D had negotiated a deal to handle much of the backstage security duty. The staff at the Theater at Madison Square Garden would control the crowd, but in the backstage area, which had proven at previous Source Awards shows to be the real trouble spot, D Security would be working the hallways, to try to squash beef before it spilled onstage. D had outbid the Nation of Islam for the contract, a matter of considerable pride.

As the staff was discussing the deployment of forces for the bodyguard and club gigs, an unfamiliar face appeared in the doorway of the conference room. He was a sour-faced Hispanic in a Phat Farm denim outfit and a red, white, and blue Clippers cap. He had a doughy face that testified to his love of black beans and pork. "I'm looking for D Hunter," he announced. Eyes darted around the table.

"And who are you, dog?" Jeff asked.

"I'm a man doing his job," the Hispanic man replied roughly. He surveyed the several large black men in the room. He didn't want to tip his hand, but clearly, no one was going to identify D for him. If he'd known he was walking into a staff meeting, the matter would have been handled very differently. So he made a choice. He walked over to Danny, who had the oldest-looking face, reached into his jacket, and pulled out a white envelope. "D Hunter," he said, "you have been served with an official notice," and then took out a camera, held up the watch on his wrist, and made sure Danny, the envelope, and the watch were in the frame.

"I'm D Hunter," the real D Hunter said from the other side

of the table, "and you have not served me officially. Sorry to cost you a check, but that's life."

Defeated and embarrassed, the process server backed out of the conference room with all eyes save D's on him.

"Should I open it?" Danny asked D.

"No, give it here. Since it hasn't been officially served yet, I can read it—no harm, no foul." D opened the white envelope, which was filled with several legal pages. Reading the first two paragraphs made D's face sag. Leafing through the following eight pages didn't brighten his day either. He put down the paper on the table before him and then put his face in his hands. No one reached over to touch the papers.

D sat anxiously in the lobby of A.S.S., awaiting an emergency sitdown with Dante Calabrese. Next to him sat Emily, who used her right hand to rub D's muscular neck. He sat forward with his elbows on his knees, head down. His right hand clutched the letter that had sent his life into a tailspin. Emily spoke to D soothingly, as if he were a little boy with a skinned knee. "It'll be all right, my lovely. I'm sure Dante will help. He knows how loyal you've been to Bovine."

D just sat there silently, staring balefully at the floor and squeezing the papers in his huge hands. It was a $10-million civil suit against Dervin Hunter, D Security, Emily's Tea Party, and Emily Anekwe filed on behalf of Tom Brookins, the Washington Wizard, who'd just gone on the disabled list for a damaged wrist. On ESPN it had been reported that he hurt it falling during a game. In the lawsuit D, and D alone, was to blame. Moreover, the suit suggested that D had injured Brookins at the behest of his old friend Bovine Winslow, a ploy to weaken the Wizards for the playoffs.

This was a classic nuisance suit, but D couldn't laugh it off. Neither he nor D Security had the time or money for this. Legal fees could be a nightmare and would cut into whatever profit they'd receive for the Ivy Greenwich gigs. It was Emily who suggested Dante Calabrese could help. He was about the last man in New York D wanted to ask for a favor. Still, D had only moved on Brookins to squash Bovine's beef. Once again he'd had Bovine's back—even Dante would understand how that obligated him.

"I can't help you," Dante said firmly after he'd read the papers, plopped them on his desk, and gazed at the sad faces of D and Emily.

"D has been such a good friend to Bovine," Emily said. "You know that."

"Are you saying you can't make a call to Brookins or his lawyer or the league office for us?"

"It's difficult, D," Dante replied.

"Listen," D said back, "I was damn near the boy's maytag when he got to New York. I showed him where to go, who to talk to, and what not to say."

"The Knicks provided that service, D, as did my office."

"Please. Half your clients are getting high in their cars before practice and the other half have babies by chicken-heads coast to coast. You don't help these kids do anything but cash a check. I protected D from all that. Not because I wanted anything but because I like helping people."

"That may have been true once, D. But you know you owe Bovine Winslow several thousand dollars for investing in your business."

"You know I'll pay it back."

"Oh, you will, I'm sure. Someday. And that is one of my problems. Technically speaking, Bovine Winslow has a piece of D Security, which means Tom Brookins is, technically speaking, suing another NBA player for an off-court altercation. That's some Allen Iverson–like behavior that would hurt Bovine deeply in the endorsement market."

Emily raised her voice, saying, "We're the only reason that incident didn't make Page Six or Rush and Malloy. It was my contacts who kept that quiet."

"Look," Dante replied, "I'd love to help you but this suit isn't Bovine's problem—unless you go to the press and make it our problem."

D stood up, fuming but still under control. "You know I would do nothing to embarrass or hurt Bovine. But this lawsuit is designed to put Emily and me out of business. I can't let that happen."

"So you're gonna call Bovine?" Dante asked.

"If I have too."

Dante hit a button on his phone. Through its speaker came the sound of a cell phone ringing. "Hey, Dante, what's up?" Bovine's voice was surrounded by the sound of a shopping mall.

Dante said, "Sorry to bother you before a game, Bovine. Where are you? Phoenix?"

"That's right. Hey, why am I on speaker?"

"Well, I'm sitting here with D Hunter and his lovely girlfriend, Emily. As you know, they are being sued by Tom Brookins for injuries sustained at their club."

"You know about this suit?" D's question was aimed at Bovine.

"The NBA is where we make our living, D," Dante answered. "It's my job to know shit like this. Bovine, tell D what your lawyer advised."

Haltingly, Bovine spoke. "Well, D, it's like this. My attorney feels I need to stay away from this situation. He's affirmed it might be construed that you injured Brookins, not simply to cool down that situation at Emily's Tea Party but to hurt him in a malicious act against Tom Brookins that I ordered."

"Bovine, that was like listening to you do a fucking commercial!" D shouted. "What are you doing? Reading off cue cards? Just call Tom Brookins and get him to squash this thing and then call the league to tell them Emily's Tea Party is a safe party. You got that?"

The sound of Bovine breathing into his cell phone came out of the speaker like bad breath. "I wish I could, D. The timing's bad for me right now. You know Brookins don't like me anyway. So a call might be the worst thing I could do. As for the league, Dante will cool that shit out for Emily."

"Sure," Dante agreed, "when the time is right."

D closed his eyes and opened them again. His chest heaved. He didn't speak.

"D?" Bovine asked through the phone. "Talk to me, D."

After a long pause D spoke slowly and softly. "I treated you like my brother. But I guess that was a mistake." He turned on his heel and walked out of the room with Emily in his wake.

"D?" Bovine asked again. "Come on, man. You are like my brother."

"He's gone, Bovine," Dante said. "So how's the knee?"

CHAPTER NINE

Music videos are mostly the province of nerdy young men who know more about the telecine, focal lenses, and camera equipment than women, love, or emotion. Reared on endorphin-pumping edits, video-game storytelling, and a disrespect for cinematic meaning, music-video directors are shapers of perception with very little perspective. Often, instead of aspiring to cinematic mastery, they live to emulate the lives of the "cool" stars they photograph. Mostly that's a lost cause, since video directors will always be the guys upstaged by musicians at the MTV Awards.

Fortunately, that bittersweet fate wasn't suited to the temperament of Bee Cole, music-video diva director and entertainment-industry sex symbol. She was as beautiful as a pop star and as commanding as a mogul. Moreover, in a medium in which sexuality is defined by a girl/woman gyrating in a bikini, Bee's work had an adventurous sensuality that reflected her personal predilections. Night, for example, had been a personal muse even before he began recording. In numerous videos, Bee had cast Night as a male object of desire, the camera lingering over his dark, taut skin, festishing him as if he were her personal fertility symbol. Bee knew Night had been a black American gigolo and often picked his brain, using his twisted tales of sex for profit to inspire music-video scenarios and MTV iconography.

Bee generally preferred doing videos of male singers; she was reluctant to share her visions with other women, especially white ones. But Ivy had been wooing Bee for months. "If you can transform Bridgette Haze by remaking her appeal with a video, you'd absolutely be making history," Ivy told her. "It'll be your crowning achievement." It was a good rap, but what finally convinced Bee was Ivy's commitment to back her film debut, a sexual thriller called *Show & Tell,* about the consequences of lying about sex.

Finally seduced, Bee was hooking up with Bridgette for a night of erotic club crawling "to crack open her head and see what demons pop out." Per Bee's request, only D and a driver would accompany them on this nocturnal quest. They knew each other through Night—she had been the singer's sponsor/concubine and he'd been the singer's friend/protector—but weren't close. Each knew the other was discreet, a quality they both respected greatly.

"So," Bridgette asked Bee as she slid into the backseat of Tony's SUV, "where are we going tonight?"

"Oh, just down the rabbit hole," Bee replied with a naughty smile. When D settled into the passenger seat, Bee reached over and squeezed his shoulder. "We're going a few places you probably know well, D."

"I don't know," D said in response. "You may have been all the places I've been but I'm pretty sure I haven't been all the places you have."

Bee flashed the icy smile that was her trademark and told Tony, "We'll start downtown and work our way up. Let's hit Tenth Avenue."

As soon as the car pulled off, Bridgette asked Bee, "So, how long have you known D Hunter?"

"You're curious about D, huh?"

"My sister has a crush on him. She likes that strong silent type."

"Silent? D isn't really silent." Bee added, "I find he often has quite a bit to say."

"No, I'm joking. From what I've seen, D definitely speaks his mind."

"Well," Bee said, "I mostly know D through Night, who's a good friend. Night loves D. Says he's a person you can rely on, which, in New York, is a very big compliment."

"Yeah, D's a good man," Tony chimed in. "I've seen him save the ass of a lot of people."

Now D couldn't take it anymore. "There's no need for all of you to exaggerate," he said. "I just try and do my job. That's all."

"Are you embarrassed by all this attention, D?" Bridgette said teasingly. "I'm sorry, big, scary black man."

Bee loved this and started cackling. Tony laughed too, and even D's angry gaze didn't stop him. Feeling for D, the director redirected the conversation by asking to hear some of the tracks Bridgette had been cutting in New York. The singer pulled a CD out of her purse and had Tony play it.

The track she'd recorded that first night with DJ Power filled the car and then, unprompted, Bridgette began singing along. Hearing a familiar voice up close and unencumbered by technology can be either quite exhilarating or completely deflating. That familiarity, born of repeated radio and TV exposure, makes no allowances for a sore throat, congestion, or plain old poor pitch. In comparison to the official version, a singer's real voice can seem puny, almost inauthentic in its imperfections.

To D's surprise this wasn't the case with Bridgette Haze. Her voice was strong—he could feel the back of his seat vibrate from the force of her vocal cords. He'd thought she'd be reedy and nasal like so many of the chick singers out there. Instead there was an engaging thickness to her tone that he hadn't anticipated. He wasn't quite ready to say Ms. Haze had "soul"—that would be like pimp-slapping Aretha Franklin—but this little white girl had chops.

About the backing track, D was considerably more dubious. All Power's shit sounded alike to him, but then most things on the radio these days could be described that way. Bee and Tony were raving that this was another hit for Bridgette, when D's eyes rested on the passenger-side rear mirror. About two blocks back was a Yamaha. D smiled slightly to find that his motorcycle study was bearing fruit. If this was one of the kidnapping crew, at least he'd have some warning.

"Ignoring me, huh?"

"Excuse me," D said, startled.

"I was asking you what you thought of my song."

"Oh, yeah. You can sing."

"Thanks for that revelation," Bridgette said. "What about the song?"

"Should I be honest or just do my job?"

Bridgette got a little flutter inside. Was her bodyguard going to dis her? Everybody around her usually bit their lip when it came to her music. This was going to be interesting. "Oh, go ahead and do your job, why don't you?"

"It's a number-one hit with a bullet."

"And what do you really think?"

"It's a number-one hit with a bullet."

"Fuck you, Mr. Strong Silent Type."

D deadpanned. "Did I say something to offend you?" even as he kept an eye on the progress of the bike in the rearview mirror.

Their destination was in the Meatpacking District, not far from Pastis, but a world away from the faux-Parisian glitz of that bistro. Penny's was a vestige of the neighborhood's older character, when the air stank of carcasses, the bars weren't filled with yuppies, and transvestites ruled the streets. Penny's still had that raw, tawdry flavor, which was why Bee adored it.

It was an old-fashioned S&M bar for people who loved being led around by chains attached to studded dog collars, and the height of style was still reflector shades and heavy, thick-soled black boots. But even in this uninhibited crowd, the presence of Bridgette Haze caused a stir. Her eyes roamed Penny's, taking it all in but saying little. Walking through the black rooms, illuminated solely by crimson light bulbs, the pop diva from Virginia kept her own counsel.

While she'd worn her share of faux dominatrix gear over the years onstage, being confronted with people who meant it overwhelmed Bridgette. No smile and wink here. These folks took all of the rituals of bondage very seriously, and she felt very much like a sex tourist, which, actually, she was. After a half hour of whips, studs, and associated gear, Bridgette turned to Bee and said, "Let's go."

Outside Penny's, D lingered by the door as Bee and Bridgette entered the SUV. He peered both ways, catching the glint of street light on the grill of a Yamaha, partially obscured by a U-Haul truck. D could feel a cold set of eyes assessing the situation. From behind a wall or inside a car, D knew he was being measured and he was determined not to be found waiting. Back inside the SUV he was silent. He wanted to ask Tony what he'd seen but didn't want to alarm the ladies. Bee was talking about their next stop in excited tones. "I know that Penny's was a little extreme, but I think you'll find this next move more familiar."

"No," Bridgette said defensively, "it was cool. It was just quite a bit to take in. They weren't playing in there, you know. It was kinda moving, in a way, to see people so into what they were into."

As the car pulled off, Bee, an experienced guide on the wild-side life, pulled out a joint that she shared generously with America's sweetheart. In the mirror D spied two Yamahas, not one, cruising two blocks back. Cruising. Not blasting through traffic. Not bursting through intersections. Not a nasty, loud pack of riders. Cruising. Bad sign. D pulled out his Motorola two-way pager and wrote Tony a note. At the next light Tony felt a buzz in his jacket pocket and slipped out his BlackBerry. After reading D's message, Tony glanced into his side-view mirror and nodded at D.

On the west side in the Thirties, a few blocks behind the huge post office on Ninth Avenue, Tony pulled the SUV in front of the Purple Petal, a nondescript bar holding its weekly ghetto-dike extravaganza. Unlike the glamorous lipstick lesbians of music videos, the Purple Petal was where hard-core ghetto girls who had men in jail, or who'd been treated badly by men who weren't in jail, or who just plain never felt much need for a male companion traveled from the BK and the BX, from uptown and Queens, to meet like-minded women for kissing (and no telling). At Penny's, the crowd had been too engaged in their own rituals to sweat a celebrity, but the Purple Petal was all about hooking up. If Bridgette Haze stepped into their world, well, she was just another tenderoni to spit game to. The clientele felt, Well hey, if she's looking to "experiment," why shouldn't it be with me?

So D didn't have time to contemplate any ad hoc motorcycle gathering in the street. He was busy regulating the flow of burly autograph seekers with round bodies and short-cropped hair at the booth Bee had commandeered. This was not the easiest gig D had ever had. These ladies were insistent, willful, and not at all intimidated by his size or his glare. He was the intruder, not they. Bee, happy denizen of many alternative worlds, gladly introduced her many acquaintances at the Purple Petal to Bridgette with a chatty conviviality. In contrast to Penny's, where Bridgette had clearly been overwhelmed, this crowd placed her in a position she well understood—sex object. Lust was lust to a girl who'd been ogled with desire since she'd worn her first pair of tap shoes. That these women were what her very southern mother would have labeled "bull daggers" didn't faze Bridgette one bit.

There was a provocative moment when a big-eyed beauty named Pamleasha sauntered over to the table and Bee embraced her with such intensity that D felt he was intruding just being in the same room. Bridgette was intrigued by this interplay but kept a neutral look on her face. The two stood next to the table, locked into their own world, before Bee introduced her friend to Bridgette. Turned out that Pamleasha was one of Bee's favorite dancers, the lady's taut, wiry body having graced many a video. At one point Bridgette touched D's thigh and leaned over to whisper, "Bee's pretty intense, huh?"

"That's why she's so good," D observed casually.

"Yeah. That must be true," was all Bridgette could muster. Then she gave D's thigh a squeeze. "Hmm," she said, "my sister will be impressed." D slid away from the singer and looked at her as if she were crazy. Could it be that this little white girl was the one checking for him? No way, he thought. The very idea made him blush.

Back outside the Purple Petal, two other black Escalades were lined up with Tony's, one in front and one behind. Tony was standing next to his car, talking to the other drivers, Rob and Eric, both black men in their mid-thirties.

"What are the extra cars for?" Bridgette inquired.

"Oh," Tony said, "I just needed to have a meeting with

some of my men. That's all." The man was a fine driver but a very unconvincing liar.

"So let's get in the car, Bridgette, so we can head off to Bee's next spot." D herded the singer and the director into the middle car and shut the door. Instead of entering on the passenger side he walked back to the third car and surveyed the block for lingering motorcycles. About two blocks back he spotted one of the two Yamahas with a driver on board. D went back around the cars on the street side and looked up the block for signs of surveillance. He spied a young, light-brown man in a black-and-blue oversize Pele jacket, smoking a cigarette. D got in on the passenger side of the first car.

"Eric," he said to the driver, "did Tony brief you?"

"Yeah, man," the driver replied eagerly. "Is this gonna be a car chase?"

D looked at him hard and answered, "No. This is more in the area of a car scare. I'm gonna drive."

"D, I don't think Tony—"

"I'm driving," D insisted. "Don't get out of the car. Just climb in the back."

"D, I'm too old to—"

"Get in the back."

When the switch, much to Eric's consternation, had been made, D two-wayed his instructions to Tony. When Tony hit him back with confirmation of the plan, D counted to ten and then gunned the Escalade out of its stasis, followed closely by the two other SUVs. The brown-skinned spy threw down his cigarette and began to dash. D flicked his Escalade's left tail-light. Tony caught the signal.

"What's going on?" Bridgette shouted.

"I'm sure D knows what he's doing," Bee said.

Tony just kept his eye on the road.

The brown-skinned spy made a left at the corner. Traffic at the intersection was going right. At the corner D turned his Escalade left, while Tony and the third SUV went right. As D turned the corner his quarry was just revving the engine on his Yamaha. The bike was parked next to a fire hydrant about a third of the way down the block. To say the least, the biker was quite surprised to see the Escalade barreling up the street, as were a taxi and two sedans. All three began swerving and blaring their horns. D was undeterred. He wheeled the car down the block and made a hard left that drove the front of the SUV into the Yamaha's front wheel, sending the bike backward and the would-be rider flying to the sidewalk. D leaped out of the Escalade like a linebacker on a blitz. The beleaguered biker, who, on closer inspection looked Latino, scrambled to his feet and made a mad dash for safety. D pursued for half a block, realized he wasn't fast enough to catch the rider, and gave up. Eric was inspecting the Escalade for damage when D walked over.

"Man, you are crazy. You could have got me killed!"

D replied, "And you act like that would have been a bad thing." D bent and tapped the glove compartment of the motorcycle. "This job does have its perks."

When D walked into the main room of the Golden Lady, near Bruckner Boulevard in the South Bronx, ninety minutes later, the long, straight bar-length stage of the biggest black/Latino strip club in the city was bursting with talent. There was Rita, a dynamic Dominican girl whose large, powerful legs were wrapped around the center pole like A-Rod's hands around a bat; there was Chante, a small-breasted but prodigiously bootylicious Brooklynite who could make her butt cheeks clap, applaud, and scoop up change; and at the far end, a top music-video director and a huge singing star feigned cunnilingus in their La Perla bras and panties. Missy Elliott's classic "Get Ur Freak On" blasted from the speakers at the one-third-full house. Few in the room recognized Bridgette Haze. To most of the working-class customers she was "the white female dancing with that fine-ass black freak." A few of the men at the bar were in fact a little irritated, since neither woman seemed interested in either baring all or accepting the one-, five-, and twenty-dollar bills being offered to them. "What's they problem anyway?" one man muttered as D walked over to where Tony sat nursing a beer.

"Full night, huh?" Tony said.

"So the other bike followed the other car?"

"Yeah, that's what it looks like. He had to make a choice at Forty-second Street. We made a left toward Times Square and he followed Rob up the West Side Highway and right over the GW."

"Ivy's gonna cover the time of the two drivers, the gas, and the minor fender work on Eric's car."

"How about throwing in the Yamaha?" Tony inquired.

"To the victor go the spoils," D said. Bridgette now spotted D sitting barside, sauntered over, stripper style, and then broke into a dance move right off the last MTV Awards. Tony and D applauded politely. Thus provoked, Bridgette strutted over to where D sat and bent down, pushing her face close to his.

"Is this a full-service date?" she asked.

D caught the movie reference and replied, "No. But if you're hungry I'll make sure you get fed."

D wasn't completely opposed to being seduced by Bridgette Haze, but there was something ridiculous about her little-girl vamping that made her seem funny to him. Bridgette read the amusement on his face and, suddenly, dirty dancing on the bar at some godforsaken strip club didn't seem like fun. In fact, she felt incredibly self-conscious, which was unusual and disquieting. She held out her arms, D took them and then slid his arms down around her waist, lifting Bridgette up and then putting her down lightly on the floor. She looked at his eyes. He said, "Let's go," and motioned for Bee to join them. Bee came over, put a hand on one hip, and said, "I know I better be getting picked up too!" D obliged her and they all left the Golden Lady.

At Jimmy's Uptown Café everything was back to normal. Everyone at this uptown celebrity hangout knew who Bridgette Haze was and treated her accordingly. People gawked and pointed. Little girls and waiters were photographed with her. Free drinks came from the bar. People ran up their cell phone bills telling friends and family they were breathing the same air as Bridgette Haze.

To D's surprise, neither Bridgette nor Bee had yet inquired about what happened with the motorcycles and where D had disappeared to. In the ride over to Jimmy's and in the ensuing

conversation, the two creative women had been talking excitedly about creating a video that captured the kaleidoscopic nature of the night. "This is what it needs to be," the director said
passionately. "It needs to feel like *Alice in Wonderland*."

"Yes, that's it," Bridgette agreed and then sipped on her
second mohito.

"Little Bridgette sits at her suburban looking glass and
then walks right into an edgy urban wonderland. First you're
in a world of leather queens and, for a moment, you assume
that identity. Then you're being trailed by a posse of lesbians
and you do a hot dance that would make Madonna blush."

"Yeah, I like that," Bridgette said.

"Then you're at some uptown strip club being stared at
by black men old enough to be your grandfather."

Bridgette shouted, "Ooh, that's hot. We'll have a room
full of guys who look like D."

D just smiled at the crack and surveyed the room. When
creative people, particularly clients, were brainstorming, he
knew there was only one mode for a security person—silence.

"That's the video, Bridgette!" Flush with the night's activities and her potent drinks, Bee was as animated as D had
ever seen her. Usually she had the chilly demeanor of a very
relaxed pervert. Now there was something bright and child-
like about her. She was almost adorable, a word he'd never
have thought could apply to Bee Cole. She was already for-
mulating shots in her head.

"We'll have dancers, but they'll reflect these environ-
ments in the dances we do. We'll get a Broadway choreographer, someone who did a show like *Contact*."

"Did you ever see *Pennies from Heaven?*" Bridgette asked. "It was this really dark musical with Steve Martin as a killer and Christopher Walken as a pimp. He does this pimp dance on a bar that was just rad."

"Really. I've got to watch it."

Bee and D were impressed that Bridgette knew of a film that the director didn't. This started the conversation on a tangent about musicals. They were debating the merits of the film versions of *Cabaret* and *Funny Girl* when D felt someone staring at him. Not at the table. Not at Bridgette or even Bee. Eyes on D Hunter. By the bar, next to the overweight Goya-products salesman kicking it to a half-interested legal secretary, was the kid from Emily's Tea Party. When their eyes met, he raised his shot glass in salute to D. This was awkward. He wanted to rush over and have a word with his new pal, the man he was sure was behind Night's kidnapping. But leaving Bridgette Haze alone at that table was not an option. If they were gonna make a move inside Jimmy's, he needed to be right by her side.

This was feeling like a real Kevin Costner moment when Ivy Greenwich entered the room with a most unusual posse. Next to him and, in fact, holding his hand was a fair-skinned black Wall Streeter named Kirby Turner, who liked to hang out when she wasn't negotiating deals. Behind them was Mercedez Cruz, looking as sexy as she was surly. Now D's antennae were quivering like crazy. Mercedez's presence was a plus, but the level of risk in the room had risen exponentially. D looked past the arrivals at the table and ignored their greetings. All his attention was aimed at the bar, where the kid put some money down and headed toward the door.

"Where are you going, D?" Ivy asked, but D was too preoccupied to answer. In six strides he was out the door, standing in front of Jimmy's, looking to his left and right. Tony, who was typing in his two-way, rolled down his window.

"D, what's up?"

"You see anybody come out here in the last few minutes?"

"Sorry. I've been two-waying my wife. Is there another problem?"

"No, my man. It's cool."

There were cars and people and the low mumble of New York voices. In the distance D heard a motorcycle. It wasn't close, and, in fact, it was fading away. Tony heard it too.

"You wanna get in and try and chase it down?"

"No, not tonight," he replied. "But soon. Real soon."

CHAPTER TEN

"TELL ME AGAIN why we aren't calling the police." D was sitting in the men's Jacuzzi at the plush Reebok Sports Club. Ivy was across from him, on the other side of the Jacuzzi, his head back, his eyes closed, his gray, kinky hair covered by a red rubber swimming cap.

Without opening his eyes, Ivy asked rhetorically, "You know how common extortion is becoming in the record business? Last year an A&R man for Sony was kidnapped for not signing an act. I know a major singer working out of a studio in Jersey who got snatched when he stepped outside for a cigarette."

"Any connection to what happened to Night?"

"No," Ivy said firmly. "It turned out to have been by his cousins, who he'd refused to lend money to."

"Do you think Night was kidnapped because of some family affiliation? His sister has been known to date some rough Negroes."

"No." Ivy opened his eyes and looked across the churning

water at D. "You are missing my point. Ever since hip-hop brought the street into the music business, this kind of gangsta behavior has grown, and now it's out of hand. If I bring in the police every time a situation arises, I'll never have time to do business."

Now D was irritated. "Ivy, you talk like gangsters" (he made sure to pronouce the word properly) "haven't been working this game since Frank Sinatra was a pup. I read Dwayne Robinson's book, Ivy."

"It's different today," Ivy asserted. "We weren't like this group around today. We wanted to make some money. These kids are into intimidation just for the sport of it." Ivy clearly knew more than he was telling D, but the bodyguard felt he wasn't in a position to press his employer. Perhaps a little manipulation would help.

"The police know something happened to Night." When Ivy didn't react, D continued, telling the manager the gist of his conversation with Detective Williams, except for the crucial detail that he'd known the cop since he was a boy.

"All that means is that they see smoke," was Ivy's response. "But in New York there's smoke somewhere every day. It's only a fire if we tell them where the flames are. Eventually they'll see a bigger fire elsewhere and move on."

"This is a sexy case, Ivy. They're gonna stay on me until I give them some love."

"You think they're feeling it like that?"

"Ivy, there was a motorcycle chase through Union Square, down Broadway, and right over the Williamsburg Bridge. That's not a fire, Ivy. It's a blaze."

Ivy put his head back and closed his eyes. "Let me enjoy this, D. We'll talk about it some more later."

D lifted himself out of the Jacuzzi and moved through the glass doors to the showers. Ivy looked ridiculous sitting with his little red rubber cap on, but D knew it was a bad idea to underestimate the old man. You didn't survive as long as Ivy had being either naïve or loose-lipped. Still, it seemed prudent to gather some additional information on his benefactor. D showered quickly, put on his black and white Phat Farm tracksuit, and then made a call on his cell. Afterward he took the elevator up to the sixth floor where a hip-hop dance class was under way. D stopped outside one of the two entrances to the mirrored room. At the other was Hubert, who acknowledged D's presence with a nod. Since the incident at Pastis, Hubert had kept his distance from D. Apparently he'd been impressed with what he heard about the night Bridgette had spent with Bee, but he hadn't shared his thoughts with anyone. D thought Hubert's knowledge of Bridgette would be helpful, but he didn't want to press the issue.

Inside the mirrored studio were fifteen women and a couple of adventurous men working through the shoulder shakes and robotic instructions of a spry, brown-haired teacher. In the back row, but far from inconspicuous, was Bridgette, and next to her, dancing gamely, was Mercedez. This was her night off, but Bridgette had taken a liking to this tough New York lady and invited her to tag along while she worked out. In the row before them was Jen, who actually moved more gracefully than her younger sibling. Bridgette was flashier, but there was a pleasing flow to Jen that stirred D a bit.

Bridgette and Mercedez spotted D gazing at them. He put on his trademark glare and then, with all the style his six-two, 250-pound frame could manage, he wiggled his hips in his best approximation of a music vide-ho. Both of them burst out laughing but D didn't stay to milk his joke further. It was very out of character for him. He was as surprised as they were. But he felt good about it. Stress had to escape somehow.

Outside the Reebok on Columbus Avenue, Tony stood next to his Escalade, talking on his cell. "Yeah," he was saying, "Cameron Diaz will be landing at 11:00 P.M. Take her from JFK to the Trump Tower and then wait because she may wanna go to Bungalow 8. All right then." He clicked out and smiled when D approached. "I've only seen one bike today and it was one of those little Vespas. No self-respecting bad man is gonna ride that."

"Cool. I'm gonna break out and then meet you guys at the studio later. Hit me on the two-way if anything jumps off."

"Well," Tony said quickly, "something's already jumping off. The Haze sisters are beginning to get concerned about what you're concerned about."

"Come with it."

"Today in the car they were asking me about what went down the other night. Whatever Ivy is telling them is not hitting the spot. They've been around enough to know a cover-up when they hear it. They're a little too busy now to—oops, you better turn around."

Jen exited the Reebok, still moist from her workout but determined to have a private word with D. Her face was still flushed from the dancing. D imagined that's how she'd look during sex. They walked over to the window of the Reebok store. As they talked, a poster of Venus Williams grimaced over their shoulders. "I know you work for Ivy," she began, "but he pays you with our money."

"Relax, Jen, you don't have to strong-arm me. I know you're nervous about the other night but you and your sister shouldn't worry too much."

"Just a little, huh?" Jen's tone was sharp. She was clearly displeased with his answer, but she was going to hear him out.

"Well, I'm not gonna lie to you," he said. "Everybody wants to be safe. Everybody in this city wants to be safe and everybody in the whole damn world wants to be safe. But the truth is there's always gonna be danger out there. All you can really do is be careful and make sure all the things that can be done are done. That's my job."

"All that's what worries me, D. You and your people have never done this before, not for someone as important as my sister. Besides, your responsibilities are about to grow. Against my wishes, Bridgette has gotten our father to recall Hubert. He's going back to Virginia in the morning. I have my problems with him but I know I can trust him. I'm not sure about you."

Now D was rocked. He had no idea Jen could be this straightforward and tough. Nor did he think it was a good idea for Hubert to disappear. And what about all this talk that Jen liked him? For a woman who allegedly had a crush on him she sure was having no problem crushing D's ego.

Fumbling for his words, D replied, "Well, Jen, I don't know what to say. If you are dissatisfied with my work or that of my people, you can certainly have us removed."

"I've discussed that with my sister, but in light of Hubert's recall, she and Ivy think it would be counterproductive to bring in a whole new New York team at the same time. They both feel you and your people have done the best you can under the circumstances. But I remain concerned." Jen's voice was heatless. Whatever anger she possessed was subsumed in a classically American bureaucratic voice—the voice of a woman used to judging workers and not very interested in nuance. It was a voice that said you were either up to the job or not. D excused himself and turned on his heel and headed up Columbus Avenue.

D cursed that little dance he'd done upstairs. It had probably killed any lingering respect Jen had for him. He felt he'd gotten caught up in the hype—just like any kid who suddenly found himself around stars. Letting Mercedez dance with her was equally bad. None of it was professional. He had fucked up this job just like he was messing up D Security. Now he couldn't even go back to being a gofer for Bovine. His mother had a life. His brothers had God. He just had scrambling, and, he thought, he was doing a weak-ass job of that.

D crossed to the north side of Seventy-second Street and hooked a left toward Amsterdam Avenue. Midway down the block he entered La Dinesta, a Cuban-Chinese diner with the best black beans and yellow rice south of Washington Heights. He traded greetings with Mike, the headwaiter with the spiked hair and round black yazuka shades, and headed to the booth where his friend was already enjoying the boneless chicken and black beans.

D had first met the author Dwayne Robinson at a Prince concert in the early nineties. People were standing all over and grooving to the sounds of "Let's Work" when D noticed a lean, bearded man sitting and scribbling in a notebook with a pen that had a tiny light in its tip. A curious D intercepted the scribe after the show and wondered if the guy was a music critic. Turned out he was a critic at *The Village Voice* and D had read many of his pieces. After that D became a fan, following his writings so closely that he was one of the first people to purchase the updated edition of his twenty-year-old classic R&B history, *The Relentless Beat.*

They finally became friends two years later when Dwayne did a profile of Bovine for the *Voice*. Turned out they were both from the Brownsville section of Brooklyn, though D was about ten years his senior. An older brother–younger brother relationship developed, and it was to Dwayne, more than anyone, that he came closest to telling his family history. Dwayne knew more than most, but no one knew everything—except D, his mother, and Fly Ty.

D wanted some specific info from Dwayne but didn't press for it, instead listening first to Dwayne relate the tortures of screenplay writing and the pleasures of his wife, Danielle, a love story he never tired of telling. He had a house way out in Jersey ("Whitelandia," he called it) where he doted on his son and tended to his bushes. It made D feel optimistic about his future. Here was another Brownsville boy, another product of a place the city didn't care about, who was respected for his work, had a family, and was still a good, down brother. D knew his life was different from Dwayne's—he was older and smarter—but the similarity always cheered him up. Dwayne then prodded D to tell him about his life, which was pretty much composed of D Security's financial difficulties and his troubled relationship with his sudden savior, Ivy Greenwich, the mention of whom ignited Dwayne's memory just as D had hoped.

"He came in and out of *The Relentless Beat*," Dwayne said between bits of crackling chicken. "At one time or another he managed many of the great soul stars before escaping into the big money in pop and rock. He and Clive Davis are the only old lions left from the sixties who are still active. Everybody else either has made big bank or been put out to pasture."

"Why has Ivy survived?"

"Well, Clive has made it by being all about songs. Your man Ivy is all about voices. He has a knack for managing people with distinctive voices that somehow cut through on the radio. From Adrian Dukes to Bridgette Haze, music has changed, but the quality of the voices he hooked up with have kept him in the game."

"Adrian Dukes. 'Green Lights.' "

"You've been listening to too much oldies radio, D."

"My mother loved that song, man. But, believe it or not, that old song is somehow tied in to this situation. Listen to this." Over his own plate of rice and beans and sweet banana, D related the story of Night's abduction and how "Green Lights" was used as an instrument of torture. "Why that song, Dwayne? Is there something in Dukes and Ivy's history that connects to the kidnapping? Something so bad Ivy won't go to the police?"

"Well, you know how Dukes died, don't you?"

"Suicide, right?"

"Jumped out of the window of the Theresa Hotel. Had been in the same suite Castro stayed in when he visited the U.N. in '62. Landed on 125th Street just down the block from the Apollo. Left no note. All they found was 'Green Lights' playing on the turntable. The official story is that he was frustrated with the lack of response for his subsequent singles, that he couldn't take being a one-hit wonder."

"Come on with it, Dwayne. I know you know the unofficial story."

"Rumor has it Ivy was having an affair with Dukes's wife. Based on the photos I've seen, the lady was a brick house, Commodores' style. While Dukes was on tour supporting his one hit, Ivy was laying pipe to his woman. When he got back home and someone peeped him to her infidelity, he rented the room at the Theresa, got prissy, and tried to be the first black man in space."

"Do lots of people know about this affair?" D wondered.

"You'd have to be from the ancient school or know someone who was."

"That would explain Ivy trying to ignore the song's importance. It was definitely a message to him. Plus Night is an R&B singer like Adrian Dukes. But what was that message saying? I guess it was a warning of some kind."

"Or a reminder that the past doesn't always stay in the past," Dwayne suggested.

Afterward they walked across Seventy-second Street toward the Broadway subway station. "There's one more thing I can tell you about your boss," Dwayne said.

"Sure. Whatever you know I wanna know."

"Well, it won't help you figure out what's going on, but it might come in handy. Before he was Ivy Greenwich, big-time talent manager, he was Irv Greenfield, barbershop owner in one of the black neighborhoods of Brooklyn."

"A barber?"

"Yeah, when those areas went from Jewish to black, Irv owned a barbershop. He liked the music and he loved the women, so he trained himself to cut black hair and got the best jukebox he could. Next thing he was cutting the hair of singers who needed a white man to navigate the business. That's how Ivy ended up with his uninhibited white Afro."

"Damn. Everybody's got a story."

"That's how I eat, D. Collecting them and telling them. Anyway, I'm gonna take my black ass back to Jersey. I'll take the train down to Forty-second Street and the Port Authority. What are you doing now?"

"You know me, Dwayne. I love the night life."

"Okay, man," Dwayne said and gave D a hug. "But watch this vampire shit. Do it too long and you'll be sucking your own blood."

CHAPTER ELEVEN

IN THEORY, GETTING into a modern recording studio should be harder than entering a bank vault. There are private phones and closed-circuit TV cameras and security codes on many of the doors. Within a modern studio are hundreds of thousands of dollars in equipment, master recordings that will generate millions, and artists, producers, and musicians who earn the gross national product of a non-oil-producing third-world country.

So the area inside a studio should be one of the safest places in any American city. In truth most big-city recording studios are rife with drugs, guns, and more than their share of indiscriminate sex. That's because studios are no longer—if they ever were—a creative oasis. The posse rules at any studio in New York, Chicago, Atlanta, Miami, and places in between. It's the rare young urban musician, black, white, or Latino, who doesn't allow friends, acquaintances, and friends of acquaintances to hang, as if studios were the rec room at a community college. It's not that some artists aren't sticklers, allowing no unauthorized persons into their sessions. The problem is that at any large facility, with many rooms, each artist or producer will have a different policy regarding access. In one room James Taylor could be cutting a folk-pop ballad, while next door DMX could be laying down a testament to man's inhumanity to dogs. In the common area, a place of vending machines and flat-screen TVs, where people lounge as engineers tweak drum sounds, everybody has to interact. It can make for some very strange bedfellows.

Around 12:30 A.M., D arrived at Right Track studios, where Power was producing Bridgette Haze's vocals in room A and RZA was cutting tracks for the Wu-Tang Clan in room B. Pop songbird next to hard-core posse. D was a little concerned that when he arrived he'd see little Bridgette surrounded by herb-smoking, rowdy Shaolin MCs. And to his dismay, he was right. Out in the main lounge there were Bridgette and Jen on a black leather sofa, squeezed in between six young black men sprawled around them on the sofa and floor. The singer and one of the black men, who looked vaguely familiar from a music video, were battling in a furious game of John Madden football. Bridgette had the Redskins and the young black man had the Steelers. The space possessed the pungent smell of marijuana, Chinese food, and the funk of Wu posse members who wore heavy jackets indoors but no deodorant. The young man closest to Bridgette wore a red bandana, a red Iverson jersey, and enough bling bling to illuminate Times Square. A few of the collected group nodded when D entered, but otherwise their focus stayed on Bridgette Haze's display of vid game dexterity.

Mercedez was nowhere to be seen, which irritated D, since it seemed to confirm Jen's concerns. Then, from the direction of the studio, he heard her voice. "Absolutely. There's not a night life situation that D Security can't handle."

"Is that right?" a man said, clearly humoring the speaker.

From around the corner came Mercedez with the publicist Rodney Hampton, whose left hand held a digital camera that rubbed up against his wedding ring. "Hey, man," Rodney said, extending his free hand to D. "It's a pleasure to meet you again, D. I couldn't say this the other night, but any black-owned enterprise that lands a contract with Ivy, I salute. I know how difficult that can be."

D was a little put off by the brothers-in-business rap. Not that he didn't believe in it—it was one of his bonds with Tony at TZL—but he detected a glibness about Hampton that put him off. For D, every utterance by the publicist seeking common ground was suspect. Hampton brought his digital camera up and snapped a photo of Bridgette and the homeboys.

"This is gold," he said, with an emphasis on *this*. The publicist held the camera at an angle so that D could see the digital images stored within. Photo after photo showed Bridgette huddled up and happy with thugged-out young black men. To D, all the shots looked like the box cover from the porn series *Black Dicks in White Chicks*, but he kept that insight to himself. Hampton continued, saying, "In a few hours these shots will be all over the Web, repositioning Bridgette Haze, opening her up to the hip-hop audience, and setting the stage for this new record."

"Bridgette Haze, Hip-Hop Queen, huh?"

"No," Hampton corrected, "Bridgette Haze—Queen of Pop. This trip to New York isn't just for her to hang out with the Wu. Ivy is also gonna have her do some classic New York music."

"One of the songs wouldn't happen to be 'Green Lights'?"

"Whoa!" Hampton exclaimed. "Ivy really has brought you into his confidence. He sees that as the second single. A great but obscure song. We'll do the video from the stage of the Apollo. Did he tell you that, too?"

"No, that's a surprise to me, too. Hey, has it always been the plan or is that something that's come up recently?"

"Oh," Rodney said. "I believe he called and told me that last week."

Power popped his head out of the studio. His eyes were red and Buddha blessed but there was a determined scowl on his lips. Despite (or perhaps because of) the controlled substances in his system, the man looked ready to work.

"Yo, Bridge, you ready to blow for me, hon?"

"Born ready, boo," she replied. She stood up and handed off the controls to Jen, who handed them off to one of the Wu posse and got up herself.

Someone cracked, "Where the white women going?" and everybody laughed.

"Must be your stank breath," someone else said, and suddenly the room turned into the *Def Comedy Jam*, with snaps flying around the room. On her way to the studio, Bridgette stopped in front of D and gave him a hug and patted his thigh. "Quite a dancer, aren't you?" and then headed into the studio. Jen came up to D as well but offered no hug. Hampton excused himself and followed his client.

"Could I speak to you, D?" Jen asked.

"Sure." Jen looked at Mercedez as if she wanted her to leave, but Mercedez didn't budge and D didn't instruct her to.

"Look, I'm sorry about what I said before. I may have been a little harsh. You understand, of course. Bridgette is my little sister. I have to be protective."

D eyed her coolly and replied, "No problem, but in the future, you should bring any complaints to Ivy. Until then my staff and I will do our best to provide your sister with the best security we can."

"Fine then, D. Okay." A couple of the Wu posse wondered if Jen would rejoin them on the sofa, but she demurred and joined her sister in the recording studio.

"You know," he said to Mercedez, "Bridgette told me Jen liked me."

"Yeah," Mercedez said with a shrug. "Well, I think that must be some kind of game they play. I don't think Bridge is that comfortable letting people know what she thinks. She's young and all, you know, despite all the hype. I think she's the one who likes you."

"She's way too young for my old ass."

"Please," Mercedez said sharply. "My baby's father was ten years older than me. All you men are pedophiles, whether you admit it or not."

CHAPTER TWELVE

D'S MOTHER'S FUTURE HUSBAND sat across from his future son-in-law and sipped nervously on his Jack Daniels. Zena Hunter's son was a big man with a hard, full face that reminded Willis Watson of Deacon Jones, a vicious defensive end who had played for the Rams in the sixties. Deacon Jones had been part of a defensive line known as the Fearsome Foursome, and to Willis, D was part of a fierce foursome—Zena's four sons.

Zena didn't mention her ex-husband much unless prompted, but those boys dominated her life in ways that Willis was still coming to terms with. Willis had his own crosses to bear—an estranged daughter and an ill-tempered former wife—so he didn't feel comfortable judging Zena's feelings. They were both adults with long histories that couldn't be forgotten or ignored. The best you could do was commit to making more history, to living life as if there were new feelings to experience. You had to believe life hadn't been used up yet. After all, Willis figured, neither of them was sixty-five yet, so they still had plenty of time.

"Yeah, she was just the sweetest thing," Willis said as Zena beamed and D forced a smile at the story he told. "I'd been going into that FedEx for years, but I'd never had anyone like your mother take my package before."

"Sounds romantic," D said flatly.

"Well, Zena made it so for me. Playing Marvin Gaye in the FedEx office. Shit, I was stuffing interoffice envelopes in FedEx packages just to have a reason to stop by."

Zena chuckled. "I knew you didn't have all those packages to ship."

"Shit!" Willis exclaimed. "I was stopping people outside and giving them five dollars to let me drop off their packages for them."

Now the happy middle-aged couple laughed together and traded goo-goo eyes, acting as if they were sure romance was wasted on the young. Only someone who'd lived a bit could enjoy it this much. Sitting and watching, D had to admit he hadn't seen his mother look so happy since, well, maybe never. So what if Willis Watson struck him as a corny, Bama-ass Negro in a green suit and matching Gators. D had either forgotten or ignored what he did for a living. Something for some data-processing concern located in downtown Brooklyn near his mother's FedEx office.

Willis Watson wasn't as dashing or as important to the world as Fly Ty. Nor was he handsome or smart. But he carried no baggage—at least no Hunter-family baggage—and he seemed to be crazy about Zena, and that's all that mattered. So D sat and forced a smile, despite the jealous palpitations of his heart. At a Federal Express office on Court

Street, right across from the courthouses and the seat of municipal power in da BK, Zena Hunter had found a mate, something that had eluded her son, who traveled in the most glamorous, celebrated circles of the juicy Big Apple. She had moved on. He had not. So when D offered his toast to the happy couple there was a hollowness to his voice, the echo of the vast empty space below his left nipple.

Detective Tyrone Williams lived in the Midwood section of Brooklyn in a two-story building with an extremely clean stoop, an American flag draped out of a second-story window, and a well-manicured little garden where he sat on warm summer nights and smoked Cohibas purchased from a Cubano he knew in Union City, New Jersey. Tonight, however, Williams had been drawn away from his bachelor pad to Flatbush and DeKalb, just a few blocks from the Manhattan Bridge, to Junior's Restaurant, a local landmark since the fifties.

The menu was caught between cheese blintzes and barbecued spareribs. This once-Jewish diner was now a multicultural center full of ethnic groups Junior's founders had never even heard of. Fortunately for the businesses's survival there was one unifying thread—cheesecake. Whether the customers were off-duty transit-authority workers, corpulent couples, or bejeweled bad boys, it was this dessert that kept the cash registers ringing at Junior's.

In an orange booth in the restaurant's main room Williams was poking his fork into a huge hunk of strawberry cheesecake as D sat updating him on the latest developments surrounding Night and Ivy Greenwich, as well as the worrisome shadowing of Bridgette Haze. "This song stuff is interesting," Williams said meditatively. "What I'll do is pull the file on Adrian Dukes's death and see if anything pops up. You didn't wanna be a cop, Dervin, but I see you have a fine future ahead of you as a snitch."

D, who was having a chocolate shake, pushed his straw around in the thick brown liquid while deciding to ignore Williams's crack. "Okay," he said, "now what are you gonna do for me, Fly Ty?"

Williams reached inside his jacket and pulled out a folded white piece of paper. It was the flyer for an event that Saturday in Brooklyn. "I was gonna send a man over to check it out, but I'm gonna give you this lead instead. It'll make you look good with that Ivy cat, and if you turn up something, you write me up a full report and put my name on it."

D had to smile. "Good looking out, Detective."

"What, no Fly Ty? Damn, are you softening toward me or is that just fear your mother will actually marry a man who wears Versus suits? I mean, come on, that's Versace's ghetto line. Shit. What is she thinking?" D just sat back, nodding sympathetically as Fly Ty vented, while he began to formulate a plan of action.

CHAPTER THIRTEEN

F AR FROM THE SPIRES of Manhattan, closer to Jamaica Bay than the Hudson and a quick fifteen-minute ride from where Night had been carjacked, a cornucopia of Hondas, Yamahas, Suzukis, and the odd Harley-Davidson poured exhaust fumes and mechanized noise into the Brooklyn sky. Affiliates of the Brooklyn Kings, the Rough Ryders, the Latin Kings, and sundry other black and Latino motorcycle clubs filled a long, flat straightaway next to the huge housing complex named Starrett City.

The urban road warriors of New York City and surrounding areas were gathered to trade stories, show off custom modifications, and set up some *Fast and the Furious*–style down-low showdowns for later. There were Jeeps with their rear doors open to dispense barbecue and beer; there were card-table-based vendors hawking T-shirts, key rings, and flyers for transmission shops and subscriptions to *Black Gold* and other sepia-flavored men's magazines; there were two scantily clad, round-hipped women selling copies of their calendar featuring them draped over various pieces of gleaming chrome. And from everywhere—bikes, Jeeps, and boom boxes—hard-core beats rocked the boulevard.

D drove onto the street as conspicuously as possible, gunning the Yamaha's engine, blasting DMX's "Get At Me Dog," and wearing a bright red biker ensemble sure to attract or inflame every Blood in the vicinity. He'd had the motor checked, but whatever scratches and dents he'd made smashing into it with the Escalade a few nights ago were left intact. Someone would recognize the bike or D or both, and whoever they were, he welcomed their attention.

D parked at the far end of the dead-end street right next to a Jeep selling mix tapes out of the back. To his right and behind him was grass- and swampland that would lead an adventurous walker in the direction of the Belt Parkway. To his left was a hilly, grassy area and then the closest of Starrett City's twenty-plus-story buildings. He could see people looking out of their windows at the gathered bikers. Some had cameras, others binoculars. D imagined that one or two of them were New York City cops looking, just as he was, for a connection to Night's kidnapping. That Fly Ty had said no one else was coming was no reason to believe him.

D got off the bike and stretched his legs, straightened his back. Unlike the cruisers he'd had some experience with in the past, rides where you sat back as if the bike were a motorized easy chair, these superfast Japanese racers forced you to sit with your butt high and shoulders hunched over. Aerodynamically it was a speed racer's dream—nothing took a corner like these machines—but for a big man, the ride was deeply uncomfortable.

D went down on one knee to check his tires, though what he was really doing was checking to see who was checking him. About halfway up the block was a crew called the Harlem Warriors. They were about twenty deep, and in their number was a new member named Ray Ray, sitting on a secondhand Honda that D had leased from the garage mechanic who'd repaired the Yamaha that D was riding. As instructed, Ray Ray didn't attempt to contact D. He was supposed to be just another homeboy biker on a whack-ass ride trying for his bit of road-running glory, and that's what he looked like. The kid was struggling not to look at D, knowing there was no reason to if he didn't know him, but this undercover shit, well, it wasn't easy. The Harlem Warriors weren't much of an outfit—it had only been around about five years and was composed primarily of young men who purchased their rides after watching too many DMX videos.

A few of them were hustlers—a little herb selling, cell phone scams, low-level pimps with underage hookers up at Hunts Point in the Bronx. Most were scramblers, kids like Ray Ray, who didn't have much but sought a time to shine. Ray Ray was working hard at his Harlem Warrior role, so his back was turned when two old heads rolled down to where D sat on his bike, smoking one of Fly Ty's Cohibas.

Both men were right around thirty, heavyset, and very working class. They didn't strike him as gangsters, though they both had the same make of Yamaha that D sat on. "Beautiful day to ride, isn't it?" he said to break the ice.

"It is," the rider on the left said. He was a light-brown man with freckles and an American-flag bandana on his head. "My name is Petey and this is Z-Rock." The other man, browner, smaller, and wearing a sky-blue metal and matching jacket, just grunted a greeting. No one offered his hand.

"We thought it was interesting that we all had exactly the same make of motorcycle," Petey said.

"Yeah," D agreed, "where'd you get yours?"

"We were wondering the same thing about you," Petey answered. "We got ours out in Hempstead. In fact we bought it with a pal of ours. All on the same day."

"Sort of the black Musketeers, huh," D cracked. Petey smiled but Z-Rock didn't, D noticed. "Something bothering you, sir?"

"Yeah, pardner," Z-Rock said in an unfriendly tone. "Our man had his bike jacked two weeks ago by some kids in Queens. It looks like the bike you're riding, pardner."

"Right down to the license plate," Petey added.

"So what's your game?" Z-Rock asked. "No real rider would knowingly bring a hot bike around here unless he was looking to sell it, looking for a fight, or just a fool. Which are you, pardner?"

"First of all, there are other options. Lots of them, actually. But the one that's relevant right now is that I might have taken the bike off the original thief and, pending some verification of ownership, that I'd return it in exchange for money or something of equal value, such as information."

Both men were bewildered by what D had said. "If I get you right," Petey said, "you're admitting that this is Derek Johnson's bike and—"

"And that's enough proof for me." D got off the bike with

the keys in his hand and handed them to Z-Rock. "You can give the bike back to your friend, but now you owe me."

"We don't have any reward money," Petey said, still trying to figure out what was going on.

"But you were with Derek Johnson that day he got knocked off his bike on Jamaica Avenue and you got a look at those who robbed him. However, you wouldn't give the police your names, so you weren't that useful."

"You a cop?" Z-Rock asked, his confusion deepening.

"Hell no. I'm better than a cop. I'm not about the law. I'm about justice. You let me know if any one of the men who ripped off your friend's bike shows up here, then the debt is paid. You don't have to testify in court or watch a police lineup or any of that. Just give me a heads-up and I'll take care of the justice."

Z-Rock laughed. "What, nigga? You some damn vigilante? You Charles Bronson or some shit?"

D wasn't fazed by the sarcasm. Not one bit. He leaned over toward Z-Rock. "I'm who you want me to be. Now do we have a deal?"

Not long after this conversation a posse rolled onto the street in three disciplined rows four across. The first row came in doing handstands on their seats, looking more like circus monkeys than men. The second row had their front wheels in the air and rolled in, totally in control, on their back wheels. The third row was surprisingly conventional—they just sat on their bikes with their arms folded, like an old-school MC, looking calculatedly bored with their beautiful balance. One rider put a leather-gloved hand to his mouth as if he were yawning.

Though he was a couple hundred feet away and his view

somewhat obscured by the two lines of bikes in front of the yawning rider, D recognized him as the young man who'd been clocking him at clubs for months and haunting his dreams for weeks. And though there were no women in any of the three lines, D was sure these were members of the posse from Union Square. The bikes were all different. So were their clothes and helmets. But it was them.

His phone rang. "Yeah, is this them?" he asked evenly. He could hear the roar of the bikes loudly in his ear, since Petey was standing up the street abreast of the incoming riders. "The guy in the back and a couple of those other guys look like the guys who jacked Derek," Petey reported.

"Hey, I'm not asking you to testify, so you don't have to dance for me, man. Does your man Z-Rock agree?"

"Yeah. He says that's them too."

"Cool. You have the keys. I'm gonna leave the bike down here. Pick it up at your leisure."

"So," Petey asked anxiously, "what's your plan?"

"I'm leaving. No use for a man around here without a bike." D clicked off his phone, got off the Yamaha he was sitting on, and walked to his right. D didn't look back, he just moved quickly across the grassy hill toward the Starrett City building, getting out of sight as swiftly as possible. He'd hoped to run in to one of Derek Johnson's friends today, and actually, things had gone better than he'd anticipated. Petey and Z-Rock had dropped Johnson off at Jamaica Hospital but hadn't stayed around to give the cops a description or corroborate his story. Apparently both men had priors for minor drug possession and wanted nothing to do with Five-O. Still, they now had ID'd the thieves for D, and that's all he needed. He hadn't expected it to come off so easily. If his two friends hadn't tried to step to D, hoping to assuage their lingering guilt, D might have had to sit and inhale exhaust fumes all day.

Once D saw the showboating bikers he knew his presence was suddenly a liability. Once hidden behind the corner of the apartment building, D called Ray Ray. "Yo, dog," his coconspirator assured him, "I got you. I know you must wanna know about the crew that just rolled in. That's all everybody's talking about."

"Well, what's the word?"

"They known as STP, or the Speed Tribe Posse. They not from any particular 'hood. Their members are from all over the area and are recruited by this girl called Sunrise, who only goes after certain riders based on their skills."

"Is she there now? I didn't see a woman with them."

"Nah, she not here today."

D peeped around the edge of the building and saw that everybody was still jocking STP, who'd parked and were now being surrounded by other bikers checking out their rides. Ray Ray was standing a few feet away from the crowd watching everything. D smiled and asked, "Who was the guy in the back yawning?"

"They call him I-Rod. Apparently he's got some connect for them to get the freshest rides. Some say he's a fence; some say he has a slave selling them legit. I do know this: People are a little afraid of STP. Sounds like niggas who step to them tend to get fucked up. Not wet up but just having accidents on the road and shit like that."

"You sure you're not making this up? That's a lot of info to pick up in such a short time."

Ray Ray turned to look in the direction of the building. "C'mon, dog, I'm doing my job. Besides, soon as these niggas rolled up that's all people be talkin' about. Everybody told me to keep my distance."

"So, you know what I want you to do?"

"Get up in there, right?"

D laughed, "Yeah, yo, do that. Call me tonight."

D took one more look out at the road covered by brown-skinned bikers, wondering how this particular insular little world, far removed from showbiz, intersected with that of Night and Ivy and Bridgette Haze. Why target Ivy's acts? None of it seemed random. D had already checked with Fly Ty about whether there had been other motorcycle-based abductions around town, but nothing similar had occurred. Motorcycles were regularly used in criminal transactions to transport this or that. There were no records, however, of the kind of massive swarm of bikes used in the Night case. This just raised more questions: If, for argument's sake, STP was involved as drug couriers or moving stolen goods, why the dangerous escala-tion? From where he stood, D could see Ray Ray moving through the crowds around the STP members, admiring bikes and talking trash. A little quiver of guilt ran through his body. He'd definitely put Ray Ray in harm's way, but then, what was new about that? A poor, big, beefy black boy in New York City was in harm's way from the first time his mama let him out of the house. D turned and walked away.

Chapter Fourteen

Outside Emily's Tea Party, things had changed some. The crowd was still waiting to get in, though perhaps not as anxiously as before. The crowd was still good-looking, but not quite as hip as it used to be. D Security was still handling the door, but neither Jeff Fuchs nor Mercedez nor his original staff members were visible.

When D walked up to the velvet rope, a burly white man in his mid-twenties with a twenty-first-century blond crewcut and a headset stared at him. "Can I help you?" he asked D. Clearly he had no interest in letting D in.

"No," D replied, "I can help you."

Not impressed by D's answer the young bouncer said, "And how's that, bro?"

"I can make sure you get paid tonight and the night after that and so on. My name is D Hunter, and no one may have told you, but you work for me." D opened his leather jacket and flashed the "D" button on his black jacket lapel—one that was similar to, but bigger than, the one the young bouncer was wearing. The young man blinked, knowing the name meant something, yet not ready to give in.

"Just let me check," the young man said uneasily. He took a couple of steps back and began whispering into his little microphone. After a bit of back-and-forth, the young bouncer pulled back the ropes, saying, "Sorry Mr. Hunter," while trying not to sound too kiss-ass.

"What's your name?" D asked.

"Kirk Robiski, sir."

"Good work," D said. "If you don't know what to do, check with a higher authority. That was Emily, right?"

"Yes, sir."

Inside Emily's Tea Party the spot was jumping but he didn't recognize any of the swells. Models, yes, but mostly girls living in models' apartments just off the plane from Helsinki or Lexington, Kentucky. Musicians, yes, but just wannabe rock gods from Williamsburg. And not one athlete. Not even a member of the Mets. And where was Emily, the empress of this soiree? A bartender had seen her walking into the manager's office, which seemed odd, since Emily usually didn't venture in there until the end of the evening to tally up. He wondered if his Chester Himes book was still stashed safely away.

D didn't knock—why should he? So when the two faces turned toward him, D was as startled as they pretended to be. Emily stood facing a tall, fit black man with dreads and a mustache. He was in his mid-twenties, brown-skinned, and dressed in a beautiful gray Roberto Cavalli suit. Emily's right hand was on his arm. Didn't look like they'd been kissing but it sure felt like they were about to.

She said, "D, I wasn't sure when you were coming by." Yet she knew he was here because she had been on the other end of young Kirk's walkie-talkie. As she spoke, her hand moved down to her thigh. The brother in the Cavalli suit slumped slightly and looked down at the floor. Emily moved over to D and kissed him lightly on the lips. D glanced down at her but all his energy was channeled toward her friend.

"D," she said, "this is Pierre Mbuwe, an old friend of mine."

Pierre finally looked at D. It was a guilty, sneaky look that said everything about his intentions. They shook hands politely. Pierre spoke a brief greeting in French-accented English and then turned to give a receptive Emily a hug. He murmured something to Emily in French, which made her smile, and then she kissed him on both cheeks. Pierre made sure he was arm's distance away from D as he exited the room.

Before D could ask any questions, Emily said, "I'm so glad you came tonight, D. Something bad is going on here and only you can stop it."

D now had a decision to make: Ask the old "Who is he and what is he to you?" question or simply ask, "How can I help you, baby?" Because he knew he'd been neglectful, because he knew she'd been more than understanding about his medical status, and because he knew he'd never truly give her his all, D asked the second, safer question.

Emily's answer was, "The drug use is getting obnoxious in here, D. I mean, I can feel the energy has changed. It's all these damn trust-fund kids getting out of hand. And none of this has been helped by saddling me with your second-division security. None of these new men would make a real football club in Britain."

"C'mon, Emily, stop with the soccer references. Besides, you always wanted me to expand the business and I have," he said defensively, somewhat amazed that he was the one having to answer to her. "I have to use my best people on Night and Bridgette Haze. Now we have a chance to make real money."

"I finally got served," she said.

He sighed and said, "They still haven't gotten me yet. Not that it really means anything. The suit's gonna happen. Have you seen an attorney?"

"Yes. And I've been talking to Dante."

D felt a flash of anger run through him. This information pissed him off more than catching her with Pierre. "Dante? Okay. And what's he been saying to you?"

"Things he doesn't want me to tell you."

"Funny," he said, not laughing. "I think those are the only kinds of words he knows."

Emily, who'd been standing near D, took a step back and sat on the edge of the desk. "He thinks he can get my name and the club out of the suit."

"In exchange for—?"

"He didn't lay down any terms, D," she said, trying to disarm D with charm. "He just thought it was unfair that I was being included when I really wasn't a part of what happened."

"And, as my woman, you told him to kiss your fine yellow ass."

She giggled. "Not exactly. I told him how I felt about you and that it would be wrong to help me and not help you. Especially since you two had history."

D shook his head and his voice got deeper. He couldn't believe how casual she was about all this. "Emily, you know I don't like Dante. And I don't like how you're bringing this to me, and I sure didn't like walking in here and seeing that dreadlocked French fry pushing up on you."

"What are you talking about?"

"Emily, you knew I was coming to find you. Yet you still didn't get rid of him. You know I could have hurt him easily. Easily. You know the kind of man I am."

Now she got off the chair and moved right into his face. "What kind of man is that, D? I've been with you for two years and I still feel like you're a stranger. I've put up with more shit than anybody else would. So why don't you tell me what kind of man you are?"

D was contemplating that question an hour later as he stood near the VIP booths, sipping a Coke. His stomach was still churning as he watched a redheaded waiter deliver a bottle of Dom to a table peopled with two bottle blondes, a real brunette, and a duo of spindly young men wearing too much mousse. There was nothing unusual about that table. Rich kids buying bottles to ensure a table at a hot club was, in fact, the backbone of New York night life. Not long after the bottle arrived, so did a second waiter, black-haired with a thin mustache, leaning over to talk to the rich boys. D saw a little brown package passed off by the waiter, but instead of tightly rolled bills, he was handed a credit card. The black-haired waiter walked over to the wait station to where the redhead stood. They exchanged some words. Then the black-haired waiter walked away as the redhead rang up a bill that said table one had ordered Cristal.

"Can I help you?" the waiter asked as he suddenly noticed D peering over his shoulder.

D aimed his trademark glare at him and asked evenly, "Isn't table one having Dom Pérignon, not Cristal?"

"Excuse me, sir. You are not supposed to be here."

"And you're not supposed to charge people for something they didn't order. Unless, of course, the difference is being made up by a different stimulant."

The redhead fumbled a minute before responding. "Sir, I know my job, thank you, and don't appreciate you coming over here and bothering me. I'm going to have to call security."

D smiled, showed his D Security button to the redhead, and told him, "I am security, white boy. Do we have a motherfucking problem?" D flashed a false smile that dissolved into a real serious scowl. "All joking aside, I saw what you and your partner just did. Don't try to run away after your shift. Just come see me." He took the waiter's arm and squeezed it very hard. "We cool, right?"

The redhead nodded, his face not quite as bright as his hair, but pretty close. As soon as D had gone out of his sight, the redhead went to the ladies' room. He cut past the line of women, opened the door, and stuck his head in, oblivious to the consternation of everyone around him. The restroom attendant, a Hispanic woman, mid-forties with very dramatic eye makeup and jet-black hair, came outside and spoke to him. She calmed him down and sent him on his way. She looked around for security before smiling at the women in line, and went back inside.

An hour later, Mercedez Cruz, looking very sexy in low-cut jeans, big belt, and a stomach with more cuts than a ghetto barbershop, entered Emily's Tea Party, had an apple martini at the bar, and brushed off the advances of two men. Eventually, Mercedez went into the ladies room, where she encountered Rosa Valdez, a Mexican national who'd been in the United States three years, ten months, and a few days. By the time she'd used the toilet, freshened up, and tipped Rosa liberally, Mercedez knew more than Rosa's travel history.

"The restroom attendant is the middleman on the deal," Mercedez said as she sat in the manager's office.

Emily, now sitting behind the desk, was still trying to understand how the scam worked. "But it's my party," she said, bewildered. "I still don't understand how I could be so unaware."

"Well, unless you're counting the bottles, it would be hard for you to know," D said, sitting on the same edge of the table Emily had leaned against a few hours before. "The customer wants to buy drugs for him and his pals. Instead of paying cash, they put it on their credit card along with a legitimate purchase. Since these kids are college age their parents may still monitor their cash advances and purchases. So it looks like they purchased a fine champagne and not E or Vicodin. The bottle delivered is cheaper than what's on the receipt, and the dealer keeps the difference. In this case the dealer is the house."

"But I'm the house, D."

"Well, it's your party, but the bartenders or one of the managers of the club or someone else who has access to inventory and receipts has set up a little business catering to the trust-fund crowd."

"Rosa is holding the drugs in the ladies' room," Mercedez said, "but I couldn't figure out who else is in on it. That would take me buying a lot of champagne and hanging out more and, quite frankly, I'm tired. I been hanging with Bridge and Jen all day."

"Bridge and Jen?" Emily said, and then, displaying an acute understanding of ghetto style, the Brit sucked her teeth like a welfare mother on a park bench.

Mercedez asked, "What's that about?" and stepped toward the desk.

"This is a perfect example of why you and D should be here and not hanging out with some little girl who can't sing."

"Wrong," Mercedez said, "Bridge sings very well. Right, D?"

Ignoring the question, he asked Mercedez, "Is there anything else you found out from Rosa? We'll have to put someone in here to check out what's going on anyway, but any other info would be great."

"Well, yeah, there is one other detail." Mercedez looked sheepish, an unusual expression for her. D urged her to continue and, reluctantly, she did. "Rosa said she'd been recommended for this job by that nice man, Señor Fuchs. Yes, Jeff Fuchs."

This rocked D and made Emily excited. "D, I have told you many times not to trust that man. He has a record and a very childish attitude. He might be behind this whole thing." Jeff had a drug background and he had urged D to tax the dealers at the party. But he was also a loyal friend. The idea that Jeff might be behind this scam made D feel physically ill, as if he'd forgotten his HIV cocktail and the virus was spreading. It hit him that hard. He valued all his friendships deeply, because he didn't let many people in. Now, in the course of this night, he was feeling distrustful of Emily and Jeff, and he had found out a serious crime was going down in a place he'd deemed secure. He said to Emily, "What you need to do is get the security tapes that cover the VIP section and watch them. Go back about two weeks and watch for any champagne transactions. You should be able to spot what's going on and who's doing what."

"Will you watch them with me?"

"You need to start without me, Emily. You know how busy I've been lately. Besides, the other thing you need to figure out is which one of the floor managers you work with is involved. One of them has to have been filing false inventory reports."

There was a knock on the door.

"Who is it?"

"It's Kirk, sir."

D walked over and opened door. Kirk said, "This man says he's an old friend and you were waiting on him," and then stepped aside.

"Dervin Hunter." Standing happily in the doorway was the Latino process server from his office. He was wearing an expensive-looking silver cross and a slick outfit that made him look like uptown royalty. He handed D the legal papers and snapped a picture of D with them. He grinned, said, "Good night," and walked away.

"Kirk," D said, "why didn't you use the walkie-talkie?"

"Oh, man, I'm sorry. But Ramon said it was supposed to be a surprise."

"Second division, D!" Emily shouted from behind him, and he had to agree.

CHAPTER FIFTEEN

PLANET HOLLYWOOD IS ONE of those heinous additions to Times Square designed to make tourists more comfortable than the peep shows of the past. Certainly it's infinitely more kid-friendly. Still, the idea that what passes for New York City entertainment is glass-enclosed replicas of Hollywood memorabilia, multiple TV screens, and generic hamburgers is repulsive to a great many natives, D Hunter among them. As much as he disliked the atmosphere at this huge barn of a restaurant, D bit his tongue and did his job, which, this morning, was to intimidate.

He stood next to a temporary stage as photographers clicked, TV crews shot video, and entertainment journalists (an oxymoron if ever there was one) asked insipid questions. From behind dark, green-tinted shades, D stood close enough to Bridgette Haze so that he could smell her lemony perfume, yet far enough away to be framed out of the shot by the *Entertainment Tonight* crew.

The Source had decided to hold its press conference an-

nouncing the return of its awards show to New York at Planet
Hollywood. Considering the show's checkered history of high
ratings and rap violence, bringing it back to hip-hop's home-
town would have been news on its own. But that Bridgette
Haze was to cohost with Treach, well, that was truly juicy. On
the dais, Bridgette sat next to Treach, actress/cohost Lisa
Raye, various *Source* higher-ups, and sundry hip-hop lumi-
naries. The sides of the stage were packed with members of
the permanent entertainment industry (managers like Ivy,
publicists like Rodney Hampton) as well as dates, mates, and
hangers-on of various descriptions (like Jennifer Haze).

D Security had coordinated security for the event along
with the Planet Hollywood staff and the NYPD. In his earpiece, D had three channels on which he could hear reports
from Mercedez, Clarence, and Jeff Fuchs, who was outside
working with the cops. Today the general populace of the
New York metropolitan area would find out that Bridgette
Haze was working in New York and hanging with the rap
scene, so her manager and publicist had pulled out all the
stops. Right after *The Source* press conference, Bridgette
would sign copies of her DVD video collection next door at
the Virgin Megastore and then walk across Seventh Avenue
to1515 Broadway for an MTV appearance. It was to be a big,
busy, and somewhat dangerous day of high-powered hype.

"I am so proud to have been asked to cohost the Source
Music Awards," Bridgette said with perky charm. "I know I
am not the obvious choice, but I believe in hip-hop as a
music and culture, and hope all those fans who love it will
accept me because I love it too!"

There were many questioners, but they basically all wanted to know the same thing: "You must be kidding, right?" No one could believe that Bridgette Haze was stepping into the rap world. It was one thing to have an MC lace a track or even prance around with one in a video. But this would connect the pop princess of the day with hip-hop in an unprecedented manner. While the journalists tossed questions, Rodney Hampton smiled like the Cheshire cat as he stood next to D and Jen Haze.

"Page Six. *E.T.* MTV. Quite a few five o'clock local news shows and sure repeat airings on CNN," Rodney whispered, partially to D, but mostly to himself. Then he began quietly counting down from ten. "Nine. Eight. Seven . . ."

"You got a bomb going off?" D asked.

"I'm just gonna detonate this press conference," he said and then resumed counting. "Four. Three. Two. One." As soon as he reached the ultimate single digit, Rodney moved behind Bridgette and whispered in her ear.

"Oh, okay," she said reluctantly. "I've got to go over to the Virgin Megastore to sign some DVDs." As photographers clamored for one more shot and flashbulbs popped like automatic-weapon fire, Bridgette made her way off the dais and into the Planet Hollywood kitchen, led by D. Into his lapel mike he announced, "Pretty package on the move to position two."

D led the Haze sisters, Rodney Hampton, and two members of the Planet Hollywood security staff through a door and down a staircase to the ground floor where a door stood open and two Virgin Megastore guards stood waiting. D greeted them and followed the two men down a long, well-maintained alley that connected the rears of Planet Hollywood and the Virgin outlet. "We're gonna wait here fifteen minutes," D announced.

"You have it all covered, huh, Mister Man," Jen observed.

"I hope so," he replied.

Bridgette leaned back against the alleyway wall as, like a gust of wind, her poised public persona blew out of her. She sagged against the wall and looked moodily down at her shoes. "Let me have one," she said tartly to her sister, and Jen pulled out an open pack of Kools from her shoulder bag and handed the cigarettes and lighter to Bridgette, who ingested the smoke greedily, as a hungry baby does a tit. D had never seen this side of the singer, and it surprised him more than her dirty dancing in the Bronx. She felt his gaze. "I only smoke at moments like these," she said, feeling slightly embarrassed. "Appearances always make me tense. It's not like singing. It requires a different part of me, you know. I could really do without it."

"But," Rodney added, "you really can't."

"I know," she said, and then dropped the cigarette and ground it out with the toe of her black high-heel sandal.

D looked at his watch, then asked into his lapel mike, "What's it look like outside?" There was some static and then Jeff Fuchs's voice filled his earpiece.

"Well, it's almost lunchtime in Times Square and in ninety minutes, the matinees start. So, while the whole damn area is not as crowded as on New Year's Eve, it's pretty damn close."

D switched to another channel. "Clarence, are you guys ready in there?"

"Sure," he said. "Other than keeping maybe a thousand teenagers and horny old men in an orderly line, we are ready."

The two Virgin guards took the lead, walking the posse down the alleyway to a black door, which one of the men opened with a long, flat key. He held the door open as his partner led them down a staircase to a room packed with CD and DVD boxes. The high-pitched voices of teenagers could be heard just outside the walls.

"Give me another cigarette?" Bridgette said to Jen.

"Sorry," the second guard said sheepishly. "We have smoke detectors in here."

Ignoring the guard, Jen handed her sister a Kool, which Bridgette fired up and took two puffs from, sucking in the smoke deep. "Sorry," she told the guard, "but a girl's got her needs."

D listened to the chatter in his earpiece as the Virgin Megastore guard weighed whether to dispute a superstar or incur his bosses' wrath. The guard's quandary was resolved when he heard the words "bring her in" in his earpiece. D and the first guard got the same message.

"You ready, Bridge?" D asked Bridgette, to which Jen replied, "Give her one more minute." Bridgette took one last, long drag, looked at the Virgin guards, and blew the smoke upward in the direction of the smoke detector. After she'd tossed her cigarette to the floor, Jen handed Bridgette three sheets of Listerine breath mints. Then Bridgette looked at D and nodded. The tension in her jaw, the furrows in her forehead, and the wrinkles being incubated by her tired, squinting eyes remolded themselves into a bright, professional mask of amiability, the same one that had graced countless posters and promo shots. It was a fake face that captured none of Bridgette's humor, true innocence, or growing weariness. Bridgette had discovered this face on a contact sheet of head shots taken when she was thirteen. It wasn't the biggest smile she could project or the most suggestive. There was just something particularly accessible about this smile, and Bridgette spent her teen years perfecting it before brushing her teeth at night. It was a face that said, "I love you, so love me too," a face that fed people without offering one bit of nourishment. It was Bridgette Haze's money face and it made cash registers ring.

As they walked out into the lowest of the Virgin store's three levels, cameras flashed, people cheered, and the balance in the huge space shifted as everyone's weight tilted toward a girl who weighed only one hundred pounds on days she ate too much. The ropes holding back the crowds bent back. The security guards braced their feet. Bridgette waved to her fans and wore her face like a shield. D surveyed the crowd—schoolgirls, teenagers, a couple of diligent mothers, and a man or two fearless enough to face his desires. No apparent problems. It was the nonfans, people leaning over the railings, looking at but not loving Bridgette, who concerned D. At a desk decorated with posters, videos, and DVDs, the star sat armed with three gold Sharpies.

"How is it outside?" D asked into his mike.

"Crowded," Jeff reported. "The matinee crowds are heading toward the theaters and the lunch crowd is looking for lunch. In twenty minutes or so Times Square will be packed like a mall during an after-Christmas sale. Homie, it's only a block and a half, but I'm still not sure it's a good idea."

D grunted, but there was nothing he could do. This was Ivy and that hypester Rodney Hampton's idea. It was way out of his hands. "How's it look over by the MTV studios?"

"Building, baby. Getting in won't be a problem. But getting her out we should just drive her via the Forty-fourth Street parking lot."

"Are the police cool?"

"Oh, man, they love this. Say it beats chasing after ragheads."

D switched to another channel. "Mercedez, I'm concerned about those people leaning over the railing up there."

"Roger, D," she said from her post near the main exit. "I'll get the Virgin people to move them back."

Grudgingly the heads of Virgin shoppers disappeared from the railing one and two floors up from where D stood watching. So far so smooth. Bridgette was managing to sign memorabilia, make a little conversation, and maintain that money face with no sweat showing. Her fans, though youthful, weren't hectic. Most were just bubbly little bundles of estrogen seeking a bit of validation from their role model.

Watching Bridgette work her fans actually made D relax. He wasn't chasing larcenous bikers or dealing with lawyers. He was helping make someone safe, which was what satisfied his soul. Over the next hour, D stood near the stage, occasionally receiving updates from Jeff and Mercedez, but generally enjoying this nonstress duty. The singer was to be at the store only ninety minutes, but D had put a thirty-minute cushion in the schedule to allow her to wrap up with her fans, move her out of the store, and walk her across Forty-fifth Street to 1515 Broadway and the MTV studios.

That was the tricky part. Rodney Hampton had convinced Ivy to have Bridgette walk through the midday throng followed by cameras documenting this "impromptu" moment. D had advised against it but Ivy saw this as a dramatic way to redefine his act. There were at least fifty people still on line when Rodney Hampton took a microphone and announced, "Bridgette has to go on MTV right now. Carson Daly is waiting. I'm sorry." There were groans from the crowd. "However, everyone left on line will receive a free T-shirt and a promo CD of her mix-tape appearance with DJ Power."

She waved to her fans as the two Virgin guards, her sister, Rodney, and D all took positions around her. They went past the CDs, up the staircase, and into the alley again, where Ivy and Mercedez stood waiting.

"How you feeling?" Ivy asked.

Bridgette sighed and let her face drop. "I need a smoke," she replied and waited for her sister to hand over a Kool and the lighter.

"Bridgette," Ivy scolded, "you know you can't be seen smoking."

"I thought this was all about redefining my image," she said, half facetious, half serious. She took a drag and blew smoke into the air. "Can't be more adult than cancer sticks."

Ivy pressed on. "You know with the telephoto lenses the tabloids have, it's easy for them to catch you. Isn't that right, Rodney?"

Rodney was supposed to pipe up and support Ivy, but he clearly didn't want to get into a conflict with his star client. He stammered, "Well, Ivy, I'm—" but before he went any further, Bridgette cut him off.

"Listen, Ivy," Bridgette said with an edge, "I want to smoke a cigarette. I know it's bad for my lungs, bad for my singing, and may disappoint the mothers of eight-year-olds. But I'm tired of worrying about all that. You wanna worry, you worry." She turned to her sister. "Give me a smoke, Jen."

"But," Jen replied, "you already have one," motioning to the cigarette burning brightly in her right hand.

"Oh." Bridgette giggled. She dropped her lit cigarette to the ground, rubbed it out, and then held her hand out to Jen for another. Ivy saw where this was going and turned to D.

"How much longer before we move?"

D looked at his watch, "We're already running late. They're ready for us. Whenever the lady wants to roll, we'll roll."

Ivy didn't say anything. He just turned and looked at Bridgette, his silver hair thinning by the second. Bridgette refused to return his gaze, turning from Ivy and taking some leisurely puffs as D, her entourage, a squad of media folk, a fleet of NYC police, and the staff at MTV waited. She leaned back against the wall and Jen joined her. The two began whispering. Rodney very much wanted to be part of their huddle but he clearly feared Ivy's anger. Mercedez stood close to the sisters and laughed when she overheard some comment from Jen. The sisters didn't seem to mind her listening in.

D found the whole episode very revealing. It was his first time seeing Bridgette in diva mode; his first time seeing Ivy back down from a client; and the first time he realized that Rodney Hampton wasn't simply trying to do a good job but, perhaps, was even seeking Ivy's. D was analyzing all this info when Bridgette laughed and then walked toward him with a sneaky grin.

"Hey, Mr. D, you wanna escort me across the street?"

"That's what I'm getting paid to do."

"No, I mean really escort me." She took his arm.

"I'm your security, Bridgette, not your date," he said with harsh professionalism.

And she replied in a voice of privilege, "And you work for me, right? And I say let's go."

So it wasn't simply the sight of Bridgette Haze strolling casually across Forty-fifth Street that led cars to honk, sightseers to gawk, and denizens of Nueva York to gaze in surprise. Bridgette Haze had her left arm wrapped around a grim-looking black man dressed in black and three times her size. A flotilla of photographers jockeyed with the E! channel, *Entertainment Tonight*, and sundry other infotainment camera crews to capture this odd moment at the crossroads of the world.

If D had only been a few feet behind Bridgette or just in front or watching from a distance with his earpiece on, he would have been as comfortable as he'd been just an hour before. But now he was being photographed, digitally taped, and recklessly eyeballed with a petite, famous little white girl on his arm. First of all, Emily, his nongirlfriend girlfriend, would freak out. Then his mother, an old-school southern woman who liked white people as long she could keep both eyes on them, would lash out. Then he would see himself in the paper, on TV, or on some damn website and know that someone from the Ville would remember his family, remember him, and put it all together about that traumatized little Dervin Hunter he'd banished years ago. All these thoughts made D want to seep into the potholes on Seventh Avenue and flow down into the subway. Making this public unveiling even more uncomfortable was the running commentary in his ear from Mercedez and Jeff.

"Yo, yo, yo, here comes the groom, looking like a goon," Jeff cackled.

"You two make a great couple," Mercedez remarked. "Can't wait to see you two on the cover of *Teen People*."

When they reached the corner of Forty-fifth and Broadway, by the Marriott hotel, D looked up and saw his image on the huge TV screen at One Times Square. D was so distracted he was slow to notice the long-haired white male in a SMELLS LIKE TEEN SHIT T-shirt coming his way with great determination. The guy's eyes were wide and giddy with mischief. His manner was focused, yet unbalanced. He held his hand low. D thought he saw a black object in it. When he was just four feet away and squeezing between two cameramen, D made his move. He swung Bridgette behind him, sending her knocking into Jen and then Rodney who, like a bowling pin, tumbled to the ground. The T-shirted young man jerked up his left arm, but D quickly snatched his wrist and swung it violently around. The young man yelped in pain. D pulled the young man back and then drove his knee into him, sending the young man's body onto Forty-fifth Street.

There was a wild frenzy of screams, police sirens, and people running from the center of the action. D sat in the middle of the mayhem with his knee on the young man's back, smiling as he watched Mercedez and Jeff hustle Bridgette and entourage into 1515 Broadway. D was so satisfied with his staff's performance that he wasn't overly upset when two uniformed cops rushed up to him with guns drawn. "No problem, officers," he said, raising his hands above his head. "No problem here."

CHAPTER SIXTEEN

THE DETECTIVE SAT looking at the reports in front of him, with wire-framed glasses perched on his wide, reddish nose. He was in his early fifties, balding, and looking forward to dinner at home. His wife was making her best dish—meat loaf. He said, "There was no gun found."

"I never said I saw a gun." D had his hands in his lap, clasping his fingers together to keep himself calm.

"But you acted like you saw a gun," the hungry detective responded.

"No," D corrected him. "I reacted like I saw a threatening object. It's not my job to wait and identify the make and model number of a weapon. It's my job to protect my client. I think we all agree with the president that the best way to deal with imminent danger is to eliminate it with overwhelming force."

The detective sighed and said, "You know how often I hear that these days, fella? It's like we got a whole country of cowboys."

"You know," a voice from behind D said, "this young man is not a very original thinker."

"I see," the hungry detective replied. "Well, I'm through with him. Knock yourself out."

D sat there, his back straight, his eyes steady and focused, just as they had been for many hours in police custody. When the hungry white detective left the room, D allowed his body to sag and his hands to come to his face, covering his eyes as his forehead dipped forward. Detective Tyrone Williams pulled his chair up to the table next to D. "Well," he began, "you know I don't give a damn about this nonsense."

"I know."

D removed his hands, raised his head, and looked at the man he called Fly Ty. "Still, it doesn't make me look good to have subdued a kid in the middle of Times Square with no evidence that he was a real threat."

"Listen, you wouldn't have moved on him without feeling he was dangerous. I'm sure someone will believe that."

"Thanks for that ringing vote of confidence."

"So what do you have on the Night kidnapping?"

"Nothing concrete yet. I have a guy inside a bike posse that I think might have supplied our riders. He's supposed to get back to me today. He might be calling right now."

"But you're in here."

"That's right."

"Okay."

Williams stood up and buttoned his beige jacket.

"That's it? You came all the way into the city to ask me that, Fly Ty?"

"Son, it's Detective Williams, and no, I didn't. You ever think you're being set up?"

"Excuse me?"

"You got a new security company. You handle keeping drunks from vomiting on the dance floor and stickup kids from rifling the cash register. Noble work, of course. But not like securing a major pop star hanging out in the biggest city in the world, particularly when your employer knows, or at least suspects, that his acts are the targets of kidnappers."

D stood up now, slightly pissed. "You saying I'm not up for the job?"

"I'm saying your much-sued, now-notorious ass is in a bad position if something happens to that little white girl. I know you understand that. Otherwise you wouldn't have overreacted to a cell phone in the middle of motherfucking Times Square."

"How do you know it's a cell phone, Detective?"

Williams reached into his pocket and pulled out a long black cell and laid it on the table. "This look familiar?"

It was an old black Nokia. D closed his eyes and remembered and saw the SMELLS LIKE TEEN SHIT T-shirt and the long-haired young man's hand, and then he opened his eyes and looked at the phone again. In a small voice from a very big man he said, "Where did you get this?"

"That crazy white boy with niggeritis who works for you picked it up. Guess he figured it might be wise if he gave it to a friend." Williams picked up the phone and put it back in his pocket. "People like you, D," the detective said.

"I guess I should be more grateful to my friends."

"No," Williams said and headed for the door. "Why do that? You have a lot of new friends anyway." The detective was almost out the door when he said over his shoulder, "You coming?"

There were new friends waiting for D to be processed. No charges had been filed against him, and Jeffrey Lebowitz, Ivy's attorney, noted it was "unlikely" he would receive any criminal charges. "Civil charges," Lebowitz advised, "will depend on Mr. Swanson." Mr. Swanson, better known as Pete Swanson, was the young man D had subdued, a nineteen-year-old Columbia University student and member of the postpunk band whose T-shirt he sported.

"Don't worry about that kid," D's other new friend assured him. "I've already arranged for him to get a picture taken with Bridgette and a signed poster. It's mop and glow, my friend." Sure, he'd met Rodney Hampton before and spent some time around him. Still, his presence at the precinct and his squiring of D down to his office in a black town car suggested their relationship was going to a new level. As they rolled down Broadway, D responded, "So you got it all covered, huh, Rodney?"

"Yes, I do, D."

"You are a very efficient publicist."

"Well, thank you, but I see my role in this situation as more than just that of someone who handles the media. I feel like I'm a conceptualist and an expeditor. I know how to get things done, D."

"Sounds like you're ready to manage a big star, Rodney."

Rodney smiled. He was real charmer. There was something quite boyish about this L.A. native. Yet there was no mistaking his focus on business. Adolescent enthusiasm meets business acumen. A shrewd one, this Hampton. D saw his wedding ring, but suspected that Rodney might have let it slip off a time or two. "Well," Rodney said finally, "you just have to be ready. You never know when an opportunity will present itself. Kinda like how you just jumped into this situation after Night's kidnapping. I know you're looking into that for Ivy. How's it going?"

"I have a lead or two," D said vaguely. "Nothing concrete yet."

"You know Ivy wants Bridgette to do that 'Green Lights' song."

"Only because you told me," D replied, and wondered where this conversation was going.

"It's a good idea. Good for Bridgette. Good for Ivy. Good for Adrian Dukes's widow too. You know she lives out in Hollis, Queens, right there where Run-D.M.C. and L.L. Cool J rocked their first mikes."

"You are just a fount of information, Rodney. You wouldn't happen to have a number and address on her, would you?"

"Unfortunately, no. But I do know she works part-time at an arts center out there, where she helps kids hone their musical skills. I hear it's a nice thing. I tried to get Ivy to contribute to the place—thought it might be good PR—but he wouldn't do it. Got the feeling she was a sore spot in his life."

"So, Rodney what's in this for you?"

"Someone is messing with Ivy and his acts. We both know that. He doesn't want the cops involved, but I got the feeling he's not telling you everything. Don't you have that feeling, too?"

The town car pulled up in front of 580 Broadway. "Thanks, man," D said as he prepared to exit the ride. "But you know, I have the feeling you're not telling me everything you know either."

"Just like you, D, I tell people what I know for sure. What I suspect, well, that's my business. At least for now."

D nodded good-bye and exited the car. When he entered his office he found Mercedez sitting behind his desk and on his computer. She looked up and smiled. "Hey, how was Oz?"

"Better than the show," he replied. "What's up?"

"I'm checking out Bridgette's fan site. Damn, they already have your picture up there. They move as fast as the *Post*. You wanna see?"

D shook his head and slumped into the chair that faced his desk. It was good to be back in his dark office, though he would have preferred to be alone.

"Since I've been here a woman's called three times." She handed him a piece of paper with a number scrawled across it.

"Laurita Grayson?"

"Says she's Ray Ray's mother. She said it's an emergency."

D grabbed the phone from his desk and began dialing the number.

"I know it's been a long day," Mercedez said, "but I just wanted you to know, I think you did the right thing."

D just stared into space, as motionless as a monument and just as grim. The voice that answered was black, female, and very ghetto. "Who this?" Laurita Grayson asked. He introduced himself, listened, and then almost cried.

CHAPTER SEVENTEEN

KINGS COUNTY HOSPITAL is one of the oldest in Brooklyn. Its central hub is an old brick structure that dates back to the 1930s and Franklin Roosevelt's WPA. Once a noble example of can-do American spirit, it's now an ancient relic in desperate need of a modernization that's unlikely to come. There are newer parts to the Kings County complex (across the street is Downstate Medical Center), but the overall atmosphere is of a place where old illness hangs in the air, infusing new patients with a sense of lingering disease.

Ray Ray hadn't been there long enough to have had any of the building's lingering maladies seep in. Besides, his system was already pretty busy with new ones he'd acquired in the service of D Security. "You looking good, my man," D said with a fake smile to the young man sitting in a crowded ward with his broken right leg elevated and his right wrist covered in bandages.

"You a funny nigga, you know that?"

D reached over and took Ray Ray's good left hand in both of his. "Son, was this an accident?"

"Yeah. I think so. We was out on the Conduit in Queens and I took a curve too fast, yo."

"I spoke to your mom on the phone and told her I'd definitely help with the bills."

"That's cool, yo." Ray Ray's eyes shifted toward the door of the ward and a deep smile curved his lips. "Yo, what's up, Areea?"

Areea ("A-ree-ya") Lucas came walking toward the bed in black leather pants, jacket, and boots and a white turtleneck. There was a large vintage cross dangling around her neck and nestling between her ample breasts. Golden-brown skin, like butter rolls fresh from the oven covered a face of dramatically plucked eyebrows; small, intense eyes; a flat nose; and round, authoritative lips. These were lips that never pouted. They were used to giving orders and having them executed.

"The real question," she said when she'd reached his bed, "is how are you?"

"I'm good," Ray Ray said eagerly. "I'll be back riding soon. Believe that." Ray Ray, who'd been grateful that D had come by, was anxious speaking to Areea, sounding both smitten and intimidated. Ray Ray introduced D to Areea, who said, "I saw you on MTV news this afternoon. Did they ever find that gun?"

"Gun?" he said warily. "Is that what they said? There was no gun. The man just acted in a threatening manner and I couldn't take chances."

"Yo, D, what's up with that?" Ray Ray asked. "You in MTV rotation now?"

"Oh, yes," Areea answered as she studied D's face. "D Hunter is famous. I'm impressed you know someone who hangs out with a real American idol."

"Yo, Areea, I don't know about that. I just know I was in a situation at a nightclub where some niggas was about to do some dirt to me and mine and D stepped up and handled his, you know." It was a beautiful falsehood. There was a kernel of truth in what Ray Ray said, but also enough quality deceit to truly impress D and, perhaps, cool Areea's suspicions.

"A guardian angel, huh?" Areea said as she continued to survey D. It wasn't a sexual gaze but the wary look of one warrior sizing up another.

"Angel, no," D said. "But a guardian if the opportunity allows. Unfortunately, I can't keep young men from crashing bikes."

"No one can do that," she replied. "Boys will be boys. All a woman can do is suggest what road to take and be supportive. Boys will fall down all by themselves."

"Areea runs the motorcycle club I was riding with, STP. Not only is she a hottie, but she is probably the best rider in the crew."

"Impressive. What do you do," D asked, "for a living, Areea?"

"Oh," she said coolly, "I keep it moving. Nothing regular. Just enough money to keep gas in the tank. You know how that is."

D said, "Yes, I do," realizing this woman was not going to make anything easy for him.

Areea turned her attention back to Ray Ray. "I know you didn't ride with us long, but you got a lot of love from the members, so we decided to help you a little with your bills." She reached inside her jacket and pulled out a manila envelope that she placed in Ray Ray's good left hand. Ray Ray squeezed it and felt the flat rectangular thickness of bills stacked and wrapped in rubber bands on his fingertips. "Whoa!" he said.

"It won't pay all your bills, Ray Ray," she said, "but it'll help a little." Ray Ray thanked her profusely. The polite young man under the thuggish demeanor that D had peeped before was now completely out in the open.

"Damn, Areea. I got much love for you and all the riders, yo."

"Okay, okay," she said. "You're welcome. I just ask one thing of you, Ray Ray."

"Whatever. Whenever."

She leaned closer toward him, and D asked if she wanted him to leave.

"No," she said softly. "You're a friend. What I have to say is no big secret. Ray Ray, I just want you to remember to treat us right, okay? Me and everybody in the club just want to be treated right in whatever you do or say. You do that and we'll all stay cool. That's all, Ray Ray."

Ray Ray felt a chill when she spoke, so he opened the envelope and looked inside to recapture his sense of comfort. Seeing the money certainly did the trick. "How much is that, Areea?"

"As Tony Soprano would say, 'Five large.' "

D said, "That's quite generous. Your club must win a lot of prize money."

"We do the best we can, Mr. Hunter." She leaned down and gave Ray Ray a kiss on the forehead. "Gotta go, Ray Ray." She stuck out her hand and held D's in hers. Her grip was solid and supple at the same time, an exciting combination but, again, no sensuality flowed from her to him. She was just seeing how easily he could be macked—should the need ever arise. "Mr. Hunter, do you ride?"

"It's D, Areea, and while I've been on a couple, I wouldn't say I was a rider."

"You should take it up. Nothing gets you through city traffic faster." She actually winked at D when she spoke, a cockiness that made the blood rush to his face. Both D and Ray Ray watched her leather pants swish out of the ward and then turned toward each other.

"Well," D said accusingly, "did she just buy your loyalty and silence with five thousand dollars or am I mistaken?"

"No, D, you my dog. No doubt." Ray Ray's mouth said one thing but his face suggested sudden, unexpected confusion.

"So, dog," D wondered, "what are Areea and the crew into?"

"From what I could see, and I didn't get that close, yo, I saw a lot of guys carrying packages around town. You ever see that flick about the English dude who drove shit and protected that fly Asian shorty?

"*The Transporter*?"

"Yeah, that's what they are—transporters. They get a fee and, depending on the situation, a cut. They roll up and down the East Coast as far south as VA."

"They go that far on those speed bikes they had out at Starrett?"

"Nah. Seems like they have access to all kinds of bikes. I saw some Harley Roadsters a couple of times. You know those bikes are like chillin' on your sofa. When I asked about them, guys would say they were loans or leased. They'd say that Areea and I-Rod hooked them up."

"Is that the guy who was grandstanding that day?"

"Yeah. That dude loves an audience. He talks loud. He talks all the time. He has to have everyone paying attention to him."

"How does he get along with Areea?"

"You saw her, dog," Ray Ray said with a smile. "He talks loud but she's in charge of every situation she's around."

"So what about Night's kidnapping? Anything?"

Ray Ray fingered the money in the envelope, agonizing over what to say. "I wasn't in their inner circle, D. I'd just got there, you know." Ray Ray fell silent. D just stood by the bed looking at the young man, awaiting his move. "All I heard was some guys joking about being chased by the police and about how someone they had riding with them looked like he'd shit a brick."

D's face got red. "That's it?"

"I'm sorry, D. That's all I heard on that."

"Cool," D said. No use pushing the boy. He'd gotten a

broken leg on D's behalf, so why alienate him? "You did a great job, Ray Ray. I put you in a dangerous position and you handled it. I don't have a package for you right now but I will." D leaned down, gave him a hug, and headed out of the ward.

Back outside Kings County D mulled over the info he'd gleaned: This Areea was definitely the woman on the bike and that I-Rod was likely to be the one whose bike D was on. If those guys were transporting, someone in the crew probably had a jacket—something to run by Fly Ty. The easy availability of bikes suggested either I-Rod or Areea worked for or had a tight relationship with a dealership, bike-repair shop, or manufacturer. Ray Ray had given D a lot. Even Ray Ray's accident was a plus—if he hadn't gotten hurt it would have taken D a lot longer to encounter Areea. Still, that five thousand dollars was a lot of cheese for a young ghetto boy and seemed to have put a lid on Ray Ray's memory. Even though it had been a long day and the sun would soon be setting, D decided to follow up Rodney's lead.

When D entered her parked car, Mercedez asked, "How's your cousin?"

"He's good," D said, lying smoothly. "Just messed up his leg playing ball. Young men can be reckless."

"Can I tell you that I feel honored?"

"You just did but I have no idea what about."

"Everyone at the company says no one gets to meet your family. In fact no one's even sure you really have a family."

"Oh, I got family. They have really left their mark, too."

He got quiet a moment. Mercedez thought he might say more. When he didn't, she asked, "Back to the city?"

"No, let's take a ride out to Hollis, Queens. Take Linden Boulevard out."

As Mercedez pulled out of the lot, a black-clad motorcyclist on a Kawasaki Ninja coasted by.

"Nice ride," she observed.

"Yup," he said, as the bike idled at a red light before taking off.

CHAPTER EIGHTEEN

HOLLIS, QUEENS, was the first of the many obscure black working-class enclaves to become internationally known via hip-hop. Before Run-D.M.C.'s emergence in 1983 with the twelve-inch "It's Like That" b/w "Sucker M.C.'s," Hollis was the harder cousin of the more bourgie St. Albans. In the sixties and seventies, the adjoining 'hoods were a mecca for blacks from Brooklyn and Harlem seeking homes within the city limits that afforded their families a backyard, a parking garage, and a wood-paneled basement. Several generations of musicians called the Hollis/St. Albans area home, including James Brown, Count Basie, Roy Hanes, and Ivy Greenwich's first client, Adrian Dukes. Dukes had purchased a nice two-story house in St. Albans just off Linden Boulevard for his wife, Rowena, himself, and their anticipated family a year before his suicide. It was there that the R&B singer wrote songs on the living-room piano, barbecued in the backyard, and hoped to conceive a son he planned to name Roderick.

This comfy, aging, yet well-maintained home with plastic covering the living-room furniture and renderings of Dr. King and a blue-eyed Jesus in the dining room was empty this overcast early spring night as D rang the buzzer. While he waited to see if anyone was home, D recalled how much his mother had yearned to move to Queens after his father had split. This was just the kind of house she had dreamed of. A place where her boys could play on grass, not concrete, and where the basement would be a playroom where she could monitor them at night. It never happened for the Hunter boys. They spent their lives stranded on the unforgiving streets of Brownsville.

"Nobody's home," Mercedez observed.

"Yup," D said, still caught up in his thoughts.

A woman shouted from their left, "You looking for Rowena Dukes?" She was in her late fifties, carrying a Macy's bag in one hand and pushing a shopping cart with the other as she came up the walkway to her home.

"Yes, I am, Miss. I'm a record producer. My name is D Hunter. This is my associate Mercedez. We'd sure like to talk to her about music."

"Well," the woman said, "every day about this time she's usually over at the center. It's a few blocks away, right across from what they used to call Andrew Jackson High School."

"Thank you very much," he said. Then he walked over to the woman and took the heavy Macy's bag and carried it for her into the house.

In the car later, Mercedez remarked, "I've never seen you so sweet."

"You act like I'm a mean guy or something."

"Well, you kind of are a mean guy, D. I know it goes with the job and shit, but you definitely aren't the warmest, most welcoming person."

"I'm as nice as the next man," he said defensively.

"To an old black woman you are warm. To everyone else you can be chilly."

"Then they must have had a cold when I met them."

"Yeah," Mercedez said, "that's the D I know."

The car rolled down Linden Boulevard, past two-family homes and small, modest commercial strips of grocery stores, pharmacies, and take-out food. D took a left at the old high school and spied a storefront that had a hand-painted sign that read HOLLIS HAIR. But stenciled on the window in graffiti-influenced lettering were the words HARPER'S SCHOOL OF RECORDING ARTS. A thick burgundy curtain hung behind the glass. In front of the building, chained to a fire hydrant and right under a streetlight, was a spanking new Suzuki bike.

As he crossed the street toward the bike, D planned to open its glove compartment and take a look inside. But he dropped that idea when a solidly built and familiar young black man came outside. It was the man whom D had encountered in various places over the last few weeks. They'd exchanged many a glance—most of them unfriendly. It was time for a showdown, D thought, and felt the muscles inside his shirt tighten and flex.

"This your ride?" D asked.

"And what if it is?" the surly young man answered.

"It's a beautiful thing. Must cut through city traffic like A-I through the Knicks."

The young man didn't reply, just looked at D and Mercedez and pulled on his cigarette. D could see the guy's gears were turning and was fully prepared for the young man to bum rush him or even reach into his pocket and squeeze off. D was about to try another conversational gambit when music came from inside the building. It was a live band playing the bridge to Slave's "Just a Touch of Love."

Just as quickly as it began the music stopped and a woman yelled, "Roderick, are you through with that cigarette yet?"

Roderick, aka I-Rod, turned his head and yelled back, "Almost."

"Hey, Roderick," D said and moved toward the younger man. "I didn't introduce myself. I'm D Hunter. I work for Ivy Greenwich, the talent manager."

Roderick's face grew harder. He knew damn well who D was and who he worked for. He was highly offended that D was going to play it as if they'd never met before. He didn't respond to D's outstretched hand. Ignoring the dis, D continued, "My associate Mercedez Cruz and I are looking for your mother, Rowena Dukes. We were told we could find her here."

Roderick closed the door behind him. "You were told wrong."

"Really," D said with false innocence. "You mean to tell me that Rowena Dukes, widow of the singer Adrian Dukes, doesn't run a cultural center at this location?"

Roderick gazed at D with that petulant sneer young men employ to intimidate their elders. It was nowhere near as effective as D's battle-tested glare but one day it might ripen into something truly threatening. The testosterone both men were emitting through their flared nostrils was counteracted by the arrival of Rowena Dukes at the door.

"What is going on here?" She was five-foot-four, about fifty, with graying dreads, dark, almond-shaped eyes, and hellacious curves in a number-eight Sprewell T-shirt and Baby Phat jeans. What if Angela Davis had Betty Boop's body? That was Rowena Dukes.

"Hello," D said with an incandescent smile that stunned Mercedez. Her boss was showing her some heretofore un-known dimensions to his game. D moved past Roderick and introduced himself as "an employee of Ivy Greenwich but not his representative."

"Mr. Hunter," she said, bemused, "I don't get told too many riddles during my day, so I'll give you a minute more than I'd originally intended, but don't waste my rehearsal time."

"Well, Mrs. Dukes, it's a little complicated. If we could come in and chat, I think you'll find what we have to say interesting."

"This man is full of shit," Roderick spat. "Ivy Greenwich is a thieving snake. This man works for him, so you know he's got some trickeration up his sleeve."

"Enough," she said firmly. "If this man wants to speak to me, and he's been respectful, then he'll get five minutes of my time. Now why don't you all come on in."

Roderick stood aside as Mercedez introduced herself and then followed the older woman inside. Roderick continued to stare hatefully at D as he passed him by. Inside were two electric keyboards, a drummer behind a kit, and bass and guitar players.

For decades the site had been a barbershop that served as social center, haven, and gossip central for three generations of black Queens residents. It had gone out of business in the eighties and the site had subsequently been purchased by Derek Harper, a St. Albans native son; scion of the owner of Harper's, the area's largest black funeral home; and, briefly, an R&B star with his one hit, "Black Sex." Derek had never enjoyed a follow-up success, so after beating his head against the record-biz wall (and his father's death), he'd transformed the barbershop into a cozy little rehearsal space/demo studio that also served as a nonprofit community music school. It all looked inexpensive and cozy, some state-of-the-art equipment mixed in with old fixtures and echoes of its barbershop origins. In the corner was an old jukebox filled with ancient 45s, artifacts of a bygone musical era that made D happy. "Can this still play?" he asked Rowena.

"Oh, yes," the lanky, bearded man behind a Roland 808 answered. "Every now and then we plug it in and jam like it's 1979."

"You're Derek Harper, aren't you?" D asked. When Harper agreed he was, the security guard continued, saying, "I loved your hit, man. It's a classic. My man Night sang the melody on a mix tape and then recorded it on his first CD 'cause I stayed on him about it."

"Well, then," Harper replied, "thanks for helping me get that ASCAP check. So what do you do, D? You a producer, a songwriter, or a manager?"

"No, sir," D said humbly, "I'm a bodyguard."

The roar of a motorcycle taking off came from outside. D and Mercedez exchanged looks. Rowena opened the front door and watched her son blast off into traffic. Her dreads shook sadly and she came back inside.

"Damn, Rowena," Harper said, "guess we won't be rehearsing with him anymore tonight."

"Whatever," Rowena said and walked over to the electric piano and sat down. "Why don't you wait a minute, D, and let us finish this piece. We're supposed to be playing a wedding next week and the groom is a Slave fan."

"No problem," D said and sat down on the floor against a wall near Rowena. Mercedez joined him.

"This has been an intense day, D," Mercedez said.

"Oh," he said, and nodded toward Rowena, "it's not even close to being over."

D savored the iced tea in his mouth. Sweet as a sixteen-year-old on her first date and tart as a mouthful of lemons, D let the liquid roll around the sides of his teeth before it slid down his tongue toward his throat. Rowena sat at the head of her table with a Parliament cigarette burning in her left hand. Mercedez nibbled on a large piece of corn bread, trying hard to keep her hands off the candied yams sitting succulently on her plate. D put down his glass and began again.

"There's been a lot of tragedy in my family, and my mother always went back to 'Green Lights' whenever she was troubled. It was kinda like a hymn to her."

"Like a hymn, huh," Rowena said.

"For real," D said earnestly. "She'd play it over and over to give her comfort."

"Do you like the song yourself?"

"Do I like 'Green Lights'?" D stared into space and, with a frown, replied, "Well, it's hard to say if I like it or not. It's not about passing judgment on that song. It's way past that. I know for you it's just one of the songs your husband recorded, but to me it's connected to my life in a real deep way." D's voice trailed off. He felt silly being this emotional around an employee, but he was sitting with Adrian Dukes's widow, which put his inner life up on the surface.

"No, D, it's funny about 'Green Lights.' It wasn't just a another song for Adrian either." She puffed on her Parliament and laid it in a plaster ashtray promoting an Atlantic City casino. "His father was a minister and his most popular sermon was about how embracing Jesus Christ was 'like driving a brand-new Cadillac to heaven, having green lights all the way.' The way he preached it, people would all fall out and shout 'Amen.'

"So one evening after a late Sunday service Adrian wrote that song. He told me, 'The good Reverend Dukes ain't ever gonna make a dime off it, so I better help him out.' His father wasn't too keen on it. 'Green Lights' wasn't a praise song, so it bothered him, you know. It wasn't like today when there isn't one bit of difference between church music and what someone in the street listens to. What Adrian made of that phrase was kinda dark and bluesy. But when those royalty checks came in you better believe the good Reverend Dukes definitely took his share."

She picked up her cigarette, used a puff for a pause, and then resumed the narrative: "I guess what I'm saying is that 'Green Lights' isn't your typical song, Dervin. It's got some history to it. It moved from a father to a son, like a family legacy. That song comes from a deep place. I suspect that's why your mother felt it so. When Adrian sang from that particular place nobody was better than him. Not Otis. Not David Ruffin. And sure damn not Elvis." As D and Mercedez laughed, she took a last drag and then squashed the life out of her cigarette. "My husband wished he could have sung through life instead of having to talk. Talk always got him in trouble. Me too." Her smile was wan and melancholy, and Mercedez didn't know if she should laugh or not.

D nodded and said, "I hear you."

Rowena got up and went over to a closet in the hallway. Inside were various outmoded pieces of technology—eight-tracks and a reel-to-reel tape player along with a dusty, cardboard Carnation milk box stuffed with tapes. With D's assistance she placed the reel-to-reel player on the dining-room table. "I'm gonna play you something you should enjoy." Rowena spooled a tape onto the player and clicked on the ancient machine. She picked up some dishes and left the room as the sounds of a crowd murmuring and the tinkling of glasses filled the room. Mournfully pitched horns, sad like a late-night drink, sounded first, followed by

the piano, bass, drums, and a steely guitar riff that counter-
pointed the horns. Finally Adrian Dukes stepped up to the
mike at some smoky club and started singing the words D
knew by heart, yet interpreted here in a way he'd never
heard them. More twists. Trickier inflections. A lower, huskier
range.

"This," D told Mercedez, "is Adrian Dukes."

"What a sexy voice," she said. Sexy, sure, D thought. It
was also a dead man's voice. Then he caught himself and
realized it was really a voice from the dead. He listened with
his eyes closed. And then, before the third verse, a single
tear dropped from his right eye. And then another and then
another and then many more from both eyes in an involun-
tary spasm. Mercedez looked across the table and asked him
if he was all right, but D had no words. He just sobbed quietly and lay his head on the table. It wasn't until the live version of "Green Lights" was over and D had pulled himself
back together that he noticed Rowena standing in the
kitchen doorway, smoking and looking at him.

She turned off the tape player and sat down next to him.
"I see you weren't lying to me about how you feel about this
song. You really feel it."

"I do."

"I like that. I like you, D. But you come in here and tell
me you work for Irv Greenfield and then you want me to
believe that my son's a kidnapper. Well, Irv's a thief and a
nasty old bastard. He probably set this whole thing up to
force me to release these tapes."

"These tapes have never been released before?"

"No one's heard them but Adrian, Ivy, the man who engineered the live taping, and me."

"Well," Mercedez cut in, "I hate to say this, Rowena, but that only makes it seem more likely it was your son. Why else would he play 'Green Lights' to torture Night? Why else would he have kidnapped Ivy's new R&B star?"

"That's not enough," D cut in, surprising both Mercedez and Rowena with his answer. "I don't believe he started all this to punish Ivy over some old songs."

"Well, there's the money," Mercedez added.

"Listen," Rowena said, "I've heard you talk about all this stuff my son is supposed to be involved in and it does worry me. He used to be serious about being a performer but something has changed. I do know that."

"It probably started when he hooked up with Areea, didn't it?" D said.

"You know her?"

"I've spoken to her once and encountered her a couple of times too many. My impression is that she's the kind of woman who changes men."

"Hmm," Rowena said wistfully. "People used to say that about me."

"Maybe that's why your son is drawn to her. She's a weak imitation of you," Mercedez said.

"But she's younger," Rowena said and looked over at Mercedez. "All men like 'em young."

"But it doesn't mean they're right," Mercedez replied.

"You sure right about that," Rowena said. "So you think my son was behind that kidnapping?"

Mercedez tried to be diplomatic. "Well, as D said, we really have to get at his motives for doing it. He did seem bitter about Ivy when we talked."

"Just think about it," D said. "I haven't told the police any of this yet but I will eventually have to. Now I have one more important question."

"Okay."

"Mind if I take home some of these biscuits?"

CHAPTER NINETEEN

Zena Hunter rolled over in her bed and looked at her fiancé, who slept with half his face buried in the puffs of pillows and the other half visible to his future wife. After confirming that the ringing phone hadn't awakened her future second husband, Zena turned back over and clicked a button on the mobile phone cradled in her right hand.

"Boy," she said in a harsh whisper, "do you know what time it is? It's one in the morning. You know we have to get up for work at 6:30."

"Ma," her son said with reverence and exasperation, "I have no idea what time he goes to work, but I know when you do and I'm sorry. I just wanted to hear your voice."

Zena, registering the strange tone in her son's voice, rose out of bed, put her feet into her warm, fluffy, powder-blue slippers, and shuffled into her bathroom. After she shut the door, Zena sat on the edge of the tub and asked, "Okay, did you have that dream again?"

"No. Not tonight. I just missed you."

Zena wanted to smile. It was nice to hear that from him, but she knew Dervin hadn't called to woo her at this hour.

"So I heard you were on TV today walking arm in arm with the little white girl."

"Yeah. I think I ended up in a couple of shots. There was a commotion. Nothing serious. I handled it."

"You always do, D. You've always been good about that," she said and then failed to stifle a yawn.

Zena pushed the door open a little wider to gaze at her bedmate's walnut-colored back in the dim light.

"I met Adrian Dukes's wife tonight, Ma."

"Is that right?" she replied. "She must be older than me."

This observation made D laugh, and for the first time in the conversation, Zena noticed the faint sound of drums and bass in the background. She didn't ask where he was. Ever since college he'd been around music—a club, a concert hall, a studio, that crypt he called an apartment. She didn't blame her baby boy for being a little weird. Nor did she blame herself. When life intervenes all that other stuff (plans, parenting, philosophy) don't mean shit.

His mother told him, "D, I love you, but I can't have this conversation right now. Okay?"

"If you can't, you can't." He didn't try to hide his disappointment. "It's late. We can talk about all this when you're awake."

"That's right, D." She stood up and stepped into the bedroom. "Call me this afternoon. Love you, son." Then Zena clicked off the phone and went back to bed, fitting her body against her fiancé's back, his warmth removing the chill from her body.

D flipped his cell phone closed and gazed out through the glass that separated the control room from the studio where Night sat talking excitedly to a drummer, bassist, and keyboardist. D picked up his can of Coke, sipped a bit, and belched. Got to give this shit up, he thought. He didn't drink coffee, cappuccino, or any other caffeine-based beverage, but he'd always had a fondness for carbonation and artificial flavoring. Lately, however, his stomach had been getting acidy. He knew he really shouldn't have been guzzling that sugar water. It was bad for him. But damn, he thought, I've denied myself so much else I need to get a little sweetness from something. So he tried to blame the Coke for his stomach problems. Life had gotten fizzy all on its own. He crushed the Coke can in his huge brown hands, digging his fingers into the soft metal and then squashing the top and bottom into each other.

"Yo, dog, you look tense as a motherfucker!" Night entered the control room with a fat Philly blunt in his right hand. "Normally I wouldn't share this fine, expertly wrapped, smooth-burning package of illegal medication with someone as tightly wound as you. I've just never seen anybody who needed a hit more than you."

Night thrust the blunt into D's hand and flopped onto the leather sofa next to his friend.

D said, "You know bodyguards are not supposed to get high on the job."

"When you're with me, you're just D, my friend, and my friends get lifted when I do."

D acquiesced, letting the smoke flow down into his lungs and rise high into his brain. He remembered the night he had met Night. They were hanging at the bar at Cheetah with Bovine Winslow, who'd introduced them. Both had taken shots at these two bodacious mahogany sisters from Newark. D had gone down in flames with the sour older sister (within three minutes),while Night had established a beachhead with the nicer, younger one. Turns out the sour sister had pissed off some very nasty young Nubians on her way out. They followed Night and the sisters from Newark to their car. Words got exchanged and things got hectic. The gigolo was in the process of catching a critical beat-down when D interceded, leaving the nasty Nubians bloody and carting Night to the St. Vincent's emergency room. D pulled on the joint and marveled at how Night had truly turned his life around.

"Play that back for me, Dan," Night said to his engineer. The sound of raunchy, old-school funk burst out of the speakers, with Night riding the groove as if he were Sugar-foot of the Ohio Players. "I'm bringing it back to the root," he crowed, and began singing along with himself. D just nodded to the beat, took another hit, and luxuriated in the moment. "Yo, D," Night said, "I'ma overdub this thing to death like Michael Jackson on 'Rock With You.' "

Again D nodded and was in the process of filling his lungs when Bridgette Haze, Jen, and Rodney Hampton entered the studio. Bridgette and Jen were chatting about a color of

MAC foundation, but when Bridgette heard the music, the singer began bopping her little head and gyrating her lithe body. "Oh, we getting funky in here," she said, and then without hesitation or forewarning, plucked the blunt from D's hand and dropped her butt into his lap. "My hero," she said, and hugged him.

Night watched this and decided to withhold comment. Jen and Rodney had taken up positions next to the control board, seemingly wanting to say something but laying back to see what developed. If either one had anything to say to or ask D (and both did), Bridgette's embrace of the bodyguard had silenced them for now.

"You like this?" Night asked about his track.

"Oh, yeah. Sounds like the Neptunes," she said.

"Fuck the Neptunes."

"Whoa, let me finish," she said. "But it's more organic, more real than what they'd do."

As the two singers discussed music, D sat with Bridgette in his lap. What a surreal day, he thought, and put his head back with his eyes closed. What else could happen?

The Sub-Mercer was a tiny pocket club buried in the sub-basement of SoHo's Mercer hotel, just two blocks from D's office. There was a short bar, a minuscule DJ booth, and a couple of dark corners where one could drink inconspicuously in the shadows. It was in one of those corners that Bridgette, Jen, and D sat sipping champagne from the bottles in the bucket before them. Rodney stood a few feet away, discouraging any curiosity seekers, silently pissed that he was having to do security for a security guard. A track from Portishead's *Dummy* was creating an atmosphere of intrigue in the club. It felt like a time for confidences and confessions.

"So," Jen said after a sip, "you walked into a volatile situation. When Ivy brought you in we had no idea you would be so passionate about the job. Honestly, I just thought he'd hired you to spy on Bridgette and me."

Bridgette piped up, "Unlike my sister, I knew you were a good guy from the start."

"Anyway," Jen continued, "we are seriously considering signing a management deal with Rodney, who's been great in advising us on repositioning my sister."

"But I'm not sure," Bridgette said, glancing over at the publicist to see if he could hear her. He could not, so she continued: "It's a big change. Then Night got kidnapped and it threw us. We're not sure where that fits in."

D sipped the champagne and wondered who he should sell out first—Ivy or Rodney. There was plenty of evidence to suggest Ivy knew everything about the kidnapping and was hiding that fact from his most important client. Yet if you followed the money it seemed clear that Rodney, clearly an ambitious and smart man, could have set Ivy up. If he knew about the links between Ivy and Adrian Dukes's wife and son (as he obviously did), why not break it to Bridgette himself? That info, coming from a bodyguard hired by Ivy, would surely result in Ivy's exit and Rodney's ascension.

"Listen," D began, "Ivy's a legend and a very well-connected man. He's done a great job for you. Is he getting old? Does he

have too many skeletons in the closet? No doubt. As for Rodney, he seems like a nice guy but I really don't know him, other
than it's clear he's got game."

"That's certainly helpful," Jen said sarcastically.

"Well, there is one other thing. There is a motorcycle
posse out in Queens that may be behind all this. I passed
along what I know to the police and they're gonna follow up
on it. If my hunch proves right, it may have some effect on
your management decision."

"Stop fucking with us, D," Jen said. "What do you know?"

"I'm not gonna play any games with you, Jen. I could have
it all wrong. So just be patient and let's see what the police
come up with."

Jen was unsatisfied by D's remarks and told him so. But
Bridgette cut her off. "Look, I came to New York to make
changes. That was the plan. I guess we didn't know the city
had its own plans for me."

Happy the subject was shifting, D suggested, "Why don't
you get out of the city for a few days? The Source Awards are
at the end of the week. Go away and come back for that."

"Good idea," Jen said, "except that she has a video shoot
with Bee Cole set for Tuesday and we want that video at
MTV on Monday for airing on the Tuesday after the awards.
Plus she has to do press for the taping."

A thought occurred to D, and he decided to test it out.
"Hey, Jen, why don't you manage your sister?"

A flash of excitement filled Jen's blue eyes, but her face
remained stoic. D could see it was absolutely what she

wanted, even as she tried to hide her desire from her sister. He suspected that was part of Rodney's pitch and the reason for the intimacy he detected between them. "Well," Jen said, trying to sound only half interested, "it's come up. We just have to see what's best for our family."

D wondered what Bridgette thought, but now she was zoning out, as if all her vitality was being sapped out of her. Champagne didn't usually make people withdrawn.

"Maybe it's time we all went home," he suggested.

"Bridgette," her sister said, "you do look tired."

"I am tired," Bridgette admitted, "but I like this place. It's small. There's good music and I'm having champagne with some of my favorite people, not a retailer or a program director or a reporter. No one is sweating me. I'm just a girl at a club having a drink. If we were back in Virginia, Jen and I would be sitting somewhere with some cute guys, though we'd be drinking Buds, wouldn't we?" She leaned over and placed her head on D's shoulder. She slipped her arms around his arm and got comfortable and closed her eyes. D looked at Jen, who shrugged, poured herself the last of the champagne, and walked over to where Rodney stood.

With her eyes still closed Bridgette asked, "Did you play football, D?"

"Only touch. My family was a basketball family. We didn't wanna face mask to cover our pretty faces."

"I lost my virginity to a football player."

"When? Last week?"

"Ha, ha, ha," she said without shifting. "His name was Tad Wilson. He was the center on my high school's team.

Everybody was trying to hook me up with the quarterback, but Tad was wide and very strong and had a great ass. I used to watch it all game long through my daddy's binoculars. All the squatting, I guess. Had a better ass than me."

"No way."

"Oh, yeah, D. I'm just keeping it real. You have a nice ass yourself."

"Thanks."

Bridgette opened her eyes and sat up to look at D. "Have I been making you uncomfortable?"

"Extremely."

"You probably wouldn't have crushed that guy today if I wasn't all over you."

"There's something to that."

"Well, good then." She resumed her previous, quite comfortable position. "My mother taught me never to let a man be too comfortable. I know she was right about that."

"Shouldn't you be dating Justin Timberlake or some VJ on MTV or maybe the guy from *The O.C.*?"

Bridgette ignored his question and fell asleep in the Sub-Mercer with her head against D's broad shoulder.

CHAPTER TWENTY

IN THE MURKY LIGHT of D's apartment it could have been late morning or early afternoon. Glancing at his cell phone, D grunted and pulled his big body out of bed. In the bathroom he gazed into his face, noticing the bags under his eyes getting deeper and that his left eye still got a little redder than his right (courtesy of a punch from his brother Jah when he was eleven). Once in the shower, D began contemplating a day and night filled with meetings. He tried to focus on what he had before him and not on Bridgette Haze. Was he really going to do this?

His ego, of course, wanted to own the heart (and booty) of America's sweetheart. Being hooked up with Bridgette Haze would definitely be good for business. Look at the props he'd receive being the bodyguard boning the pop star.

But there were many negatives. Like, for example, the fact that he was HIV positive. He had been fortunate that Emily was so sensitive, curious, and willing. Risking infecting someone doing so well to satisfy his own lust was like asking for a first-class ticket to hell.

And then there was the attention. Being tabloid fodder was not fun. Already reporters had been calling D Security's office seeking quotes, a bio, whatever bit of info on D they could get. And if they were calling him, they sure were calling others, offering money for dirt. No one in Manhattan knew anything substantial about D Hunter. But the phones worked in Brooklyn, out in 'hoods where the name Dervin Hunter would sound familiar. His family's past was his secret. It belonged to him and his mother. He didn't want sympathy or understanding or to see a counselor. He'd done all that and all it did was make him feel hopeless. Secrecy empowered him, allowing him to create an identity and to define himself by his own actions and not by those of his family.

Being a semi-celebrity would definitely be a pain, though it did have some benefits. "Tom Brookins has dropped his suit." Those wonderful words were spoken by his attorney, Stephen Barnes, at his small lower Broadway office. Barnes was a smart, sharp-witted black man with a graying beard and a round, authoritative face. D looked at him as if he were lying. "Did you hear me, D? It's over. His attorney called this morning and said Brookins had had a change of heart."

"Well, as much as I hate to admit it, Dante Calabrese came through for me."

"I don't believe that's true, D. I'm not sure he made one phone call or lifted a finger for you. What changed this equation was the *National Enquirer* and *US* magazine."

"What are you talking about?"

Barnes opened a file on his desk, pulling out tear sheets he handed to his client. "You need to read more, D."

The clips were from several magazines and newspapers. All centered on Bridgette Haze and her "ebony protector," "her bronze guardian," and "D-licious bodyguard." The reporters were skimpy on details about D—from Brooklyn, close to black celebrities (model Beth Ann, basketball player Bovine Winslow, singer Night), ran a small security company in New York—but mostly dwelled on Bridgette Haze's love life, including her predilection for "weighty Romeos." They detailed alleged trysts with offensive linemen, roadies, and, most infamously, a roly-poly Cuban gardener when she was just seventeen years old during a visit to Orlando, Florida.

"It's because of this shit that I can stop paying you?"

"It appears that you're too visible now. Before you were just some club security guard Brookins could crush with his wallet. Now he's afraid people will find out about the case and how he was really injured—he's missed a bunch of games because of his wrist—and that Miss Haze will help you fight the case."

"You gotta be kidding me. What a sucka."

"There is one condition."

"Hit me."

"That you promise to provide Brookins with free security the next time the Wizards are in town."

"Fuck him."

"It's not unreasonable, D. Besides, I've already cleared it with Mercedez."

"What are you talking about?"

"He wants the young woman who knocked him down to protect him."

"Oh, he wants to hang with the bitch that knocked down his bitch ass. Fine by me if it's okay by her. I used to do security. Then I became a bodyguard. Now I'm running a dysfunctional dating service."

From that meeting, D headed up to Union Square East and Zen Palate, a two-story vegan eatery overlooking the park. Upstairs at a big round table by the window he sat with Bee Cole, dressed remarkably ordinarily in low-riding jeans, big belt, and a clingy, white cashmere sweater; Ivy Greenwich, looking tan after a quick trip to Costa Rica; and two male members of Bee's production team. They munched on faux food (most of it composed of either soy bean or wheat gluten) with budgets and schedules on the table around them. It was D's first time in Ivy's presence since the Times Square incident and the pilgrimage to Queens.

"For this video shoot," D said, "I want nothing to compromise Bridgette Haze's security. The Times Square event was well conceived from a PR point of view, but it was obviously a security disaster waiting to happen. I don't want Bridgette and, quite frankly, my company to be put in such a vulnerable position again."

"D," Ivy said reassuringly, "there was lots of bad judgment displayed by people who should have known better, including yours truly. Some forces influenced those events that, I assure you, will not influence Bridgette to that degree ever again."

"Okay," D said, "I know this will be a very elaborate shoot with a great degree of spectacle but I want it to be clear that all production personnel will have to check in with my staff, that only D Security will control passes, and that any major changes in the schedule will be made in consultation with me."

Bee smiled and said, "I love a forceful man," but D's face barely softened. He was in no mood to be flirted with. Seeing this, Bee pulled back her fishing rod and agreed to D's demands. After that, talk at the table moved back to the details of the two-day shoot. No problem shooting at the Apollo. No problem using that S&M club in the Meatpacking District or the strip club in the Bronx. But D was troubled by the money shot, which featured Bridgette Haze and a gang of New Yorkers she befriends on her nocturnal journey dancing at dawn on the Brooklyn Bridge.

"Couldn't it be City Hall or a rooftop or someplace more easily controllable?"

"The video is a metaphor for how the city brings people together," Bee told D, "and the bridge is an internationally known symbol of the city, sugah."

"You agree, Ivy?"

"It'll connect Bridgette with New York in a powerful way and that's why we came here in the first place."

Resigned to helping secure the Brooklyn Bridge, D took notes the rest of the meeting and wondered if either Ivy or Bee was going to bring up the tabloid stories linking him with Bridgette. But the meeting stayed professional. Only as he was leaving for One Police Plaza did Ivy suggest they talk privately later, though D detected no leer in the older man's eye. Down at Police Headquarters, D was joined by Jeff Fuchs for a meeting with a sergeant from a Brooklyn Heights precinct, a coordinator from the city's antiterrorism squad, and a rep from the Mayor's Office of Film and Television. It was very workmanlike. Question: What time would the crew start setting up at the bridge? Answer: 3:00 P.M. Question: What time would Bridgette Haze arrive at the bridge? Answer: Around 3:00 A.M. Question: Would she be giving autographs to members of the NYPD? Answer: Absolutely.

Afterward D and Fuchs strolled up Centre Street, through Chinatown, and up toward SoHo, sharing their first private chat in several days. "So are you fucking her?" Jeff asked as they crossed Canal Street.

"No. Don't believe what you read. If anything's going on, it's a little crush on her part. Nothing serious."

"No," Jeff replied. "Not the little singing stunt. That Puerto Rican bitch, Mercedez."

"Jeff, she's not a bitch. If I'm not wrong, Mercedez has been an asset to D Security."

"So you are fucking her?"

"No. I'm not."

"Oh, she's just giving you head?"

D stopped in front of the old Police Headquarters on Centre. It was now a ridiculously expensive condominium. A doorman in a brown blazer looked out at the two men with concern, sensing the tension in their bodies. "Come on, Jeff, what's with you and her?"

"I don't understand how you're giving her access to information I don't have." There was real hurt in Jeff's raspy voice. "I don't understand how you seem to trust her more than a man who's always had your back."

"Listen, Jeff, you are still my dog. No doubt. Mercedez just happened to have been around a few times when I thought a woman could be helpful. Besides, the Haze sisters like her. That's all."

"That's not all, D. I know you're a secretive motherfucker. That's your right. But there's more going on than you're letting on."

D wondered if this was the right time to bring up the drug-dealing situation at Emily's Tea Party. He could have cold-busted Jeff right there, but D realized there was another issue in play. D started walking again with Jeff right behind, anxious for his friend and boss to reply. They'd walked half a block when D turned to Jeff and said, "You and Mercedez did the nasty?"

"No." Jeff said blandly.

"Something sexual went down, am I right?"

"Kinda." All the fire had left Jeff's voice. He sounded like a little boy now. "But that's not what this is about."

"No, huh."

"Yeah."

"Jeff, you're a lying motherfucker. But, hey, that's cool. It's your business—your business until it starts to interfere with mine. Right?"

Jeff agreed and looked beaten down. D decided the Emily's Tea Party situation could wait.

It was five o'clock by the time D Security's weekly meeting got under way. First he announced the dropped Tom Brookins suit to applause, and Mercedez's assignment to laughter. Despite that lightness, there was a palpable tension between Jeff and Mercedez that D tried to ignore. He just plowed through the details of the shoot: where staff would be stationed, who the police liaison would be at the various locations, handing out the insurance forms and time sheets, and the other mundane details of managing a field operation. As usual, Jeff was assigned to coordinate with the Film and Television Office and, in a real surprise, he would have Mercedez work under him. Both Jeff and Mercedez were protesting when Clarence, the classy, always distinguished gentleman of D Security, cut in.

"D," he said, "I have a crucial question regarding the shoot." As the veteran member of the company, everyone deferred to Clarence whenever he had something to say.

"Please, Clarence," D said, "what concerns you?"

"Just wanted to know whether you are going to be doing your work outside or inside Bridgette Haze's trailer?"

D was stunned into a stutter. Clarence burst out into a deep, full laugh that infected the entire room. Whatever questions about D's relationship with the singer lingered in the room, they were diffused by Clarence with one bad joke.

"Nothing serious is happening, Clarence," D said finally. "I'll be out in the cold just like everyone else."

"Oh yeah," Clarence said next, sparking more laughter. D broke up the meeting soon afterward and gave Clarence a hug. D grabbed a backpack out of his office and headed to the elevator with Jeff and Mercedez on his heels. "Listen, you two," he said with fatherly exasperation. "I have to go handle a family emergency. You guys have a problem, well, work it out. I'm your boss, not your referee." The elevator doors opened, D entered, and, after a wave good-bye, let the doors close in their faces.

It had been a busy day and it was far from over. Downstairs one of Tony's TZL town cars was double-parked at the curb, and as soon as D entered, it rolled down Broadway. A left on Canal took the car over the Manhattan Bridge and, once in Brooklyn, onto Flatbush Avenue. As Brooklyn landmarks like Junior's and the Brooklyn Academy of Music passed the town car's windows, D checked messages on his two-way: two from Bridgette Haze wondering how his day was (answer: hectic) and whether he'd stop by the studio tonight (answer: can't); three from companies hawking security gear (wiretaps, miniature surveillance cameras, al-Qaeda–proof metal detectors) and sundry e-mails from the usual nuisances (party promoters, Viagra sellers, sex sites featuring Sepia Sluts).

By the time the car had made a turn onto Eastern Parkway, D was satisfied that he was on top of everything, so he leaned back into the leather seat, loosened his muscles, and contemplated the wide boulevard's tall, skeletal trees. During Labor Day weekend, the West Indian Day Parade filled this avenue with floats, steel bands, beef-patty salesmen, and over a million, many inebriated, mostly brown New Yorkers re-creating the carnivals of the Caribbean during one long day.

As a child, D had loved to walk up and down Eastern Parkway the day of the parade, pushing and dancing through the throngs all the way from Brownsville, at the far eastern end, through Crown Heights and all the way west, past the Brooklyn Museum and the beautiful Botanical Gardens, to the arch at Grand Army Plaza, next to the entrance to sprawling Prospect Park. It would take all afternoon to make that trek, but it was a joyful walk. When he was six he sat on Matty's shoulders and felt as if he could see over the entire vast crowd. When he was ten he held Rashid's hand as his middle brother flirted with Trinidadian girls gyrating with butterfly wings on their backs and garish makeup on their otherwise comely faces. At twelve he spent much of the day searching for Jah amid the smoky clouds emanating from the clusters of herb dealers prospecting on the edge of the crowd. When he was a teenager, D walked the parade alone, enjoying the music while searching for ghosts. He hadn't attended the West Indian Day Parade in years and had no plan to do so ever again.

The sedan made a left off Eastern Parkway near Lincoln Terrace Park and went up two blocks to an ornate, well-maintained old church. A huge video screen and a baptism tub dominated the high hall. Its long, overhanging balcony and the presence of several cameras around the room made the church seem more a concert hall than a place of worship. As D walked toward the front of the church, faces turned his way—some sitting in pews, a couple standing by the wide, brightly lit pulpit. None of them, however, was the person he sought.

"Hello, Dervin." Willis Watson stood up from a pew to address his future son-in-law. He was half D's height and yet was not a small man. He was barrel-chested with wide shoulders and a head well matched with his round, full lips. Willis was a lifter, a trait he shared with D, though attempts to bond through that activity had proved fruitless. D had no interest in the man, a fact he barely disguised. "Where's my mother?"

"She went to the restroom." Willis extended his hand. D shook it perfunctorily, as if he'd just been offered a bad business deal.

"I hear you're a celebrity nowadays, D."

"Really." This was not a conversation he wanted to have with Willis Watson.

"Yeah, people on my job were telling me you were the new Chris Judd."

"Chris Judd?" The reference bewildered D for a moment and then it sank in and made his stomach do a backflip.

"Oh, yeah. J. Lo's second husband. Listen, Willis, you can't believe everything you read, except the Bible. Everything else is a scam."

From behind him he heard his mother call his name. She came striding up toward the pulpit with purpose. "D," she said, "it's about time you got here."

He apologized, kissed her lips, and awaited his orders. Zena Hunter's reappearance made things happen. The reverend showed up. The organist sat on his bench. Willis Watson and his friends assumed their positions. Zena took her son by the hand and led him to the back of the church. As they walked, D asked, "How are you, Ma?"

"How am I? Well, my youngest boy is consorting in public with some little white girl and I have to hear about it all day at work. I understand that some fool on the radio in the morning called it 'Beauty and the Beast.' "

D sighed. He was tired of saying there was nothing going on, tired of trying to ignore or make a joke about it. Whatever his mother wanted to say, she'd say anyway. As if he could stop her.

"You remember what I used to say?"

"Which thing, Ma?"

"About white girls."

"You said a lot of things, Ma."

"Well, the one you should have remembered is that it was fine to bring them home. I'd be nice to them, serve them dinner, and make polite conversation."

"Oh," he said, trying to cut her off. "Yeah, I remember now."

"Clearly you don't," she shot back. "'Cause the last part was that I'd walk them to the door and you could take them back to wherever they lived—"

"But don't expect to be let back in your house."

"Thank you."

"Don't worry, Ma. I'm not bringing her to your home."

"I'm not worried about that," she said. "I just wanna know if she's coming to my wedding."

"No way. Don't worry."

"I'm not worried. I just wanted to know where to seat her at the reception, knowing she'd have an entourage and all."

"Oh," D said, "sorry to disappoint you. You want me to bring a white woman to your wedding?"

"It's all right if she comes. You know, she might even sing a song or two."

"Okay, Ma. I'll look into it."

The reverend had been waving for them to come down. Zena took her son by the arm and guided him toward the altar.

CHAPTER TWENTY-ONE

"To da break of dawn, uggh! To the dawn!" The sound of hard-partying young male and female voices blasted from huge speakers on the most famous street in Harlem. Twenty dancers garbed as thugs, dykes, strippers, cops, and S&M practitioners moved in freaky unison to the beat. Huge lights illuminated 125th Street as Bridgette Haze sprinted out of the world-famous Apollo Theater, clutching first place in the amateur night contest, and dashed into a waiting gypsy cab. The converted-police-car-turned-taxi was crimson and was driven by DJ Power, who, in the video, was playing the singer's whacky guide to a wild night in underground New York. The car sped off toward St. Nicholas Avenue, right past two 35-millimeter cameras. As it swished by, Bee Cole yelled, "Cut!" then turned to her DP and said, "Check the gates." The gates on both cameras were checked. Notified that the gates were clear of hair and dirt, Bee announced, "Let's print that and move on."

The music evaporated from the night and was replaced by the chatter of walkie-talkies, the murmur of mingling production minions, and the clamor of fans lined up behind barricades across St. Nicholas. The first assistant director, a stern young black woman named Jua, spoke briefly with her boss and then loudly declared, "We're wrapping location. Company move." The other ADs and the sundry production assistants and department heads began picking up, boxing up, and moving out objects and people.

Bee got out of her director's chair, took two steps from the bank of monitors she'd spent much of the last three hours in front of, and yawned as she stretched her lean body with feline indulgence. A muscular male PA walked over to her with a bottle of Evian water. She took the bottle from him and sipped slowly as she eyed her buff young employee. "I need a back rub," she announced.

"Sure," he replied and reached out to rub her shoulders.

"Oh, that's good. Strong hands," she said. "Let's move this to my trailer."

Down the block from the video village, fans screamed at Bridgette Haze as she was escorted out of the taxi by D, wearing his trademark scowl like a suit of armor.

"Yo! Yo, shorty! Whas up with you?!" a pudgy, light-skinned teen in a red Phat Farm hoodie shouted. "I know you like it big and brown!"

Bridgette ignored the jibe, though the crowd around the young man howled in response. D's ears burned and he glared at the teen, who was unintimidated. His look said, I wish you would, and D had to grudgingly appreciate the teen's badass nature.

It had been a long, exacting, but very smooth two New York nights. The previous evening they'd ventured into a Bronx strip club and dallied around Manhattan, including an S&M club and Times Square. The production had spent most of this night in Harlem, shooting in and around the refurbished Apollo. After breaking down this location they were off for the money shot on the Brooklyn Bridge. Securitywise it had been a cake gig. No sign of motorcycles. No threat of kidnapping. No kids in TEEN SHIT T-shirts. It was eerie, actually, how uneventful the shoot had been. D wasn't complaining, but he didn't trust this ease. Not one bit.

D opened the door to Bridgette Haze's trailer. Inside, a shouting match was under way. Rodney Hampton stood in the middle of the luxurious trailer looking down at a smug Ivy Greenwich. Sitting near Ivy, looking mortified, was Jen.

"Well, someone contacted my wife," Rodney was saying when Bridgette came up the staircase. The publicist struggled to pull himself together. "Hey, Bridgette, so good to see you." He came over and hugged the singer, but his efforts at affection were hindered by the rage that still filled his body. D stood behind Bridgette. Thinking he'd get some questions answered, D just folded his arms and leaned back against the door.

"Rodney," Bridgette asked, "why are you so angry?"

"Well," he said, "I believe your manager is trying to ruin my marriage."

"And," Ivy said, "as I was telling Rodney, I don't know who

sent those pictures to his wife, but it was not me. I have no beef with Rodney, and it's hard to imagine anyone having such anger at a mere publicist. But these things happen."

"Infidelity?" Bridgette wondered out loud. Then her gaze shifted from Rodney to her sister, who sat looking at the floor. Jen didn't say anything to her. Didn't have to.

"Okay," Bridgette said, "I don't think this is the time to figure this out. I have a video to finish."

"I'm sorry, Bridgette," Rodney said, "but we have to deal with this now. I can no longer work for a man of so little integrity and neither should you."

"This is not the time for this, Rodney."

"No," he replied, not backing down. "This *is* the time. You need to make a decision about your future. Your sister has told me you want to make a change. Isn't that right, Jen?"

Jen stood up and said, "My sister makes her own decisions, Rodney—just like you make your own. She'll change managers if and when she feels like it. Just like you'll change wives when and if you feel like it. Everyone does what's best for them. Isn't that right?"

"Jen." Rodney spoke softly, his voice as tender as it had been accusing just moments before. "Jen, I am so sorry."

"Yes, Rodney, that's the problem. You're sorry." Jen then walked past Rodney, her sister, and D and right out of the trailer. Bridgette watched her sister go and then stepped over to Rodney and slapped his face. He took it and didn't respond. Emulating her sister, Bridgette walked past Rodney and the sitting Ivy and went back into the trailer's bedroom, slamming the partition shut.

Someone had sent Rodney's wife some incriminating photos, and both Ivy and Jen were worthy candidates. But what concerned D was who had taken the photographs. If someone from his company had been moonlighting in the blackmail business, well, that was a serious problem. D cleared his throat and said, "I get the gist of what went down here. Actually, it's really none of my business and I'd be happy to leave, except that I need to know if any of my people were involved."

"Come on, D. Stop that innocent shit. You are capable of a lot of things, but lying well isn't one of them," Rodney said as he snatched a manila envelope off a countertop. It had the D Security logo stamped on it. D could feel photographs inside, but he didn't look in.

"Anyone could have used our stationery," D said. "It doesn't prove a thing. How long ago was this sent?"

Rodney ignored D's question and looked down at the sofa-bound Ivy, who, despite all the hubbub, hadn't moved an inch and looked quite comfortable. "I guess you win, Ivy," Rodney said.

"Oh," he replied calmly. "Was there some kind of competition going on?"

"Apparently not. You'll have my resignation in the morning and an invoice for my overdue payments."

"Whatever you wish, Rodney. Have a nice flight back to Cali."

Rodney moved toward the door, pausing at D to mutter, "Don't trust that motherfucker," and went out the door into the Harlem night. Now it was just Ivy and D in the trailer's main room. D pulled over a chair from the dining area and shifted it to face the manager.

"How was Queens?" Ivy asked.

"Like always. Little houses. Fake thugs. A little too far away from everything."

"You find out anything interesting?"

"Ivy, I just saw you break up a business deal and possibly a marriage, and you did so by apparently employing someone on my D Security team. So don't act like you don't know who I talked to or what they said. Let's skip that dance. What we need to get at is why you're letting a young man—a young man who just might be your son—terrorize your business."

Ivy looked toward Bridgette's closed bedroom door and in a whisper replied, "Let's have this conversation outside."

The crew was speedily breaking down the lights, the dancers were being corralled into charter buses, and the police were urging the remaining fans to move on. Amid this hectic activity, Ivy found a streetlamp to lean against. "Okay, it's like this. Dukes's widow hates me. She blames me for her husband's suicide. Her boy was raised with all that anger and it boiled over this year. He's young. He's got no direction. He's got no father. Hating me seems to have given some focus to his life. I've been hoping it would go away. That I could reason with her and him and keep his ass out of jail. But then he got hooked up with that crazy motorcycle woman and things have gotten out of hand. That's it."

D said, "That's bullshit, Irv Greenfield. I know what Roderick looks like. That is your son. Period. You were fucking the wife while Dukes was on the road. He found out. I guess he was tenderhearted, so instead of killing you he bailed out on life. Green lights all the way to the motherfucking ground. Tell me I'm wrong."

Ivy kept a self-satisfied look on his face but his eyelids shook like a dog being washed. It was an amazing sight. Ivy had total control of his lips and his cheeks due to years of deal making. He could make them project whatever, whenever. But his eyelids and the wrinkled area around them were determined to reflect the truth on this particular night.

Ivy sighed. His eyes watered. That last bit of slickness, that remaining level of control, disappeared, and now his whole face was in harmony with the truth. "I met Rowena first. At the Lenox Lounge, not far from here. She walked in wearing an orange dress and a bright red wig and I lost my heart to her. She wasn't really into white men. Thought I was looking for a mistress." He laughed sourly at that thought. "Anyway, she loved music so I invited her to gigs I was promoting. She met Adrian at one of them. That was a couple of years before 'Green Lights.' He was a fine singer but a bit of a mama's boy. Didn't know shit about women. I guess that's what attracted Rowena to him. They got married and I was the best man. All the while I was still in love with her."

In his earpiece D heard Jeff Fuchs announce they were moving Bridgette and Jen to Brooklyn. D motioned for Ivy to stop and told Jeff he'd meet him down there. While D was talking, Ivy started walking east on 125th Street. D caught up to him.

"So," Ivy began again, "I rolled with it. They were doing all right. Then 'Green Lights' hit and Adrian got brand-new.

He went from choirboy to cock hound and was banging everything that moved. Rowena didn't have to know this. As his manager it was my job to keep shit like that undercover."

"But, as we know, certain secrets are very useful."

Across the street was the Apollo, where staff members were putting padlocks on the famous doors and beginning to pull down the metal gates. Ivy ignored D's comment and continued: "Adrian had played the Howard in D.C. and was supposed to be on his way home. But he made an unscheduled stop at a Howard University dorm. After he left, one of the schoolgirls called Rowena. How she got the number I don't know. I mean I really don't."

D said, "Anyway."

"I got back to New York first and I caught her fall. We only had sex once. That's all."

D's fist clenched and the blood rushed to his head, but if the man wanted to testify, he shouldn't be interrupted by a kidney punch. "If that call hadn't gotten through from D.C., I'm sure they would have stayed together. But that breach of trust was never repaired. Adrian got deeply depressed. We couldn't get him into the studio to record his follow-up when he was still hot. He moved into the Theresa Hotel."

Ivy looked up and D's eyes followed. Above them loomed the large white building that had once been Harlem's most famous hotel, where the greats of black culture and even Fidel Castro had slept. Somewhere on the street before them Adrian Dukes's body had landed a few decades ago.

"So you never claimed Roderick as your son?"

"After I saw the baby it was clear what was what. But

Rowena wouldn't do it. In light of Adrian's death I'm sure she was afraid of what people would say. She placed her guilt for cheating on D on me. All that boy has ever known is that I was a thieving Jew trying to steal his father's legacy. Was that right, D?"

D didn't care and wouldn't offer an opinion. He just wanted to know. "So this Areea woman pushed him from anger to action?"

"I guess," Ivy said. "So are you gonna turn him in to the police?"

"Well, I'm working for you, Ivy, or have you forgotten?"

"But I know how close you are with that cop Williams."

"Ivy," D said, exasperated with Ivy's attitude, "I don't understand why I'm even involved in this mess. Why did you hire me?"

"To protect Bridgette Haze and spin your wheels investigating while I figured out my next move. I had no idea that Rodney and Jen would get together and lead you to all this information. I mean, I wasn't trying to fuck with you. I was just buying time with Night and his girlfriend until I could get a handle on the situation."

"So when do you tell my friend you knew all along who'd endangered his life and that of his woman?"

"I did not know the whole time, D. Believe me. It wasn't until he talked about 'Green Lights' being played for him that I knew."

"Okay," D said, "that's your story and it is your business. But Night is my friend. If you willfully let him stay in harm's way, and I find out, you're gonna have a problem."

D glared for effect but Ivy's bout of truth-telling had

passed. His regular mask of glib deception had been glued back in place. "I have two more questions for you, Ivy."

"If I know the answers, you will, too."

"Which one of my people took the pictures of Rodney and Jen?"

"That wonderful Latina woman of yours."

"Did you step to her or did she come to you."

"I don't remember."

D picked Ivy up and tossed him against the window of the fried-chicken joint. The old man crumpled onto the sidewalk and held his head. The same hacking cough that had hit Ivy at Emily's Tea Party ripped into his body again. It was a dry, nasty sound, as if all the juice had been squeezed out of Ivy's body. He reached into his pocket for pills and D slapped his hand, sending the pills to the ground. Then he moved his face close to Ivy's. "Now for my second question: Are Roderick and Areea still trying to snatch Bridgette, or did my hanging around Queens make them nervous?"

Ivy reached down to retrieve the pills, but D grabbed him by the jacket and pushed him roughly back against the wall. "I asked you a question, motherfucker."

The fear that gripped Ivy calmed his coughing a bit, and he stammered, "I don't know. I really don't know. I'm sure you spooked Roderick—the boy's unstable. But that woman doesn't seem easily intimidated."

D nodded—that sounded right—and then picked Ivy up from the ground like a garbage bag. A few remaining PAs had seen D in action and were now half picking up debris and half waiting to see what would happen next. D just stared at him, wondering if it was really worth it to vent on Ivy's aging body. As he stood there contemplating more violence, Ivy, who'd been roughed up more than a few times in his life, pulled it together. When he asked, "Do you wanna ride down with me?" D almost laughed. This man, D had to admit, was a survivor.

"No," D said as he walked away. "I'm taking the subway. Better class of people."

CHAPTER TWENTY-TWO

Suckers have been buying the Brooklyn Bridge since the day it was completed, well over a hundred years ago. It's a beautiful structure with a medley of lean metal rods creating an intricate spider's web linking several stone dominoes. It's a sweet balance of complexity and simplicity that makes the other East River bridges look, at best, utilitarian (the Manhattan) or just plain old butt-ugly (the Williamsburg). If you were going to photograph a multimillion-dollar music video on any bridge in New York, only the Brooklyn would really do. Which was why at near the crack of dawn on a Sunday morning scores of disgruntled travelers were being rerouted at Tillary Street in Brooklyn and at Centre Street in Manhattan. For a few hours this beautiful structure belonged to Bridgette Haze.

"Five minutes to sunrise! Everybody in position!" Bee Cole's first assistant director yelled into a bullhorn as dancers limbered up and the crew made hurried checks of the six cameras stationed to capture nature's magic. In Bridgette's trailer, her makeup was being touched up, her hair tweaked, and her legs massaged. Three skilled professionals were tending to Bridgette's body, tuning her like a concert piano.

Jen sat quietly, watching her sister get ready to perform, just as she'd done hundreds of times before. Aside from the professional image-polishers, the Haze sisters were the only ones in the trailer. No manager. No publicist. No body-guards. Despite all the fussy activity around her, Bridgette was outwardly calm, yet joyous inside. This was her comfort zone—her sister by her side as she prepared to rock the world. One day she would desire children. One day she'd seek out a husband. Right now, however, her only goal was to make her mark on history, to fulfill the fantasies she'd projected onto her bedroom ceiling.

There was a knock on the trailer door. "Come in," Jen said. D entered, looking refreshed by his ride downtown on the A train.

"Fifteen minutes to sunrise, Bridgette. They need you in position."

"Which position is that?" she said back, very flirty. What-ever anguish she'd felt up in Harlem was gone. She was back being the star, the ruler of all she surveyed. For her, D was a wonderful short-term addition to her life. He was tall, dark, handsome, and seemed to exist solely to keep her safe. Unlike most men around her, D's desires seemed simple. They didn't involve running her life or getting rich off her talent. He didn't even seem that enthused by her attentions. Sure, he wanted to fuck her—the man wasn't crazy. Still, he wouldn't have made a move if she hadn't pushed him. In a world of grabbing hands, slippery words, and constant flirtations, D's reticence was incredibly attractive.

"On the bridge, Bridgette," he said, smiling, and she rose to join him.

Outside, Bridgette put the crook of her arm in his and walked behind an AD who led them from the trailer past the large percolating generator, up a dark staircase and up to the walkway that led hardy pedestrians across the Brooklyn Bridge. Along the way they passed key members of D Security—the solid old-timer Clarence, his old buddy Jeff, and the lovely Latina Mercedez. Monday afternoon he'd have to sit down with all three. With Jeff and Mercedez, to determine how many side deals they'd been cutting, and with Clarence, to figure out what to do with them.

D knew once this shoot was completed and Bridgette was neatly tucked into her bed, there would be a lot to figure out: D Security's future, his relationship to the woman on his arm, and how to tolerate his mother's new husband.

Bee Cole and the choreographer, a fey black man with a woolly natural, stood awaiting the singer. Bee gave his arm a squeeze and then walked Bridgette to her position in front of a phalanx of dancers. The sun began to edge out the horizon.

"Roll playback!" Bee commanded, and then yelled, "Action!" Cameras rolled, dancers wiggled, and the sun appeared like a slice of orange peel on the horizon. All eyes were focused on Bridgette on the bridge. Bee sat behind her multiple monitors, savoring this iconographic pop moment that had come to her a week ago on the StairMaster. Ivy sat a few feet away, sipping coffee, no longer thinking about the past but of how he once again owned the future. Jen, both proud and bored, was watching her sister, while she contemplated her judgment in getting emotionally and professionally involved with a married man.

The sun was full but low as the song ended. The first AD yelled. "We're going again!" as makeup and hair staff, gaffers, and electricians scurried to do touch-ups or make adjustments. In this brief space between takes one and two, not longer than forty seconds, D heard motorcycles. Many motorcycles. As everyone else gazed toward Bridgette and the bridge, D looked away from the set.

"I just heard motorcycles," he said into his headphone. "Anyone have a location?"

"Nothing on the Manhattan side," Jeff said, "but I'll alert the police."

"I heard them too!" It was Mercedez. "But I don't see any down by the trailers."

"I'm headed your way," D said and moved back toward the steps. The playback kicked in and everyone on the bridge refocused on making MTV history. By the time D arrived down by the trailers, Mercedez, Clarence, and several other staffers had gathered to meet him. "Okay, there are plenty of cops and barricades over here. Maybe they won't make a direct attack but try to swarm us as we get ready to move Bridgette."

D was still talking when a large mobile generator exploded into orange and blue flames. His staff members dashed toward the fire, but D held himself in check and moved back to the bridge's staircase. The sound of frenzied chatter filled his headphones. Sirens wailed. People screamed. And, buried inside those sounds, was another—the roar of motorcycle engines.

"Jeff, bring Haze to the Manhattan side!" he barked, but in the chaos, no one seemed to hear him. Here it was, the moment of truth for his team, and no one was home. "Bring Bridgette Haze to the Manhattan side!" D turned and looked up the stairs where crew members, dancers, and a certain pop star were stampeding down. Jeff had Bridgette and Jen in either hand. How he'd gotten across the bridge so quickly to grab her mystified D, but there they all were.

"Follow me!" D said. Both Haze sisters were bordering on the hysterical, asking questions in high-pitched voices. D grabbed Bridgette from Jeff and led them away from the chaos under the Brooklyn Bridge.

From three directions motorcycles roared into view. The police had established perimeters, but someone had left barricades askew in several places and the bikes roared into the production area. A policeman had his knee shattered as he tried to intercept one bike. A female PA was run over when, in a panic, she tripped and fell into the path of an oncoming bike.

D didn't see any of this. Along with Bridgette, Jeff, and Jen, he was in a mad dash through the streets of DUMBO, the neighborhood of converted factories and loft living between the Manhattan and Brooklyn bridges—the same area that Night and Tandi had been dropped off in by the kidnappers. Jeff pulled out a nine-millimeter from his waistband. D saw it, but this wasn't the time to discuss Jeff's legal status.

If he could get around the base of the bridge, D figured they could head up into Brooklyn Heights where it would be easier to hide. That early in the morning in DUMBO there were no cars on the street, nothing to flag down, nothing to escape in. D wasn't letting that worry him. His adrenaline was pumping hot. He couldn't believe how good he felt.

The heel of Bridgette's right platform shoe broke and she fell to the ground. "My ankle!" D didn't hesitate. He picked her up and cradled her in his arms. Part of him wanted to laugh at this movie-poster moment but it didn't last. A Suzuki could be heard roaring in their direction. D put Bridgette down and turned to Jeff. "Give it to me!" Jeff reluctantly handed over the piece to his friend. All four crowded low against an old, yet-to-be-renovated loft building. The Suzuki had a husky male rider in a black ensemble. D aimed the nine-millimeter and fired two shots on the ground a few feet in front of the bike. The driver, properly spooked, lost control and skidded into the side of a parked van. Jeff sprinted across to the fallen driver, pulled back his visor, and slammed down his booted heel repeatedly in the driver's face. That done, D and the Haze sisters ran over. The men lifted the bike, which had some damage to the frame but was still running. D hopped on and motioned for Bridgette to join him.

"I'm not going without my sister," she declared.

Jeff grabbed her by the waist and dumped her on the seat behind D. Before the singer could protest, her bodyguard had gunned the engine and pulled off.

Jen shouted at Jeff, "Where is he taking her?"

"Somewhere safer than this."

D guided the Suzuki around the base of the Brooklyn Bridge and onto Old Fulton Street. They zoomed past the Eagle Warehouse building and then made a hard right onto the Belt Parkway entry ramp. D could feel Bridgette crying, her body jerking involuntarily against his back. He concentrated on handling the bike (which he barely felt in control of) and figuring out his next move. Where would this woman be safe? Where could he take her that he wouldn't be answering lots of police questions? An idea came to his head. A wacky idea but a damn good one. By the time the Wonder Wheel was in view, D had a plan.

Chapter Twenty-three

Going east on New Montauk Highway (aka Highway 27 on your New York State map), there's a point where the road crests and you can see the Atlantic Ocean on your car's right and Montauk cove on your left. It's a beautiful sight, one D would have loved to have pointed out to Bridgette Haze, but the Long Island Rail Road took a low approach into the town that afforded only glimpses of the cove and the backs of several low-rent beach houses. Besides, she was curled up asleep in a seat across the aisle from him.

It had taken about ninety minutes to get out to Kennedy Airport, where D ditched the bike in a parking structure. Bridgette hid in an airport hotel restroom while D purchased new clothes for her at the international departures terminal, including a cheap leather jacket, wool cap, jeans, and ugly beige boots. Dressed down and relatively inconspicuous, Bridgette and D hopped a taxi to the Long Island Rail Road station in Jamaica, Queens. There they caught the 11:17 A.M. train to Montauk, which, out of season, was a local. Lots of stops in Nassau and Suffolk County towns. A conductor thought he recognized her, but Bridgette sang off key and told the conductor she was Bridgette Haze's untalented cousin. Other than that, they'd attracted more glances by being an unusual-looking couple than for Bridgette herself. It was a sleepy off-season Sunday morning and most celebrity-watchers were apparently asleep.

D had made only one phone call, and that was to Night. "My phone's been burning up with people trying to find you and Bridgette. Everybody seems to think you'd call me."

"How stupid are they, huh? Anyway, where's the key to the Montauk place?"

"Where it always is. Ain't a damn thing changed, except you have gotten three or four degrees more out of control."

"What's the word?"

"The news is blasting that she's missing, perhaps kidnapped at her video shoot, though her PR man, Rodney Hampton, is denying it. Says she's just in seclusion."

"Rodney, huh?" D chuckled and then said, "She's with me, Night. She's safe."

"I got that. When are you gonna let other people know that?"

"Soon. I just wanna get situated out here. These kidnappers got real serious today, so I just want to keep her well out of harm's way. Any arrests made?"

"A couple, but they didn't release any names."

"Don't say anything to anyone yet," D said. "I'll shout at you soon."

"Stay up," Night said and hung up.

As the train pulled in to Montauk, D awakened Bridgette with a soft shake. "Where are we?" she asked.

"The end of America."

Passengers departing at Montauk exit onto a long concrete platform that leads to a rampway and a wide, gravel-covered parking lot. Toward the road into town is a small, white ticket station. But most incoming travelers are picked up either by an awaiting car or by one of the rival taxi companies operated by the many Irish expatriates who've settled in town. In summer Montauk is thick with the Irish brogues of foreign-exchange students who toil in a medley of service gigs (cab driver, bartender, cashier). Some, like D and Bridgette's chatty driver, Eamon, make a full-time home in this beach town/fishing village. Eamon was in his thirties, chubby, and slightly weathered, but seemingly happy to be driving his fuchsia Pink Tuna taxi for a living.

"I don't mind the winters out here," Eamon said over the din emanating from the car's radio. "The Wolf," a rock station whose signal traveled from Rhode Island, was blasting Aerosmith's "Dream On" as he said, "It's raw at times, like the coastland towns in Ireland. But it's a fine excuse to spend more time in the pubs." D was enjoying Eamon's good cheer, while Bridgette sat quietly with her wool cap pulled low, gazing at the village of Montauk. Summer days were lush and green with sweet sea breezes coming off the Atlantic. At night a cooler wind made windbreakers and pullovers mandatory during beach bonfires. Off-season, Montauk could be stark and bitter, weather well suited to the fishermen who made it their home, but a serious adjustment to those who knew it only in summer.

As the Pink Tuna taxi wound its way into the town square and made a left onto Old Montauk Highway, past Herb's grocery store and the old-fashioned Mobile station, D felt he'd made a terrible mistake bringing Bridgette out here. He could just as easily have gone up Tillary Street, and hopped the Manhattan Bridge, and taken Bridgette to her apartment in Tribeca or even to his house for safekeeping. Plus, he didn't have his meds—how long could he safely function without them? How long would it take before the virus regained its strength?

"How far?" Bridgette asked suddenly. These were her first words since the train, and they startled both D and Eamon.

"He'll be making a turn in a minute," D replied.

"You know," Eamon said, "if you stay on this road it'll take you right out to the lighthouse. It doesn't work anymore but it's a beautiful thing to see, I'd say."

The taxi made a right onto Ditch Plains Road, which led to the most popular stretch of public beach in Montauk.

"Excuse me, Miss," the driver said, "but you look familiar. Did you stay out in Hither Hills last summer?"

"No," Bridgette said, and then added mischievously, "but I have a lot of sisters and one of them might have come out. I think she might have dated an Irish cab driver. I'll have to ask her."

"Well, well," Eamon said, overjoyed at the attention, his eyes twinkling, "whichever sister it was, compliment her on her fine taste in blokes."

D interrupted by noting that their destination was coming up on the right. The taxi pulled up in front of a gray two-story house with a triangular roof. A big round window sat in the middle of it.

Eamon said, "You must be a friend of that fellow Shade."

"Night," D said, pressing twenty dollars into the driver's hand. "You mean Night."

"Yes, a fine fellow, Mr. Night. Gives quite a party, I'm told."

"Have a nice day, Eamon," Bridgette said. "You think about it and I'll bet you'll remember my sister's name."

"Oh, I will indeed try." He handed D a bright pink business card. "If you folks need any transportation during your stay, feel free to ask for me." D was relieved that Bridgette was flirting with the driver. It was the first time since the morning that she'd smiled, and he knew her cheeks needed the exercise.

It was chilly inside Night's summer house but it was otherwise impressive. There was a spacious living/dining room, a stainless-steel kitchen, and two staircases, one leading to a master bedroom and the other across the room to two smaller bedrooms. There was a long, L-shaped white leather sofa that faced a wide-screen TV, a stereo system, and a fireplace.

"Night comes this far out to party?"

"No," D replied as he went into a closet to dig out a Duraflame log. "He comes this far out to fish. The parties are a by-product of that." As D placed the Duraflame in the fireplace and surrounded it with logs from the pile lying nearby, Bridgette plucked the remote off the TV, clicked it on, and began channel surfing. MTV was playing one of her old videos, which made her frown.

"Am I dead?" she said. "They must think I'm dead to be playing this. God, do I look 'Bama." As the video ended, MTV News appeared with a goofy, gangly-looking VJ playing reporter. "There was an explosion at the New York City video shoot of Bridgette Haze that left several people injured. Police have termed the explosion 'suspicious.' Complicating the investigation was the arrival of a team of stunt drivers who were to appear in the video, at the time of the explosion. Bridgette Haze's spokesperson, Rodney Hampton, told MTV News that the singer, who's been recording in New York, is fine and will definitely host the Source Awards this week."

"Wow," Bridgette said.

"Yeah," D agreed, "that Rodney Hampton is one slick, lying motherfucker."

"Yeah, he may have messed over my sister but he's damn good at what he does. Have to talk to Jen and figure out a way to keep him around."

"Hey, did you ever think that, just maybe, your sister shouldn't be sleeping with married men?"

Bridgette shook her head and said softly, "Yeah. What can I say to that?" She turned down the sound of Nelly on MTV and asked, "So when can I go back to the city?"

"It's Sunday. I'd say we get you back Tuesday in time for rehearsal. I'll have Ivy fly a copter over to the airport in East Hampton and you'll be back in Manhattan in twenty minutes."

"Okay," she said, leaning toward D and the now steady fire. "What do we do until then?"

"Let's take a walk."

In back of Night's summer house was a tool shed filled with fishing gear, three surfboards, a Ping-Pong table whose green had faded to lime in the salt air, and a dirt path that led over a low ridge to a wooden staircase. Standing on that staircase gave one a panoramic view of Ditch Plains, a place where families and surfers (and surfing families) had gathered for decades. The water was gray and churned harshly, and the sand bunched together like mushy oatmeal. Seagulls dipped in and out of the water for lunch. Two hard-core surfers could be seen in the far distance defying high tides and frigid water. Montauk was definitely out of season, but for Bridgette Haze the insistent crashing of white foam against the shore was a melody of peace. She found a spot about twenty feet from the sea and plopped herself down, her head pressed against her hands and knees. D walked back toward the wooden staircase and made a call.

"Where are you?"

"By the dark sea," D told Jeff, knowing he'd understand and wondering if his phone was tapped.

"Cool. You straight?"

"For a couple of days. But Tuesday's the big city day."

"Yeah, I feel you. Well, motherfuckers are all over me like red beans on rice. Fly Ty. Ivy. Jen. Reporters. On and on to da break a dawn."

"I caught the news. Is there any truth I need to know?"

"Ivy and that Rodney Hampton are dancing like divas, but you really need to call Ivy."

"How's the rider who fell down?"

"His name is Antonio Douglas. He lives in Brownsville. Says he was on his way to a bike rally when he hit an oil slick. Turns out there was a bike event out in Jersey that morning, so that's the excuse he and the other bikers are sticking with."

"He hit you with assault charges?"

"Nope. He whispered some nasty shit to me but kept mum to the po po. Feels like he's got some paper coming and he's loyal. By the way, you still have my toy?"

"Can't play video games without it. Listen, my two-way doesn't work out here, so I want you to go to Ivy—don't do it via the phone—and tell him our friend will be back Tuesday. I'll call later with the details. Cool?"

"Very. Got one other thing to tell you?"

"Go."

"Mercedez and I are trying to work out our differences. After what went down, we both thought our hating was crazy and counterproductive."

"When I get back we'll all sit down and talk it out. Anyway, don't even try to get at me unless shit's real."

"Got it."

When Bridgette came back in she sat down on the sofa, watched a bit of MTV, and fell deeply asleep again. D laid a blanket over her sprawled-out body and ordered takeout from Harvest, Montauk's best restaurant, a place known throughout the east end of Long Island for huge family-style portions. He pinned a note to Bridgette's body, called Pink Tuna (no Eamon, but an Irish lass named Fiona), and picked up lobster, steak, baked potatoes, and vegetables. Back in Ditch Plains, D prepared his surf-and-turf feast, placing the food on paper plates. D had spend many such evenings at Night's, eating well, sleeping deeply, letting the waves work as a lullaby. Granted, that was usually in July or August, but even in the chilly spring, Montauk slowed his heart rate. The morning's madness seemed to have happened in another country, instead of on the other end of this island.

D was eating and watching CNN when Bridgette awakened. "I have a plate for you when you're ready. All you have to do is microwave it."

Bridgette went into the kitchen, readied her plate, and picked up the phone.

"If you're dialing the city, it won't go through. As a precaution against ungracious guests, the phone here only works in Long Island area codes. To dial the city you need a calling card or a cell. You can use mine. But I have to ask who you're calling."

"I understand. Just Jen. No one else."

Bridgette took her plate and the cell up to the master bedroom and closed the door. D put down his plate and rested his head against the sofa. He'd been asleep like that for a couple of hours when Bridgette tapped his right shoulder.

"Are you okay?"

"Sure."

"You a lying motherfucker," she said.

D laughed and said, "You should stop being so wishy-washy."

"I want you to build a bonfire on the beach."

"It's cold as a witch's tit out there, Bridgette."

"But it's a full moon tonight, D. Come on."

Ninety minutes later, after much digging, lugging of Duraflames and real wood to the beach, and the removal of several blankets from the guest bedrooms, Bridgette and D sat under a full Montauk moon. A huge, patchwork cloud floated across the sky, slicing the moonlight into hundreds of rays that illuminated bits of sand and surf. Waves scurried toward the shore like colonies of black ants. Out on the horizon, beyond the huge cloud, an oasis of soft white light fell upon the water, looking tender and delicious, tempting to the eye and mouth.

"You know I'm ruined," Bridgette said to D and herself. "When I'm an old has-been like Debbie Gibson or Tiffany, I'll lie in bed and wonder what the fuck happened."

"Sounds grim."

"It is grim. I've read up on all the teenage pop stars and it is harsh. People who want to grow up but remain perpetually seventeen to everyone else. I'll even be nostalgic for the kidnap plot, you know. At least I'll know I once had value."

"Do you really think that, or are you just being dramatic for me?"

"I mean most of it. Not all, though."

"Just know this shit will pass."

"New York's been more than I imagined."

Bridgette was going to continue with that thought when the big patchy cloud finally passed the moon and a vampire-like midnight light enveloped the beach. "Wow!" she said.

"Yeah," he agreed as he stared at the moon. She turned and looked at D, watching the light carve the outline of his brown face. He felt her gaze and, reluctantly, met it.

"You act like you're afraid of me."

"Why would I be?"

" 'Cause I'm famous and rich and, yeah, white too."

"And cocky."

"No, I'm just into the truth. Now," she said leaning closer, "are you gonna let this moment pass or what?"

"I don't have anything," he said.

"We can be creative."

"Oh yeah," he agreed. "We can do that."

They leaned toward each other and then against each other with most of their clothes on and a few pieces off. He was gentle at first, almost timid in how he pressed against her—she was aggressive, almost hungry for a body large enough to engulf her. Wrapped under blankets and bathed by moonlight, they crawled all over each other. In their blanket cocoon things got primitive and creative, and brave bits of flesh were exposed to the ocean breeze. Bridgette looked up at the bright white moon and then at D's dark skin and saw the moon reflected in his eyes. Her hands rested against D's chest. Then she put a finger in his mouth. His large hands moved around her thighs, cupping them and squeezing firmly. Something good surged through her body and she moaned loudly. It was a voice that had poured out of millions of TV sets, radios, and CD players. Now that voice floated into the air, barely audible over the sound of Montauk's waves.

CHAPTER TWENTY-FOUR

MONDAY MORNING the sky was bright and it felt warmer than the day before. Bridgette listened to the ocean for a while and turned over and looked at D's back, which was marked with a few bruises and cuts. His back suggested a life of hard knocks, of situations she'd read about in *The Source* and glimpsed in the rhymes of her favorite MCs. But D's body bore no tattoos. No jewelry adorned his neck, ears, or fingers. Aside from the marks made on him by life, D hadn't altered himself to fit any fashion. Bridgette felt as if she'd seduced a monk. There was something sacred about the man. Yeah, he was her type—broad, big, wide—but he was also very much his own man. There was something mysterious about him. He wasn't a good liar but he could easily hide his truth. Today they'd be alone together for, perhaps, the last and only time. She wanted some answers and lay there wondering how she'd get them.

Last night she'd called her sister and, after the talk of the frightening kidnap attempt and the unbelieved lies to the police (a Detective Williams was particularly contemptuous), Bridgette asked Jen whether sleeping with the help was a good idea.

"You've done it before," Jen observed dryly.

"But they were boys."

"Listen. Ever since that day in Times Square everyone thinks you've been fucking him anyway. Only a man in love acts like he did, so why not?"

"Are you jealous?"

"No," Jen said, "don't ask such stupid questions."

Bridgette took a bit of pleasure in the fact that her older sibling's New York adventure had turned messy. They hadn't planned to sleep with black men in the Big Apple, but it had worked out that way and, so far, Bridgette's adventure had been much better. Jen had messed with a publicity man and had a slick time; Bridgette had boned her bodyguard and had her life saved. Even if the sex had been lousy (and it sure as hell hadn't), Bridgette would already have gotten the better of the deal. Besides, Rodney was married, which, as D had pointed out, made Jen as culpable as the PR man was.

Somehow their affair had gotten twisted up with their talk of managing Bridgette. Pillow talk can be a dangerous thing.

D stirred, drawing Bridgette back to the here and now. If she was ever to get him to open up, it had to be now. She moved her body close to his, wrapping one arm over his torso. She whispered, "Good morning," into his ear. His eyes opened and he turned onto his back. "Good morning to you."

"So, can I ask you a question?"

"It's a little early, but I know that won't stop you."

"Why are you such a liar?"

"Why do you say that?"

"I know there's more to you than you say."

"No, Bridgette," he said, pulling back the covers to reveal his naked body, "this is it."

"Don't try to distract me." She pushed the covers back over his waist. "I watch you and I hear you. You are always biting your tongue."

D was feeling a little self-conscious. Bridgette had been paying closer attention to him than he'd given her credit for. He asked, "Why do you say that?"

"It's from experience. I bite my tongue for a living. All day I'm not saying how I feel or I'm telling a lie to smooth over something. I mean, I'm scared to death of hosting the Source Awards. I have no idea how real hip-hop fans are gonna treat me. They could boo me all night. But you know what? That would be all right too."

"You're funny, Bridgette," he said, surprised again by her.

"It's something that everyone would remember. Years from now they'll be going, 'Remember when that little white pop bitch had the heart to come to the Source Awards and fuck with the real? Yeah, they booed her ass back to VA.' And then people will laugh and slap palms and see me in their memory."

"You really are obsessed about being immortal, aren't you?"

"I think about my legacy all the time, D. Just like you think about whatever you're hiding all the time."

Bridgette could feel D's breathing change. She'd touched some spot inside with that last comment. "You all right D?"

"Always," he said, obviously lying.

"So are you gonna tell me some part of your real story?"

"No."

"But you will tell me part of it? Not every detail. Not all of it. But something that lets me know who you are."

He looked her in the eyes. He suspected he'd never be alone with her again and that she could keep a secret. Besides, he felt weak and tired and in need of a real human connection, even one sure to be fleeting. So D said, "Okay."

D's story was about his family. Fred and Zena Hunter already had three boys—Mathew, aka Matty, Rashid, and Jah—when Dervin was born. He was the "accident" child and the runt of the litter, smaller and more introspective than the rest, who were all muscular, charismatic, and star-crossed. Matty was the oldest and biggest. He strode through Brownsville's Tilden Projects with a bully's swagger. He was notorious for his brutal brand of basketball. To win was not enough for Matty. He always attempted to emasculate the competition, punishing them with his elbows and belittling them with his mouth. Rashid was the handsomest Hunter. With his prominent cheekbones and bedroom eyes framed by lush eyelashes, Rashid made girls (and a great many of their mothers) swoon. And because he was so beautiful, Rashid had a chip on his shoulder as high as the project's sixteen-story buildings, scrapping at a moment's notice when he felt dissed (which was often). Jah was a sour, bitter spirit, quick to anger and difficult to placate. Being a natural pessimist, Jah was never disappointed by the world, since he expected the worst of everyone, including himself.

So Jah was the Hunter family member who took Fred's departure the best. When Dervin was only five, his father left the family for a Jamaican barmaid named Peaches and, as far as the boys knew, disappeared into the Caribbean with her. "You know what he used to say?" D asked rhetorically, not really waiting for the singer to reply. "He used to joke that you knew you were a man when you could do the worst and accept the consequences of your action. That was manhood to him. That was his lesson to his sons. Telling that to a five-year-old boy."

"He was a monster, huh?"

"No, Fred Hunter was no monster. He was just a crazy Virginia boy who should have stayed his ass down in Newport News. My brothers were all crazy the same damn way."

"What happened to your brothers, D?"

"All three of them got themselves killed."

Bridgette's body stiffened involuntarily, but otherwise, she didn't move. Even her breath was briefly paralyzed by the horror of D's revelation. From 1987 to 1993, the heart of crack's plague years, the three oldest Hunter boys were murdered at two-year intervals.

"They were all shot," D said flatly, "and all of them died at a corner on the same block as our building."

Bridgette said a weak, "That's terrible," but otherwise didn't know how to deal.

D continued: "I was a little boy trying to figure out what death meant. I knew my brothers kept leaving but I didn't know where to. Was it with my father? Had they gone with him and left me and Ma alone?" He paused and then said with a small smile, "I used to crawl into the living room closet because I felt safe there. I'd sit in the dark on evenings while my mother played 'Green Lights.' "

Bridgette didn't want to know any more. D's story was one she hadn't heard before. It wasn't ghetto glamorous. It wasn't cool or edgy or exciting. It made her feel uneasy about every-thing, but especially about how close she lay to D Hunter.

"You don't want to know more, do you?"

"If you wanna keep talking I'll listen. I will."

"Don't worry. That's enough for me too. I talked to shrinks all my childhood and it didn't make me feel any better and never has. Talking just doesn't do that for me. It wasn't until I got into protecting people that I felt better. That's why I'm here with you. I'm keeping you safe now, so safe that in a few days you can move on, 'cause that's what people do when they feel safe. When you don't feel safe, you are stuck. Afraid to make a move. Afraid to even be. Everybody in Brownsville was like that. They lived in fear, never felt safe, and even found it hard to shake the fear after they'd moved away. They wouldn't show it in the street but my brothers felt that fear. In the street they were bold motherfuckers. I'm not as bold as they were. I know what it is to feel safe. That's why I'm still alive."

Bridgette, afraid of D and for D, found herself rolling closer to him again, her head curled onto his shoulder, tears running down her cheeks, the water falling onto the bed and onto his chest. D just looked up at the ceiling, happy to be silent again.

• • •

It was, of course, cold out on the Atlantic Ocean in March. And the water was choppy enough to make the fishing boat rock roughly at times. But the first mate, Sammy, rolled two fat joints to forestall seasickness, and suddenly Bridgette found the rhythms comforting, like a particularly potent drum program. There had never been much time for fishing when she was a child—too many dance rehearsals and theater workshops for anything so sedentary. So she savored the feeling of the rod in her small gloved hands, the challenge of balancing the long pole in the metal cup attached to the swiveling fisherman's chair, and the chuckles emanating from D.

"You should see the look on your face," he said, "like you're ready to eat the fish now if you catch one."

"There's no 'if' in it, D. I'm catching one—even if we have to sit in this boat all day."

D had retired for the day, having pulled in seven striped bass with the cool detachment of a longtime fisherman. Night and he had rented Captain Barry's boat so many times in the past few years it felt like a second home. He sat on the step that led into the ship's cabin and watched Bridgette jiggle her line just as the first mate had showed her.

"I got something!" she exclaimed. Her line grew taut and the force of the hooked fish pulled her slightly forward. D told her to start reeling. She hunched her shoulders and began winding the reel with her right hand. "Oh," she said as the first pain of strain shot up her arm, "I can't do it."

Sammy came out of the cabin and looked at the line. "Oh,

you got a good one there!" He reached back and pulled out a handheld net from a rack inside.

"Oh!" Bridgette said again.

D responded, "Just keep reeling it in. Come on, Bridgette."

"Oh," she said once again, "this is hard!"

"Yeah," Sammy said, "but it's gonna taste good later."

Bridgette tried to act as if she believed him, but there was doubt etched all over her increasingly red face. "Come on, Bridgette, you can do it," D said again, sounding like a father urging his wife through natural childbirth. Bridgette kept reeling, though her right arm ached.

"Keep your thumb on the line!" Sammy coached, and Bridgette pressed down on the incoming line with the thumb of her left hand.

Out in the water, her line bent as the fish on the other end struggled against the inevitable. Bridgette continued to reel, taking small comfort in the fact that D and the first mate were so encouraging. It was more fun just looking out at the Atlantic and not catching a fish than having to strain and struggle. Sammy moved to the stern of the boat, anchoring his feet against the low wall and clutching Bridgette's line with his right hand.

"Just keep reeling," he ordered, and Bridgette complied. Now, as Bridgette's arms burned like fire, the first mate reached down with the net. "Wow! You don't see this often!" He pulled up the line and the net and displayed three large, lively striped bass.

"Oh, my God! Oh, my God!"

"Damn girl!" D said. "That's amazing!"

Sammy unhooked the three fish, laid them on the boat's floor, and expertly sliced and diced them.

"Here, Miss Haze," Sammy said as he held the smallest of the striped bass by hooking his fingers inside its mouth. "Come and grab it like this, Miss Haze."

This was not something she wanted to do. "That's nasty!" she shouted. Still, Sammy put her hand in the mouth of the striped bass, and Bridgette held it up with pride and absolute revulsion. D took some digital shots of Bridgette and her wet trophy, which were destined to grace her website.

Three hours later they sat in Wok & Roll, a Chinese restaurant on Highway 27 in the heart of the village of Montauk that specialized in taking a day's catch and filleting, frying, and fricasseeing (as well as five other options). A crowd of teenagers had gathered in the street below the second-story restaurant, buzzing about the presence of a pop goddess in town and calling pals in the New York to brag on their cell phones.

D hadn't wanted to be at Wok & Roll. He'd expected to eat the eighty pounds of striped bass, along with the broccoli, fried rice, and string beans, in Night's stainless-steel kitchen. Instead, after their fun (and relatively private) morning on the Atlantic, Bridgette's inner superstar began to emerge. She'd been fine as an ordinary girl alone with a sexy man in a beach house for a day and a half. But when they got back from fishing, she said, "I feel all closed in, D."

"I know, he replied, "but you know we aren't here on vacation. There are people trying to kidnap you. They are not supposed to know where you are. With the exception of one Irish cab driver and two guys on the boat, no one in Montauk knows Bridgette Haze is in town. We should keep it that way."

A very reasonable argument, but one that D had lost. Bridgette wanted people to look at her. She wanted to be wanted. No fear of kidnappers would deny her a little love. D had wanted to put his foot down and forbid going into town but he did work for her. And ever since his revelations that morning, their relationship had changed. It wasn't that she was distant or hostile. It just felt as if he'd become an object again, not a person, not a lover, but some aspect of life that was to be observed, but not necessarily understood or identified with. It actually had made it simpler for him when he went back to protecting her again. It was a dynamic they both understood.

So D sat eating his striped bass sprinkled with sesame seeds and tried to ignore his roiling stomach. When she'd finished her meal, D paid the bill and guided Bridgette through the kitchen to a back staircase. At the bottom of the stairs were three Pink Tuna station-wagon taxis waiting with motors running. D and Bridgette got into the second taxi, where a blanket awaited and they climbed under. The three taxis took off as about two dozen Montauk residents armed with camcorders, digital cameras, and autograph books came around the corner. The taxi that contained the two surreptitious passengers drove for five minutes before the driver said, "The coast is clear now, boyo."

"Thank you, Eamon," D said to his new partner in personal security as he sat up and gazed out the station wagon's back window. Once it became clear that Bridgette wasn't going to budge on eating in public, D had concocted this plan. After contacting Eamon and the management at Pink Tuna (and charging a tidy sum to his credit card), D had made the arrangements. It had gone well, though Eamon, goodhearted and helpful, still didn't quite understand why everyone was so excited.

"It went well, didn't it, D?" he asked.

"Not well enough," D replied.

"No one's following us." This was Bridgette, now sitting up next to D.

"But now everybody in Montauk knows you're out here. It's only a matter of hours—no, probably minutes—before it's all over the Web. We have to leave tonight."

"Okay," she said. "If you say so. Weren't you looking forward to another night at Night's?"

D looked at her in a manner meant to hurt her feelings and then got on his cell to Ivy.

"It's about time," Ivy said.

Ignoring the manager's irritated tone, D told him, "We need to go back to Manhattan tonight. People out here just found out Bridgette's in Montauk. Not good."

"Montauk. Okay, I'll have a helicopter pick you up at East Hampton Airport. I'll get back to you regarding the time."

"Have you talked to your son?"

"No," Ivy said firmly. "Is Bridgette there with you?"

"No. But she is safe. Call me when you've made arrangements."

"Have you forgotten who you work for?"

"Not at all. I work for Bridgette Haze. You just cut the checks."

D clicked off. Bridgette looked at him quizzically. "I didn't know Ivy had a son."

"There's a lot you don't know about your manager."

"You care to tell me?"

D proceeded to do just that. By the time Eamon's Pink Tuna taxi had arrived in front of Night's house, Bridgette felt dizzy, as if the whole world had just tilted ten degrees to the left and she was right-handed. She exited the taxi without a word. D and Eamon watched her walk toward the house. When she was out of earshot, D said, "Eamon, I have a feeling something out of the ordinary could happen tonight. I don't know exactly what, but if you see someone driving one of those Japanese motorcycles —"

"Don't see many of those out here. Mostly Harleys and the like."

"Eamon, that's my point precisely. You see anything like that tonight, please call me."

"Be my absolute pleasure, D. I'll tell the other drivers the same. Heard you talking about the airport. Will you be needing a ride over there later?"

"When I know for sure, I'll give a call. But call or no call, remember what I told you earlier, Eamon?"

"Of course, D. You already paid for it."

"So that's all you need to do if it comes to it. Okay?"

"Of course, boyo."

D liked Eamon and felt confident he could handle himself under pressure, so he'd laid out a little contingency plan if the bikes showed up. But D thought that the Pink Tuna taxis were too conspicuous for a down-low exit out of town. He'd already made alternate plans for a quick exit out of Montauk. No reason to tell Eamon specifics. You can't tell what you don't know.

CHAPTER TWENTY-FIVE

AREEA READ Toni Morrison's *Tar Baby* on the ride out to Amagansett. Roderick slept with his head on her shoulder most of the journey. Filling his ears were the sweet, sweaty sounds of soul on his iPod. Marvin Gaye, Aretha Franklin, Otis Redding, the Dells, and many other giants. But no Adrian Dukes. If his head was filled with Dukes's voice, he worried it would cloud his judgment and tonight he wanted to remain cool.

Areea tapped him awake as the train left East Hampton for the seven-minute ride to Amagansett. He stirred slowly as Areea looked at her watch, which showed 8:44 P.M. "We're actually a few minutes early," she said absently. Roderick nodded, then stood up and grabbed the duffel bag filled with rope, tape, flashlights, and two Glock automatics off the overhead rack.

They exited into the gloomy chill of a March night on the eastern end of Long Island, comforted by the sight of two large U-Haul vans parked trackside. Roderick smiled boyishly and said, "It's on."

•   •   •

"A helicopter will be at the airport at 9:30 P.M. You'll be back in the city by 9:55, if not sooner." Ivy's voice was calm, soothing. It sounded as if he felt in control. Made D feel a little nervous. "Hope you don't mind but I told your friend Detective Williams about this arrangement."

"Good," D told him, not sure he believed him. After he flipped the phone closed, D leaned down and kissed Bridgette's forehead. She curled up closer to her bodyguard, though her eyes remained locked on the Avril Lavigne video on MTV.

"You think I should learn to play an instrument?"

"I thought you could."

"I mean, I can play a little piano and guitar but not enough to rock out in public. It might make people respect me as an artist."

"Well," D said carefully, "I don't know, Bridgette. If you just pick it up for one song and don't do a lot with it, I think it could backfire. If you're gonna do it, you're really gonna have to be good, you know."

Bridgette sat up. "You think I wouldn't be good? I would never do it in public unless I was great, D. Please."

She shifted away from D with her little bottom lip poked out.

"We're leaving soon, Bridgette. Back to your life where everyone agrees with what you say and everybody's on your payroll."

"You're on my payroll."

"Not after tonight." D's cell buzzed. It was Eamon.

"You told me to call if anything unusual happened."

"What's up?"

"I was driving a fare to the movies in East Hampton, and in Amagansett, I saw a bunch of those Japanese bikes being loaded off two trucks by the train station."

"How long ago?"

"Oh, fifteen, twenty minutes."

D stood up and grabbed Bridgette by the wrist, pulling her up like a bag of laundry. "Come on," he said roughly. She tried to wrestle free, to ask where they were going, to be consulted. But D was back in his favorite mode—not lover, friend, or employer, but protector. He pulled her out the back door toward the shed.

"What's wrong, D?" she cried.

He ignored her. With one hand on the singer, D used the other to open the shed's door. Once inside he took her by the shoulders and said, "This is the deal. The motorcycle kids are on their way here. If they know you're in Montauk, they surely know where this house is. So what I need you to do is shut your mouth and do everything I tell you. You got that?" She nodded affirmatively. He turned and pulled two bicycles out of a dusty corner. He put one of the bicycles in her hand and nodded toward the door. In less than a minute the duo was heading west on Ditch Plains Road.

Coming east on Highway 27 were ten Suzuki speed bikes. They were rolling down the long, relatively underdeveloped stretch of land just before the road split into the old and new

Montauk highways. Old Montauk ran low near the beach, past Gurney's resort and the streets named after presidents (Garfield, Madison, Harrison, and so forth). New Montauk went up toward the state park, with that wonderful view of water on both sides, the local recycling center, and thick woods. The old road was full of bumps and steep hills; the newer road was a smooth, well-paved ride. Aside from the LIRR tracks or a boat, these were the only ways into and out of Montauk. Areea and four riders took the old road. Roderick and four riders took the new one.

There was no reason to think D was expecting them, so they rolled toward central Montauk at a casual fifty-five. Areea noticed that a funny-colored taxi (pink? orange?) was cruising right behind them. Probably just a buster fascinated by their bikes.

As the motorcycles cruised toward town, D and Bridgette were wheeling past Essex Street and the Mobile station into the center of town. D could hear the motorcycles in the distance. Bridgette did, too. But D made no comment. He just kept pedaling and so did she. At the village square, D pointed right, guiding her past White's pharmacy on their way toward the train station. As the sound of motorcycles grew louder, Bridgette shouted D's name. All he said was, "Keep pedaling and don't look back!" It was about a mile to the station. D could feel the sweat collecting under his clothes. He hoped he hadn't gotten old Eamon in too deep.

The two Montauk highways intersected at the head of

town, so the two groups of motorcycles became one again as they rolled past the miniature golf course on their left and the small WGA supermarket on their right. Areea remembered from her map that it was a straight shot past the restaurants and stores on 27 out to Ditch Plains. The taxi was still clocking them when two other Pink Tuna taxis came from side streets and pulled in front of the bikes. Areea cut around them but half of her bikes had to stop short to avoid crashing into them. The streets were basically empty. There were a couple of cars in the distance but no one walking. Roderick pulled up next to her.

"We should fuck these clowns up!" he shouted.

"No. That's a waste of time. That's what he wants. He must know we're coming. Let them follow us. We may need them."

The Pink Tuna drivers tried to stay in the way of the bikers, but after that initial surprise, the riders got their bearings and roared around them, following Areea and Roderick. They geared up through the Montauk village square, gunning past the Mobile station toward Ditch Plains.

Adrenaline was coursing through D's and Bridgette's bodies as they moved across the gravel LIRR parking lot and onto the choppy, rocky dirt that ran next to the tracks. It was dark and there was no luminous full moon to guide them, only a flashlight D held in his right hand. Bridgette didn't say a word. She heard the noise from the center of town and knew it was all for her. She grunted and breathed heavily. Fear pushed her forward.

• • •

Ditch Plains Road was the second right, and Areea and Roderick swarmed onto it like locusts. The taxis were far behind them, straining to do eighty while the motorcycles relaxed at 110. Areea raised her right hand and they turned, creating a racket that had lights flicking on all over the area. Here's where it got tricky for the kidnappers: There were few street lights, and those that existed were weak. Areea knew the address and what the house looked like, but how to see it?

Eamon, in his enthusiasm, had made it easy. Two driverless Pink Tuna taxis were blocking the driveway to a large two-story house on the right. Areea felt it was a little too easy. It was obviously a trap, but she had no time to be picky. Let's see what's up, she thought. There was an opening between the two cars and she zoomed through. The other motorcycles followed her through and then tried to stop.

Unfortunately for them, Eamon had followed D's orders quite well. Oil had been spread on the grass. Areea had negotiated it safely, curling the bike in a careful turn, but Roderick was one of three riders who did not. The trio of bikes spilled out of control, slamming into the front of the house, the riders and their rides crumpling into one ugly mess against the front of Night's house.

Roderick was the last of the three, and his bike skidded into the debris from the two fallen machines, sending Roderick airborne. His Suzuki was stopped by the house's front wall but the man went flying through Night's front window and into the living room, landing on the same sofa D and Bridgette had lounged on while watching music videos.

From the bushes on the left side of the house, Eamon watched in wonder, hoping Night's insurance was in order. He'd seen some nasty business back in Ireland, but nothing quite this loud and spectacular. He wasn't supposed to hang around and watch, but once he had learned that he was helping to protect Bridgette Haze, he began to feel a little self-important. And he wanted to see how it would all turn out. What a story he'd have to tell his passengers.

Eamon watched as an angry, almost hysterical Areea pulled out her Glock and blasted the lock off the front door. She knew her quarry had escaped and her man was injured—perhaps even dead. What she prayed for was a clue to where they were headed. Anything.

"We'll get her, baby," Areea said to Roderick as she cradled his bleeding head in her hands. He nodded, too groggy to speak. The remaining upright bikers tossed the house. A couple of police cruisers could be heard in the distance. "Pick him up!" she ordered, and two of her posse lifted him, ignoring his moans. The two riders outside were lost causes—unconscious and broken up. She was contemplating killing them when a movement in the bushes caught her eye. Without a bit of hesitation Areea squeezed off two shots. The figure fell.

"Yo!" she shouted in Eamon's face. "Where the fuck did they go?" The Irishman screamed in agony, holding his bleeding left arm, though the gun in his face was the real reason for his tears.

• • •

At Amagansett station, D veered left and crossed the tracks. He saw the two U-Haul vans by the depot. He got off his bicycle.

"Why are we stopping?" Bridgette tried to act as if she was upset when actually the young woman was quite relieved. It was one thing to dance in videos—another to ride a bike in the dark with violence at your back. She'd never been so tired. D bent and began letting the air out of all the tires.

"How much farther?"

"We still have a ways to go. Through Amagansett, into and out of East Hampton on back roads." He looked up at her. "You gonna make it?"

"Yeah," she said, but her body language told him "No."

"Come on, Bridgette. Ride with me." She protested weakly and then agreed. D put her on the seat and was going to stand on the pedals.

"No," she said, "let's do it this way." He sat on the seat and she rode his back, wrapping her legs around his waist and her arms around his neck. It was a bit awkward at first, but both of them liked being that close again. D rolled them up to Highway 27 and then, instead of staying on it, crossed it and took to side roads that would take them around the center of Amagansett and East Hampton, and closer to East Hampton Airport. It was a shortcut you'd have to be a Hamptons regular to know. D prayed no one would tell the kidnappers.

"Drive careful but fast or I'll blow your fat Irish head all over the windshield."

"No problem, madam. No problem."

They'd glided past two police cars unnoticed. Eamon was behind the wheel of his Pink Tuna taxi with a female passenger. Just another night in Montauk. What the police didn't notice as they sped toward Ditch Plains was that Eamon's right arm was bleeding steadily onto his pants, or that the woman in the backseat held an expensive weapon against the back of his head, or that the mangled body of her biker boyfriend lay squeezed into the rear of the station wagon. No reason to pay attention to Eamon. A motorcycle gang was wreaking havoc by the beach and the police were on the case.

"What are we gonna do when we get back to New York?"

"You're gonna be a pop star and I'm gonna run a security company. Not a damn thing's changed."

"You think I'm that cold."

"Bridgette, you're not cold. You're not heartless. You're nothing hard. But I am a realist. So are you. I'm not ready to be a Chris Judd and I don't believe you're looking for one."

They were now back on Highway 27, right by the old cemetery, the gray pond, and the windmill that introduced one to the main drag of East Hampton. There were a few cars on the road. The Hampton Jitney crossed in front of them, heading into town. The Jitney was going right and D went left. His legs were weary and his back sore. But he kept on pumping. He couldn't hear the sound of motorcycles and that was all that mattered.

"D," she said in his ear, "I think I love you."

"Come on, Bridgette, we have a nice vibe. That's all. We've been in an unnatural situation. Once all this gets back to normal, you'll see. We'll both see this for what it is."

Bridgette knew he was right but she didn't have another way of defining her feelings for D. If it wasn't love, what was it? He'd protected her, revealed himself, and made love to her on the beach. That was as much love as she'd ever experienced in her young life. Sure the situation was "unnatural," but so was her life.

D made a right at the big, beautiful white house at the bend of Highway 27 into East Hampton. He loved this house. It looked enchanted, like the place you moved in to and lived happily ever after in. He often fantasized about knocking on the white house's front door and making the owners an offer they couldn't refuse. D pedaled past the house, under the thick trees that hung over the road, past the bowling alley on his left, past the street that led to Russell Simmons's summer home (D had provided security for a fund-raiser there), and, finally, up to the right turn that led to East Hampton Airport. D heard a loud, rapidly moving engine. Instead of looking behind, D looked up and watched a helicopter begin its slow descent.

The East Hampton Airport was a small airstrip designed for the private planes and the helicopters that ferried the rich and shameless from the city to their summer homes in less than thirty minutes. D was rounding into the parking lot when he heard gunfire. He threw himself, the bike, and Bridgette to the ground. But the bullets weren't headed their way. A window on the helicopter shattered, sending glass to the ground. A Pink Tuna taxi was coming up the street with a woman firing out the passenger-side window. D scooped Bridgette into his arms and began running toward the landing strip.

The helicopter floated in the air, halfway between escape and landing. D spied two people gesturing in the cockpit. He kept running. A bullet whizzed by. He kept running. Bridgette felt weightless in his arms. The helicopter came down. It landed. Dust and wind clouded D's eyes. Bridgette screamed as D fell to the ground. A bullet stung his left leg. Fly Ty jumped out of the helicopter, his police-issue revolver blazing. Bridgette scrambled to her feet and ran toward the helicopter. D rose to one knee. Fly Ty fired again, giving D some cover. D got to his feet, ran toward the helicopter, and launched himself in. Fly Ty fired again and again. The Pink Tuna taxi went in reverse. Fly Ty got in and closed the door. The helicopter elevated. Bridgette took off her shirt and shoved it against D's wound. Another bullet from the ground penetrated the helicopter, which wobbled but didn't fall.

D said to his friend, "Sometimes I love you like old-school R&B."

"Well," Fly Ty said, "sometimes you have good taste."

CHAPTER TWENTY-SIX

JEFF FUCHS SAT on the right side of the table. Mercedez was on the left. They sat looking at each other, not smiling but not hostile, either. They could hear D in the other room talking loudly on the phone. They couldn't make out the words but the anger was obvious. Finally D went silent. A few moments later the conference-room door opened and the owner and founder of D Security walked in. If you didn't know a nine-millimeter bullet had cut through his body just above the left hip, you'd think maybe D was a little tired, perhaps a little depressed. Not injured actually—just a bit cranky.

"I'm not fucking with those *Source* motherfuckers ever again," he announced to his two employees. "Life is way too short for this." D sat down in his usual place at the head of the table, his brown face red and his eyes mean. "They're making it impossible for us to do a good job. It's like the whole damn event is organized to ruin our reputation."

"I hear you," Mercedez said, trying to sound supportive.

"Fuck you, D." Jeff wasn't having it. "Stop fucking with us. Stop it."

"Okay," D said with a small smile.

"What's going on?" Mercedez was lost.

"D has been spending a lot of time with that old detective, so he's in cop mode. He's really talking about us but not saying it. Isn't that right, D?"

"Well, that's very psychological of you, Jeff. I don't know that I'm that sneaky. I am mad at *The Source*'s management. And I am mad at both of you."

"Well, bring it, then."

"Okay. You have been using Emily's Tea Party to skim money for yourself. People order champagne but get X or coke instead. Been doing it for months. Emily reviewed the tapes and caught you kicking it with the offending floor manager on several occasions. And if I can stumble into it, so can the cops. Isn't that right, Mercedez?"

"I guess so, but I'm not in it," she said petulantly.

"Yeah, you missed that one?"

"Excuse me?" she said.

"Jeff didn't put you down with that, did he?"

"No, he did not."

"Well, you had your own thing," he said, "so it was no biggie."

"What are you saying?"

"I'm saying that you've been double-dipping too," D said aggressively. "But your shit really stinks."

"I didn't do anything too wrong."

"You got down with someone in Bridgette's camp—Ivy, Rodney, maybe the old security guard, Hubert, maybe even

Jen. And whoever that was slid info to the kidnappers about Bridgette's movements. You must know that by now."

Mercedez didn't speak. She looked toward Jeff for guidance but he looked right past her toward the wall. He was exposed too, but his loyalty still remained with D.

"Jen didn't trust you." Mercedez spoke haltingly. "And she really didn't trust Ivy. She was trying to get busy with Rodney and finally did get with him, so he fed her suspicions. We, you, were hired by Ivy, so—" She stopped suddenly and sighed. "It don't matter what I say now. I know I was wrong. I made some extra money but it didn't turn out right. That's what happened," she admitted.

"So you took those pictures to help Jen break up Rodney's marriage?"

"Yes." She looked sad and contrite, but D wasn't finished with her.

"Is that why you started doing my man here?" he said, gesturing toward Jeff.

"You have no right to ask me that."

Jeff looked at her now, hoping to hear something good, but her indignant reply made his heart sink.

"Maybe you're right," D replied, "but since you betrayed me, I'm just trying to see where you draw the line."

Finally Jeff spoke up. "Don't do this, D. She was high. I was high. I thought it would be something but it never became any more than what it was." Mercedez didn't correct him, so Jeff went on being gallant. "I was under a lot of pressure, D. I was running a lot of things for D Security while you were sweating—oh, excuse me—protecting your own client."

"Okay," D said with great finality. He was feeling a little guilty himself at that moment. "I hear you, Jeff. I really do. I think we all have expressed ourselves. We all know how we feel about each other."

Mercedez stood up. D asked, "Where you going?"

"I'm leaving. I mean, I'm fired, right?"

"Sit down Mercedez," D said. "You're not leaving unless you quit. Do you quit?"

Mercedez looked at Jeff. He nodded and forced a smile. Mercedez sat back down.

D looked at her and leaned forward. "You are a valuable member of this organization. I mean that. You're resourceful and smart. But since you're staying with D Security, you owe us your loyalty and as much of the truth as you can give. Jeff and I need to know everything you know about Jen and this situation."

"What about Jeff?" she asked. "I'm not the only person to have done something wrong at this table."

D never took his eyes off Mercedez as he said, "I have no need to threaten Jeff Fuchs. I'm just gonna punish him in the way that will hurt the most."

Jeff looked at his old friend and said, "I understand."

D said, "I knew you would. Now, Mercedez, walk me through the whole thing."

When the young doorman Kirk saw D and Jeff exit a cab and walk toward him, he snapped to attention like a soldier, his chest out and his head stiffly erect. There would be no confusion this evening. "Hey, how are you guys tonight?" he asked, ass-kissing in a very subservient tone. D grunted a greeting. Jeff patted Kirk's shoulder as he followed their mutual employer into Emily's Tea Party.

The spot wasn't as hot as it had been even weeks before. A slew of large, old-school superdiscos in Chelsea had siphoned off some of the club's clientele. A bit of the falloff was due to the boredom that overcomes most New York vampire dens eighteen months or so after they open. Lots of new-generation Eurotrash filled the banquettes, buying champagne and speaking English in a variety of foreign accents.

Emily sat in a booth surrounded by three men of color, including the well-dressed, dreadlocked black man, Pierre Mbuwe, D had encountered her with before. She had her arm around his shoulders. They looked cozy. D walked over and said, "I need to speak to you."

"Really?" Emily said with an indiscreet question mark in her voice. "Since when did you need to talk to me?"

"It's business," D said.

"Why is he here?" She pointed at Jeff, who stood a few steps behind D.

"Because he has something to give you."

"An apology? That I don't need or want."

"No," D said evenly. "Something much more tangible. Now we're going to the manager's office. I think you'd benefit from joining us."

Emily turned and gave her dreadlocked companion a deep French kiss. By the time she'd unlocked lips with him, D was halfway to the manager's office. By the time Emily entered the office, Jeff had finished laying out a small stack of hundred-dollar bills on the desk. Jeff sighed and stepped away from the money.

She asked D, "What's that?"

"Your money," D answered. "Four thousand. It's how much Jeff estimated he'd earned with his little scam."

"That's all?" Emily looked at Jeff skeptically.

"Apparently," D said, "the operation was in its early stages when I noticed."

Emily picked up the money and counted it slowly. Without looking up she asked, "So when do you report him to the police?"

"I'm not going to. I'm hoping this money will keep you from doing so as well."

Finally looking up, Emily smiled, mean and self-satisfied. "I could get Eminem here in a lot of trouble, D."

Jeff really wanted to step to her but he'd made a promise to D, and he knew he had to keep it. So Jeff stood nailed to the spot, biting his tongue so hard it almost bled.

"I know, Emily," D said. He moved closer to her and she met his brown eyes with hers. "But please don't. Along with this gesture of goodwill, D Security will provide you with two free months of security."

"Five months starting tonight and another five grand."

"Three months starting next month and no cash."

"Plus, I never wanna see Jeff at any party I ever do."

"Three months. No Jeff. No money. Any other restitution will be in kind, services only. That's the deal."

Emily squeezed the money in her right hand, then slapped it against her left. "D, you must love this man a great deal to endanger your business like this."

"He's my dog, Emily."

"Did you ever love me like that, D?"

"I care about you, Emily, and I always will."

Emily didn't even get pissed at his answer. She hadn't expected anything deeper. Still, she couldn't help asking. She then said, "I heard you were shot."

"I was, but the bullet went right through. I was lucky."

"Yeah," she said, "I can imagine. Must have hit you square in the heart. That's why there was no damage."

Back outside Emily's Tea Party, Jeff lit a cigarette and stared at his silent friend. "You're like Michael Corleone right now," he said.

"Yeah," D half smiled. "Settling all family business."

"Yeah. And you're being so cold about it."

"I'm not cold," D said firmly. "I'm just trying to do what's right. I'm not into revenge. Revenge is the death of the world. If you just try to make things right, everybody wins."

"Getting philosophical and shit to boot. Damn, Yoda, what's next?"

"We need to do this Source Awards thing. Get this mess out of our lives. Make sure we get our money—"

"Amen."

"And then bring in some new business so we can keep the doors open." He paused a beat. "Legally."

Jeff nodded to show that he understood and thanked God that D was his friend.

CHAPTER TWENTY-SEVEN

THE SOURCE AWARDS hadn't been back in New York since the infamous broadcast where Suge Knight dissed Puffy (aka Sean Combs aka P. Diddy) and Snoop Dogg wondered from the podium, "East Coast got no love for Snoop Dogg?" It was a signature event in the silly spectacle that some labeled the "East Coast/West Coast Rap Wars," and others "a waste of valuable newsprint," and a wise few "just some dumb shit." All D knew was that the "war" had forced a potentially lucrative business opportunity for his security company out of town. And certainly it hadn't gotten any safer, as the mini-riot at the Hollywood awards show a few years back had illustrated.

So the Academy Awards of hip-hop was back in the culture's birthplace. Hip-hop hooray, D thought, as he stood outside the Beacon Theatre watching the early arrivals line up behind barricades and gather in front of the will-call window. Down the block a bunch of scalpers plied their trade. The early-evening sky was low and the air heavy. D pulled up the collar on his black leather jacket and surveyed the area for undercover cops. They were around all right, but D was having a hard time identifying them. It wasn't like the old days when he'd sit in the patrol car with Fly Ty and listen to the young cop describe the ins and outs of surveillance. Fly Ty would bitch about how NYPD "had all these white guys in white socks and Yankee caps hanging around Brownsville and Bed-Stuy sticking out like sore thumbs." Now the force deployed brothers in Fubu tracksuits and Timberland boots to blend in like neon lights in Times Square.

D was heading toward Seventy-fifth Street and the backstage entrance when his cell buzzed. Fly Ty was on the line, sounding as excited as D had heard him in quite a while. "The place in Brooklyn was full of bikes and equipment and old records by Adrian Dukes."

"Did you find them?"

"We have Roderick Dukes, or what's left of him. He's lost a lot of blood and broken a lot of bones. He's critical at Downstate right now."

"About Areea?"

"No sign of her. We've rounded up a few of the drivers. Some are real bangers. Most are thrill seekers who only knew a bit of what was going down. No one seems to know where she lives—only that she ran a motorcycle dealership on Long Island. We checked and that spot is padlocked. Suzuki said she'd been on suspension for several months for questionable transactions. She's on the run, D. Probably riding one of those Jap bikes straight to Cali and into the sunset."

"She's here," D replied and gazed around at the growing crowd. "She's a very determined woman. She's not leaving town without getting something done, believe that."

"You might be right. The event is well covered by the hip-hop cop squad. They have your back and they know what she looks like." Through the phone Detective Williams yawned. D wondered, "You're not coming up here?"

"Hell no," he said. "I'm going home to get my rest. I'm old. Besides, I have to go pick out the right suit for your mother's wedding."

D clicked off and sighed. Three young men came toward him, two dressed in crimson Atlanta Hawks sports jackets and the third in a navy-blue Nascar jacket festooned with the logos of corporate sponsors. That young man walked with a cane. "Hey, D," Ray Ray said, "thanks for the tickets." He came over and gave his employer a hug. The red-garbed Coo and Tone stood back, nodding at D but clearly uncomfortable with (and a little jealous of) Ray Ray's relationship with him. "I'm doing all right," he told D. "I was just wondering if you had a place for me when I'm ready."

"Absolutely, Ray Ray. And if your friends are interested, maybe something for them, too."

"We'll get back to you," Coo said, sneering.

"Fine," D said in reply.

"You buggin'. You know that?" Ray Ray said to his feisty homie.

"Don't worry about that," D said calmly, defusing the situation. "Anyway, I have something for you to do for me tonight. Most of the STP crew is in custody. We picked up

I-Rod today. But Areea, as you might imagine, has been hard to catch. I expect her to show up tonight. You have my cell. If you see her in the crowd, call me."

"Shit," Coo said. "He got you snitching again? You see what that got you, Ray Ray?"

"Don't worry, D. I'll look out."

The three young men walked toward the Beacon's main entrance, and D headed up toward Seventy-fifth Street. At the corner, barricades had been set up and the street had been blocked off between Broadway and Amsterdam, to accommodate TV production vans, tour buses, and limousines. A white tent surrounded the entrance where D Security personnel stood supporting *Source* staffers and publicists distributing VIP tags and press credentials. Standing just inside the tent, dressed immaculately in a brown Gucci suit, was Rodney Hampton.

Rodney said, "Congratulations. I heard about how you saved Bridgette and figured out who the kidnappers were." He seemed genuinely happy for him. "No matter what went down the other night, I respect you, D, and what you've done."

"I believe you," D replied. He was relieved that there were no hard feelings and that Rodney was back to his crisp, smooth self. "But this thing isn't over, and you can help me."

"Any way I can," Rodney said.

"Just one question: Who told you all that stuff about Ivy and Rowena Dukes? Was it Jen?"

Reluctantly Rodney answered, "Yes. She started telling me stuff when we were discussing managing Bridgette."

"The managing was her idea?"

"Yeah. I mean I was open to it, but she planted the seed. She had all this dirt on Ivy. It's what made her wanna make the change."

A very attractive honey-colored woman in slacks, boots, and a very sexy short beige leather jacket came up and took Rodney by the arm. "D," he said with a big smile, "this is my wife, Merry." She was not only a beauty but had a playfulness that lit up her eyes. D thought he needed to spend some more time in Cali.

"It's my pleasure," he said.

"No, D, the pleasure is mine. My husband's told me all about you. Plus, I read *People* magazine."

"I don't read magazines," D replied, trying to keep his face pleasant.

"Don't worry, D. It's not damaging," Rodney said.

"Perhaps," Merry added, "you need to hire us. I'm leaving my job to help Rodney grow his business."

"Wow," D said, and then caught himself. Didn't want to sound that surprised. Wasn't sure how much of Rodney's misstep he was supposed to know. He exchanged business cards with Merry and headed inside the Beacon, a little jealous that there was no one who had his back that like that. Despite Rodney's misstep, Merry was hanging in with him. They were looking to build a serious future. D knew he wasn't as fortunate and wasn't sure how to fix that.

As soon as he took three steps inside the old vaudeville house, all thoughts of the future receded. There was only now. These few hours. His headpiece buzzed with reports. "50 Cents's SUV is being searched by police on the corner of

Seventy-sixth and Columbus," Jeff Fuchs reported. "Diddy just walked in six members of his street team with no VIP passes," Mercedez announced. "There's a posse of Bloods harassing girls in the balcony," said Clarence.

There was a security command center set up in a dressing room near the back door. D entered and sat in front of a bank of monitors. Some were from cameras around the Beacon; others had live feeds from the various TV cameras. There was a seating chart of the Beacon on one wall and a bank of walkie-talkie rechargers on the floor. There was an hour till showtime and all kinds of people with all kinds of passes rolled past the door. Voices filled his earpiece. His cell rang. His two-way buzzed. D listened closely, gave orders swiftly, and worried about Areea. He didn't know where that woman was, but he was keeping constant tabs on Bridgette Haze's whereabouts.

The singer was in a limo winding its way up Broadway with a police escort. After that afternoon's run-through, she'd been driven down to the Rihga Royal Hotel on Fifty-fourth Street (official hotel of the Source Awards) and situated in the presidential suite until near showtime. Jen was riding up with her sister. It would be D's first encounter with both sisters since Montauk. He hoped to get a few quiet moments with them.

"Yo! Yo! Yo! What's up, Beacon Theatre!" There were cheers as Funkmaster Flex, the onstage DJ and Source Awards' official announcer, warmed up the crowd. "Welcome to the Source

Music Awards!" Then he dropped the beat from the latest Neptunes production and the energy in the old theater rose like yeast in Grandma's oven. The TV lights went up full, the music continued full blast, and Flex began running down the list of stars appearing: "Amari! Ludacris! Ja Rule! Eve!" As Flex rambled on, Bridgette Haze stood in the wings trying to hold back tears. It had been a difficult last few minutes for the Source Awards' cohost.

Her arrival at the venue had been smooth and militaristic. Police escort, lights flashing, the whole nine. Backstage had been fun at first. Lots of fans, plenty of friends, and the many lips poked out to kiss her famous white ass. In the dressing room she'd met with the producers and the writers, going over the script and making changes where she saw fit. Ivy sat through some of this and Jen, perched on a chair next to her, sat with Bridgette the whole time, just as she had since her little sister had become a star.

And then D entered the room—her protector, her hero, her lover for now (and maybe later, too). They hugged deeply and then he asked for a moment alone with her before the show. And he wanted Jen to stay, too.

Bridgette stood in the wings and gazed out at the Beacon. There was an orchestra, a mezzanine, and a steep balcony, all filled to the brim with young faces, all of them waiting to see if she could hold her own before a crowd of hip-hop heads. Yet the anxiety that filled her had nothing to do with this performance.

"So this is what I know," D began. "Your sister got a deal booking hotel rooms for a motorcycle tournament at Virginia

Beach. Crews from up and down the Eastern Seaboard attended, including several from New York. Jen even went to hang out herself. Isn't that right?"

"I was visiting friends in the area that weekend," Jen said without a trace of fear. "The promoter was grateful for my help and gave me some comp tickets."

"You met Areea Lucas there."

"I met a lot of people that weekend."

D smiled and said, "For your information, Bridgette, Areea Lucas is the lady who shot me in the hip the other night. When she's not shooting bodyguards, Areea runs a motorcycle dealership in Hempstead and a motorcycle crew called STP, the Speed Tribe Posse, many of whose members are now in police custody for kidnapping Night and attempting to snatch you."

"D," Bridgette said, irritated and alarmed, "stop being cute and tell me what you're getting at."

"I'm saying that your sister knows more about all this than she's telling and that if she admits that right now I can go to the police and cut a deal. Otherwise she's going to be charged by the NYPD as an accessory to kidnapping, assault, and lots of other embarrassing things."

Bridgette's fear bubbled up, and she asked Jen, "Is any of this true?"

"Please," Jen said from behind a very unconvincing poker face. "Your boyfriend is crazy."

The stage manager came over to Bridgette. He was a balding black man in his thirties named Jimi, who hadn't quite committed to a bald head. Patches of hair were on either side of his head in a style so retro it could never come back as cool. Jimi said, "One minute to tape time, Ms. Haze. I'll signal when it reaches thirty and then count you down from ten." Bridgette nodded, flashed her professional smile, and then returned to her thoughts.

"Jen," D continued, back in the prosecutor mode that he fell so naturally into, "I know you attended Night's concert in D.C. and hung out with him at his hotel, knowing when he'd return to New York. I know you paid my employee Mercedez Cruz several thousand dollars and promised more if she kept you abreast of my investigation of Night's kidnapping. I know that you knew Roderick Dukes, who was raised as Adrian Dukes's son but is more likely the son of Ivy Greenwich, and have met with him several times since you and your sister arrived in New York. I know—"

"Stop!" Bridgette stood up and walked to the center of the room. "This is crazy, D. You have strung a lot of items together, but that doesn't mean my sister is behind all this."

D, calm and reasonable, replied, "I think it does."

They both looked over at Jen, who gazed at D with a kind of fuzzy bewilderment, as if she were shocked by the fact that D had pulled all these pieces together.

Bridgette was trying to deny D's words. He had to be wrong, of course. But little bits of doubt about her sister floated up into her consciousness. "Jen has no reason to do this," Bridgette said, defending her sister against her own suspicion. "She has a good life."

Ignoring Jen, D stepped closer to Bridgette. He could see she was weakening. If he pushed hard enough, he knew both sisters would fall. "It's about having a better one, Bridgette. At least that's what I suspect. That's what messing with Rodney was all about, too. I think, in her mind, she was gonna chase Ivy away, end up managing you, and take her pleasure in both milking you for cash and making you miserable. I think your sister hates you the way only a family member can hate another family member. That's a deep hate. It can make you do some terrible shit."

Jen, who knew intellectually that keeping quiet was her best defense, had finally had enough of D's made-up-on-the-spot psychology. "I've had enough of you both. He's full of shit and you're dick-whipped enough to let him talk about me this way. You let him say this outside this room and your career is over, Bridgette. This will be milked by every tabloid in the world. You better put a leash on your big dog here."

D was afraid that Jen was going to stand pat. If she just denied everything and Bridgette sided with her, it could get ugly. He'd made his play hoping that Bridgette would make Jen admit her guilt and, maybe, tell him where Areea was before anyone else got hurt. He was now feeling as if he'd revealed his hand too soon and had no more cards left. What he didn't take into account was how well the sisters could read each other. What looked like a strong front to D looked shaky to Bridgette. When Bridgette said to Jen, "Fuck! You did this, didn't you?" D was the one surprised.

Jimi said, "Thirty seconds, Ms. Haze." She nodded and looked over the orchestra to the area in the back where the cue cards were situated. Across the stage Treach blew her a kiss. Her cohost was already in Mack Daddy mode and the cameras weren't even on yet. Bridgette's body was almost onstage, but her mind was still way backstage.

"I don't know what to tell you, Bridgette."

"Jen, I love you, but what D says has some truth to it. I can feel it. I trust him with my life. I've seen him risk his for mine. So just tell me which parts are true and which aren't."

Jimi said, "Ten seconds."

"Yeah, well, it wasn't my idea," Jen said. "I knew a lot about it. I guess I helped them a bit."

"Why, Jen?"

Jimi said, "Eight."

"Money."

"Money. I would have given you anything you wanted."

Jimi said, "Six."

"Give me? Why should my little sister give me anything when I could take it?"

Jimi said, "Four."

"Didn't you think at all about what Mom and Dad would say?"

"They don't care what I do. It's all about you. It's all about the meal ticket."

Jimi said, "Three."

Bridgette lunged for Jen, but D intercepted her. Jen tried to escape the room, but D stuck out his right foot, slamming his heel into the woman's thigh, which dropped her like a shot.

Jimi said, "Two."

D stood over the woman and shouted, "Where is Areea Lucas?"

"Same place you are. The Beacon Theatre."

Jimi said, "One," and then pointed with his finger out toward the stage. Bridgette walked into the spotlight, into the cheering, barking voices, into the sight lines of several thousand people, into the bull's-eye of an angry woman determined to do her harm.

"What's up, New York!" Bridgette shouted and raised both hands above her head. "The Source Awards is on tonight! What do you say, Treach?"

"I say no doubt, especially with you here, Moms! Ain't this a dime piece or what?" The MC looked down lustfully at her derriere, and Bridgette responded with her enamel whites, her glossy red lips, and big saucer eyes, projecting good cheer that was as fake as a four-dollar bill. "Now let's set this off right," Bridgette said in the shouting-talking voice that was a prerequisite of all hip-hop announcing.

"Show our first act some love—Harlem's own Cam'Ron!"

"It's impossible to know how many backstage passes have been given out." D was in the security room with Detective Williams, whom D had awakened from a sound sleep and cajoled into coming down with the promise of Areea's arrest. "Apparently someone at *The Source* made a bootleg set. So she could be standing outside this office as easily as my security team."

Williams wondered, "There's a metal detector at the stage door, right?"

"Yes, but it would be easy to slip a gat in through a garment bag or in some DJ equipment. We wanted to search it all but the *Source* people thought it would send a negative message to the hip-hop community." They both laughed sourly at that and looked at the stage monitor.

The broadcast was two-thirds over and had run smoothly. No one in the audience or on the stage had been disrespectful to anyone else, and to Bridgette's delight, no one had yet shouted anything nasty her way. Currently presenting on stage were model/actress Joy Bryant and singer Night. "In the category of best solo rap female, the nominees are Eve, Queen Latifah, MC Lyte, and Da Brat," Night said smoothly. Then Bryant ripped open the envelope and shouted, "And the winner is—!" Standing stage right, Bridgette was oblivious to the cheers for Eve. She was wondering what to tell her parents about Jen and whether, somehow, it wasn't all her fault.

In a stall in the women's restroom in the Beacon's basement, Areea plucked a piece of plastic out of her shiny pulled-back black hair. From inside each high black boot she pulled more pieces of plastic and, on top of the toilet dispenser, began assembling a weapon. It had cost a pretty penny and was a bitch to construct. She'd seen a version of it in the movie *In the Line of Fire* and had looked through a bunch of gun guides to find it. But this was actually less challenging than maintaining a high-performance motorcycle engine, so, as the sound from the stage rumbled through the walls, Areea put together a plastic gun. The bullets were the tricky part. She'd had to buy tickets to the black ghetto musical *To Love a Black Man's Sole* (the story of a lonely African-American shoe salesman) that had been at the Beacon earlier in the week.

Earlier in the week. The phrase made her face tighten and her body clench. Earlier in the week was before the star-crossed train ride to Montauk, before her lover was broken into pieces, before the police busted into the warehouse she'd leased and rousted her riders. It was before her very controlled fantasy world of speed and money fell apart. She pulled the tape off the back of the toilet and let two bullets fall into her hand. She only had two shots. Had to get close. Shoot into the gut, so you didn't miss. Had to do it for I-Rod. To honor his love and anger.

It's amazing how much stuff a woman can store between her legs, particularly if the skirt is long enough. Strapped to one leg was a blond Afro wig, a halter top, and some stockings. With the wig in place she changed her makeup, discarded her long dress for the shorter one underneath, and replaced her blouse with a tube top. Areea was a new woman when she exited the stall, looking like an eager chickenhead, a woman who'd attract attention but no suspicion. Only one item left. She placed the "All Access" pass around her neck. She moved out of the restroom and toward her destiny.

Best hip-hop group. Best hip-hop solo male. Best hip-hop video. Best hip-hop/R&B collaboration. The awards were celebrated with shouts, representin'-for, I-got-love-for, and thank-yous to God, Jehovah, Allah, and Moms alive and dead. Despite the tight knot inside her belly, Bridgette had handled her business. There was a moment or two when she'd tried too hard to be down. Treach had cut her a look once when she'd hit a slang phrase too hard. Still, she hadn't made a fool of herself. A couple of the female rappers had actually hugged her, which was nice, since most of the female R&B singers had been chilly, obviously thinking she had taken a spot they desired. She wasn't part of the culture like Eminem, but she wasn't whack like Vanilla Ice. For now Bridgette Haze was as cool as Gwen Stefani, which was a triumph for her. Backstage, Rodney and Merry Hampton were already plotting how to exploit her enhanced street cred.

D stood stage left, ready to whisk Bridgette from the podium through the backstage area to the limo. He knew it wouldn't be easy. In the hip-hop world, walking past another celebrity without an acknowledgment was tantamount to spitting in someone's face. The problem was that everyone thought they were a celebrity—from the MC's road manager to the guy who carries the DAT. Once he got Bridgette in that car he could do a Toni Braxton and breathe again. He'd been waiting to exhale for nearly three hours.

The big closing number was Bridgette singing her collaboration with DJ Power, which was to be augmented by a medley of rap stars from the East, West, dirty South, and hip-hop territories yet to be designated. Between their posses, security guards, and hangers-on there would be a lot of folks gathered around Bridgette. Happily, from D's perspective, most of them would be men.

Onstage, DJ Power's beat kicked in and Bridgette went into the intro. Power started flowing into the first six bars of the rhyme and was followed by cohost Treach.

D's cell phone buzzed inside his inner breast pocket. He pulled it out and listened to it the old-fashioned way since his head was already thick with earphones. Ray Ray spoke to him.

"I think I saw her!"

"Where?"

"There was this girl with a blond Afro wig walking up the steps from the restrooms."

"Blond hair?"

"Yeah, dog, the hair was wrong and her clothes were wrong, but she moved like Areea. It was the way she strutted. I was gonna step to her but, you know, I wasn't sure."

"You did the right thing. How long ago was this?"

"Ten minutes or so."

"Good looking out."

D announced her description into the earpiece and his words flowed out to the Beacon staff, the D Security team, and the NYPD. He'd seen at least three or four women with hair like that. It was so conspicuous. Made for a laughable disguise unless that was somehow the point.

"It went well, huh?" Ivy Greenwich stood next to D, looking older than D had ever seen him.

"Yeah, I guess. You still manage her. Her value has been enhanced and all who opposed you have been subdued. Nice."

"My son is in the hospital and under police custody, D. That isn't nice."

"At least it's settled."

"You know how family is, D. It's never settled. Not until the day you die."

"Thank you, everybody, and good night!" Bridgette shouted for the cameras, and then headed toward D in the wings, surrounded by the cream of hip-hop's hierarchy. Bridgette grabbed D's arm and walked straight toward the backstage door. Ivy was a stride or two behind. D's eyes roamed the corridor, looking for a black blond girl. He felt as if he were in a video game waiting for a shooter to pop out from a doorway. The backstage door was just ahead. Jeff Fuchs stood there holding it open.

From D's left, four young black women in blond hair emerged from a dressing room. One had short hair. One had fried hair. One had braids. One had an Afro. D did the wrong thing—he stopped dead in his tracks, trying to figure out who was who. His indecision was all the time Areea needed. Out came the plastic gun from her bag. D grabbed Bridgette and threw her behind his body. Areea fired and a bullet whizzed past D's left shoulder. Areea aimed again and fired right past D again—he thought he smelled gunpowder—and a spray of blood popped into the air. Areea threw her head back in a laugh. D leaped at her, knocking the little weapon from her fingers and pushing the assassin to the ground. Along with Jeff, D pressed her against the floor, her wig askew, her makeup a mess.

Bridgette screamed. D looked around and watched as Ivy Greenwich stood alone in a sea of frightened people, holding his stomach with both hands as blood flowed over them.

CHAPTER TWENTY-EIGHT

D SAT BEHIND HIS DESK at D Security and listened as Kirby Turner spoke. "If you agree to these terms the check will be at your accountant's office tomorrow afternoon."

"So your office will handle all the paperwork for me?"

"Just like I told your lawyer, D. All you have to do is keep people safe and keep seeking out new business opportunities. You are a famous brand in the security world now. You saved a star twice in one week. You've seen the calls you've received. Everybody wants to feel safe, especially in this world right now. You represent security."

"Tell that to poor Ivy," he said sadly.

"Well, that woman was trying to shoot Bridgette Haze."

"Maybe. Areea's not talking." He paused a minute and looked down at the papers. "Yeah, everybody wants to feel safe."

His staff was in the next room waiting patiently at the conference table when he and Kirby walked in. She sat in the seat Mercedez used to occupy. Mercedez sat on the other side, next to Jeff. D sat in his usual spot and told them that

KT Investments had put a "substantial sum" into D Security and that "effective immediately" she would be the new CFO and that all paychecks would come through her office. In addition, the staff would have to submit to new background checks and sign confidentiality agreements that would be legally binding.

Clarence laughed. "Is that all, baby?" he said to Kirby.

"For now," she said, "unless you wanna discuss more with me after the meeting."

D cleared his throat. "Okay, does anybody have any real questions?"

Clarence spoke up again. "What about Bridgette Haze?"

D got a little irritated. "What about her, Clarence?"

"Are we still working for her? I never got that autograph for my niece."

"No, we are not." D looked around the room. It got very quiet. "She ran into Will Smith at a party and is now using the same people he does—ex-Israeli–secret service folk."

"Fuck her." It was Jeff.

"Okay," D said again, "that's all ancient history. Let's go over our assignments for this week and show Ms. Turner how sharp we are."

CHAPTER TWENTY-NINE

BRIDGETTE SAT ON THE BEACH at Zuma Beach, still in a wet suit. A boogie board lay at her feet. It was a warm April morning in California. "I'm looking forward to Asia. I've always wanted to vacation there."

D lay in bed in Manhattan, his shades drawn, the blanket pulled up to his neck. It was after one in the afternoon. D was in no rush to get up.

"Doesn't sound like much of vacation, Bridgette. Tokyo, Osaka, and then South Korea and Thailand."

"I'll find time for dancing and sun, D. Believe me. So how's your side?"

"Got the bullet in a little bottle on my desk. I can't play ball for another couple of months, though there's been some discussion of me taking up yoga."

"Cool. I love yoga. We can do a class when I come back."

"Yeah," he said unenthusiastically. With real concern he asked, "So how's your family holding up?"

"My parents are doing as well as you could expect. We got

another shrink coming to see Jen. Our attorney thinks the DA may go along with a mental-illness defense—I think that's what they call it. We'll see, you know. It's been tough. Family shit. I know you know."

"Yeah," he said softly. "Bridgette, I don't think we should do yoga together."

She giggled. "The big black man is scared of being embarrassed."

"In a way. I'm still getting calls from reporters, Bridgette, and they're not asking about you anymore. They're asking about me. Who am I and other silly shit like that. I can't have that. You're just too famous for me."

There was a long silence on the line from California. "Are you dumping me?" she asked finally.

"I'm just being realistic about who you are and who I am."

"I can't believe you would say something so silly. That's kiddie talk, D. I know you're a man. Just be the man you are and it'll all be all right."

"No. No, it won't. I know who I am, Bridgette. You need to be realistic and recognize who you are. What I'm saying is for the best."

"The best?"

Bridgette clicked off her cell and tossed it onto the Malibu sand. D placed his phone on the bed and looked across the room at the photo of his family.

Four hours later he stood next to his mother in a church off Eastern Parkway in the ghetto end of Brooklyn, not that far from the street where he was born, scarred, and shaped.

His mother, Zena, held his arm. The wedding march began, with the melody being carried by the saxophonist from Night's touring band. "There's quite a few nice black girls who attend this church, Dervin," his mother said. "They cook. They have regular jobs."

"Ma, don't you think you should be focusing on your marriage?"

"I got mine, Dervin Hunter. What do you have? You have a business. That's good, but that is not a life. Besides, I want some grandchildren and you have to give them to me. You know you're my only son."

"I know, Ma."

D tugged at his mother's arm as the organ played the wedding march, and they moved forward down the aisle.

CHAPTER THIRTY

IT WAS DARK when D slipped out of the reception being held in the church's basement. He'd danced with his mother and stiffly hugged his new stepfather and even flirted briefly with one of Willis Watson's chunky but funky divorced daughters. He had a TZL car take him out of Brooklyn to Queens, to a long cemetery that twisted around an elevated roadway into Manhattan. Of course the cemetery was close, but D had done this before. Heedless of his loafers or his suit, D scaled the low wall. They were just clothes. They'd be old one day. Just be things he used to wear when he was young.

The swoosh of cars and fleeting beams of light filled the dark cemetery. There was no silence on these grounds. No sense of peace and quiet. Modern life still seeped into the afterlife for those buried here, so D felt no need to be embarrassed by this intrusion. Appropriately, he came upon Matty's grave first. Turning to his right, he knew Rashid was two graves down and Jah just three beyond him. And to D's left, three plots down, he could see construction had begun on the stone structure that would reunite the Hunter clan just as if they'd been dining on a Sunday afternoon.

He sat down on Matty's grave, plucked his pillbox from inside his jacket and the bottle of Evian from his side pocket. He took his meds, washed them down with mineral water, and then lay down, his head near Matty's headstone. One day he'd join them, he thought, and finally he wouldn't feel so guilty for being alive, so angry at them for leaving, or so profoundly alone. Until then he'd continue to live the best he could. After all, in this world, everybody wanted to feel safe.

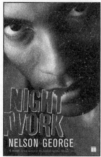

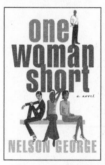